CW01211884

Crime of Fashion

Chautona Havig

Copyright © 2013 by Chautona Havig

First Edition

ISBN-13: 978-1482572254
ISBN-10: 1482572257

All rights reserved. No part of this book may be reproduced without the permission of Chautona Havig.

The scanning, uploading, and/or distribution of this book via the Internet or by any other means without the permission of the author and publisher is illegal and punishable by law. Please purchase only authorized electronic editions and avoid electronic piracy of copyrighted materials.

Your respect and support for the author's rights is appreciated. In other words, don't make me write you into another book as a villain!

Edited by: Britton Editing & Haug Editing

Interior fonts: Book Antiqua
Art font—"Smart Frocks" and Calamity Jane
Cover photos: chuvipro/iStockphoto
James Steidl/shutterstock.com
Cover art by: Chautona Havig

The events and people in this book are fictional, and any resemblance to actual people is purely coincidental and I'd love to meet them!

Connect with Me Online:
Twitter: https://twitter.com/ - !/Chautona
Facebook:https://www.facebook.com/pages/Chautona-Havig-Just-the-Write Escape/320828588943
My Blog: http://chautona.com/chautona/blog/
My Newsletter: (sign up for news of FREE Kindle promos) http://chautona.com/chautona/newsletter

All Scripture references are from the NASB. NASB passages are taken from the NEW AMERICAN STANDARD BIBLE (registered), Copyright 1960, 1962, 1963, 1968, 1971, 1972, 1973, 1975, 1977, 1995 by The Lockman Foundation.

Fiction/Christian/Mystery

~*For My Family*~

Just before Thanksgiving of 2012, I worked on retyping this book, sending each chapter off to the editor as I finished. Then tragedy struck. Thanksgiving weekend, our family lost one of the dearest people I've ever known—although I hardly knew her, really. My sister-in-law went to be home with the Lord, and my husband and I flew to Minnesota to be with his brother and our nieces. That put this book on hold for a while. Holidays came and, well, I held all of my family a little dearer this year. We forget that time with loved ones isn't guaranteed until we lose it. So, I slowed down a bit. At the same time, my publicist made other projects a priority. Alexa took a back seat.

The end of December brought another tragic accident—one that stunned us and that irreparably changed another family's lives. While reeling from the reality of more loss, I began working on the "to do" list from publicist extraordinaire, Ashley. This book was near the bottom of that list.

It seems a cruel irony that in the midst of so much loss and heartache, I had to finish retyping and editing a book that centered on that very thing—loss.

So much made 2012 a painfully difficult year for us. My three-year-old grandson was electrocuted and severely burned when he tripped over and fell on a downed power line. After several surgeries and almost a month in the hospital, he came home and learned to be his crazy, over-active self again. He has fifteen years of surgeries ahead of him. We thought that was enough trial to last us a lifetime. Then came Robin's death.

When yet another tragedy struck, I truly wondered if Satan hadn't been prowling around feeling sorry for the Lord. I could almost hear him say, "Look, last time I asked for Job—such an upright guy. That wasn't really fair of me. So, how about those Havigs? Why don't you let me have a crack at them? They're just average Joes. Nothing special about them."

And he would have been right, that old schemer, Satan. There isn't anything "special" about us—in ourselves, that is. But Jesus' blood covers us. We're bought—His. Nothing, not even the nightmare that 2012 now feels like to us will snatch us out of His hand.

God gave us an almost carefree life for twenty-three or so years. Who am I to complain when the sin and anguish around us in this world finally makes its way to our door?

The Lord gave. Abundantly. We've been refined a bit this year. We didn't like the fire, but we love the Lord. Blessed be His name.

Chapter 1

The heady perfume of blossoming lilacs permeated the rooms of Hartfield Cottage. As the sun shone across the glossy hardwood floor of the hallway, fairy dust danced in the shaft of light. Keys jingled as one slipped into the lock. Shoes tapped across the floors and down the hallway, adding music to the sights and scents of the cottage. In her guest room, Alexa Hartfield ran her hands over her spring clothing, pleased. Soft blouses, silky gowns, crisp skirts, and gauzy dresses delighted her fingertips. Moments later, she bopped through the house, crooning off-key at the top of her lungs.

A knock stopped her butchered rendition of Glenn Miller's "In the Mood."

Alexa half-danced to it and opened it, smiling at Hunter Badgerton. "Hey, I'm glad you came by. I was going to call you. Did you still want to do the pruning and yard work this spring and summer, or will you be too busy?"

"Hey, Miss Lexie. Um, yeah. I was hoping to do it again this year. My uncle is letting me buy his car—gonna show me how to fix it, but of course, I have to pay for it and the parts."

As he shuffled his feet, Alexa thought she understood the reason for his visit. "Oh, is it collection time already? Let me get my purse. I always forget—"

"Oh, no. You paid me last week, remember? It's just—oh, man. I hate this." He took a deep breath and blurted out his errand. "My drama class is doing *Music Man*, and everyone is required to sell ten tickets. I was hoping you would—"

"What role did you get?"

Hunter's face drooped. "Marcellus Washburn."

Now she understood. A boy like Hunter would prefer a role like Harold Hill or Tommy Djilas. He wouldn't see that getting a role like Washburn was a compliment. "You're going to be amazing. Not everyone can do that role justice. I can't wait."

"Yeah, I guess. He's just not going to look as good on a college application." He sighed. "And now I have to sing that stupid song."

"Well, I'll take four tickets and give you a standing ovation." She smiled. "But you have to do two things first."

"What…"

"Take two of the tickets to the chief and earn that ovation."

Hunter grinned. "I'll do it. Thanks."

She scrawled out a check and exchanged it for the tickets. "If you don't sell out before Wes gets here, come back. He might take four for him, Heather, and the kids."

Alexa closed the door behind her, reading the tickets. A plot formed in her mind as she tucked them into her purse. Despite his love for older music, Joe didn't like musicals. She might just have to find a way to bait him into escorting her — before she told him where they'd go.

Determined to make it work, she called his phone and left a message. "Officer Freidan. Citizen Alexa Hartfield here, calling to request a house visit during your lunch break. I promise to surprise you with a special gift if you can spare the time to stop by."

That done, she glanced around her and decided to call her housekeeper and arrange for spring house cleaning. Before she could dial, her phone rang. Startled, her hands fumbled the phone, almost dropping it. "Hello?"

"Ms. Hartfield? This is Silva from the Cutting Room Floor."

She found the call a bit awkward; Silva had never called her unless related to an order. "You know, I was just thinking about you today. I pulled out my spring wardrobe to see what gaps I might need to fill in and realized that I don't have anything formal—well, nothing I want, that is."

Silva sounded uncertain as she said, "You sound out of breath. Did I interrupt—"

"Not at all. I was just holding the phone when you called and it startled me. What can I do for you?"

Well..." Silva hesitated before she charged ahead with a "do or die" tone to her voice. "I have a business proposition for you and wondered if you were planning a trip to the city anytime soon."

Smiling at the New York tendency to consider only New York City as "the city," she shook her head as she spoke. "Not before fall. What kind of proposition?"

Silva briefly outlined a plan for a nationwide clothing line that would merge the best of vintage styles, modern construction techniques, and the latest in fabrics to create a classic look that, by novelty alone, would be slightly trendy.

"All clothes are rehashes of other eras—we're not pretending to do anything original—what *is* original is how closely my designer has managed to copy actual vintage dresses while keeping a cohesiveness to the line. I think you'll be impressed." A second or two passed before she rushed on, as if she'd taken a drink or a deep breath to steady herself. "I thought of you because of your interest in retro-vintage fashion. When Rhette brought me the sketches, I knew these were the kinds of clothes you'd love to see in stores."

The enthusiasm building in Alexa dimmed suddenly. This was a business proposition. She couldn't allow herself to be swept away by ideas; she had to think. "What would be the purpose in my coming to New York?"

"Well, if you thought you might be interested, we'd fax a prospectus. If you're still interested, we'll make prototypes of debut ensembles in the line and arrange a meeting for you to have a private viewing."

Alexa saw Joe open her gate, and her eyes grew wide. "Um, yeah. Hey, Silva, can you fax that prospectus this afternoon? I have to go. Thanks for calling. I like the idea. Bye."

Only vaguely aware of how rude she must have seemed,

Alexa dashed out the front door. "Joe! Where is your mustache?"

"I'm fine, thank you. It's a gorgeous afternoon, isn't it? I hope you included lunch in that message, because I'm on beat today, and I won't have time to walk home before I have to get back on the streets."

"You're not getting anything until you tell me what you did with your mustache. I almost didn't recognize you!" Hands on hips, Alexa stared at Joe.

"The annual mustache-a-thon starts next week."

Alexa hurried ahead of him, through the house, across the dining room, and into the kitchen. She pulled a retro apron from the pantry and slipped it over her neck, covering the all-white dress. As she assembled sandwiches, Joe described the annual fundraising drive—something that felt vaguely familiar to her.

"It's for the prom. There just aren't any places in town large enough to hold it other than the gym. But prom is such a big deal everywhere else, so we raise all the money we can so we can rent a nicer place for the kids—in Rockland."

"And shaving off your mustache will cut it?"

"Funny play on words there," he teased. "The businesses do what they can to raise funds, but people give more if they can see the mustached men of this town shave it off and look ridiculous for six weeks."

Alexa nodded as she grilled the sandwiches on her griddle and assembled a salad. "I don't understand the big hoopla over proms these days. Honestly, kids spend more on their proms than their parents or grandparents did on their weddings."

Joe shrugged. "I think the prom took over those formal parties of the fifties and sixties—you know, where they wore those poufy dresses and stuff. Sweet Sixteen parties or coming out parties. I think more recent generations just mushed all those into one—or two, if the kid's lucky—big bash."

She handed him a bowl of salad and put a mound of cottage cheese on each plate before transferring their sandwiches to their plates. "I can't believe I've never seen you without that mustache before. How did I miss that?"

Joe mumbled something behind his sandwich, but Alexa didn't hear. They ate with few words punctuating the quiet of the house. Alexa got up to refill their glasses and to make Joe another sandwich, but the majority of the meal remained conversation free.

At last, Joe blurted, "What is wrong with you? It'll grow back. It's just a mustache."

"What?" Alexa tore herself from her reverie.

"You keep staring at my lip! It's just a mustache."

Heat rushed to her face. She tried to hide it, rising under the pretext of grabbing more napkins, but Joe grabbed her wrist. "Sit down. I've seen you cry and blush, and I've heard you sing. Eat. Your food's getting cold."

"It's a salad. It's supposed to be cold," she muttered, retaking her seat as her face cooled. She chanced another glance at his face. His eyes twinkled with repressed laughter, making her defensive. "Well, it's just different! It takes some getting used to."

"I get it. Keep the mustache." He nudged her foot. "You know, if you were civic-minded and wanted to prove your loyalty to the mustache, you'd sponsor me with a hefty donation."

Alexa shook her head. "Oh, no. I'm not loyal to the mustache at all. Can I sponsor you to shave it back off once the contest is over?" She took a bite of salad and concentrated on finding the right lettuce, spinach, crouton, and tomato combination for her next bite.

"You don't like the mustache?"

She struggled to find an answer that didn't seem bizarre. Whether or not he wore a mustache wasn't exactly any of her business. A girlfriend could — well, possibly — expect to have something to say about her boyfriend's facial hair, but Joe wasn't a boyfriend.

He saw her glance at him and self-consciously scratched his upper lip. As her eyebrow rose, he said, "What! I don't get it. You seemed bothered by the lack of facial hair and now you tell me you don't want it back."

Alexa swallowed, took a sip of her lemonade, and grinned. "I've always said you're a very good-looking man. In that suit and hat last winter, you were downright debonair." She shook her head. "But you've been hiding an incredibly handsome face behind a swath of fuzz."

"Really."

"Really. I think it's positively criminal, which, you have to admit, is not a very good example in a police officer."

He rested his elbow on the table, covered his mouth with his hand, and stared across the table at her as if he didn't know her. She smiled and even arched her eyebrow again for effect. Joe shook his head. "If I didn't know you as well as I think I do, I'd say you were flirting, Miss Hartfield. However, I think that's irrelevant at the moment."

That flattened Alexa's comeback. How could she toss back a witty remark after his comment on relevance? "Huh?" She groaned inwardly at her stunning eloquence.

"Well, I'm curious, of course. I've never imagined the famous Alexa Hartfield flirting with anyone, so it seems unlikely. Even so, once you discover the piece of spinach in your front tooth, you'll forget about me. Leafy vegetables like that particular tooth, don't they?"

"If this is payback, it worked." She stood, untied her apron, and snapped it at him on her way to extricate the offending greenery from her teeth.

While flossing, brushing, and picking to dislodge the spinach, Alexa glanced at her face. The blotchiness that always followed a deep blush seemed nearly gone. As she rinsed her mouth, Joe called out to her. "My lunch hour is almost up, or will be if I add on the walk back. Why did you call me over here?"

She hurried back to the kitchen and removed two cupcakes from the cake dome. She cut the top off one, turned it upside down, and created a "sandwich" with it, the frosting in the middle. "Here—no cyanide."

"Wilma made them?"

She shook her head, smiling. "No, I did. But I'm sure

she'd make you some if you asked. She's convinced you're the town's very own Colombo since you caught the guy who killed her mail carrier."

"Why'd you cut off the top like that?"

"Cleaner to eat on your way back to work."

She turned to cut the top off hers too when Joe's tone dropped low and insistent. "Why am I here, Lex?" She'd only heard that tone a few times and always when concerned about someone. Sarah had declared it to be the most soothing sound in the world, "just like the shower when you're really dirty and stinky."

"Well, it's nothing serious or anything. You know that house Wes wants me to buy?"

"Yeah?"

"He got them to agree to sell, and now he's working on a price. Honestly, I don't understand why this is such a big deal to him."

"He'd be close to Heather, Zach, and Sarah without feeling like an intruder in his sister's house. It's a guy thing."

"Anyway," she continued, "I wondered if you knew who I should talk to about the place. I don't want to get stuck with a money pit. My handyman was recently arrested for killing my characters, after all, and I don't have a backup to help me."

"I know a guy who can either help or tell us who can. You wouldn't believe how many are without a handyman." Joe rinsed his plate and tossed his napkin in the kitchen laundry basket. He guzzled the last of his lemonade and checked his watch. "Oh, man. I'm going to have to hurry or I won't make it to work on time."

Alexa walked him to the door, and as he stepped onto the walkway, she called after him. "Wait, there's one more thing!"

Late, and in typical male fashion, Joe tried to expedite the leaving process. "What?"

"I need a favor."

"Anything. Just leave a message on my voicemail. I really have to go."

She watched him half-jog toward the end of the street, slowing as he neared the corner. At the stop sign, he waved before disappearing from sight. "Oh, man, he set himself up good for that one! He didn't even think to have me call and tell him while he walked to work."

Joe collapsed on his couch that evening, exhausted. Walking the beat was Chief Varney's idea of keeping a presence among the tourists that flocked to Fairbury for its excellent produce, handcrafted gifts, and small town atmosphere. For the cops, it just meant an exhausting day.

He punched his voicemail and speakerphone and listened. Jeremy rambled for half a minute, hung up, and called again—several times. Why his little brother thought he could help with dating advice when he hadn't had a real date in months, he didn't know. Two calls from his mother asked about Easter. He'd never get it off, but she wouldn't stop trying to find a way until the Monday following. He saved Alexa's message for last. As he listened, his droopy eyes widened and he bolted upright. "What! Oh, man, she set me up."

He punched her number, ignoring the side of him that knew he might wake her up. *If not, she deserves to be woken up,* he groused to himself. The moment he heard her voice, Joe pounced. "Alexa? That was low."

"I tried to ask you, but you just ran off!"

"You planned it that way!" he accused.

"Well, actually, I wish I could say I did."

"I don't believe you."

"Don't or do, but it's the truth," she snickered. "I would have if I had thought of it. I thought I'd have to beg, wheedle, beg, plead, beg—"

"Yeah, I get the idea." Seconds ticked past as he wrestled between auditory tortures and keeping his word. Integrity won. "Okay, I'll go but with one condition."

"What is that?"

"No Shirley-Jones-beauty-parlor-hair-dryer hats."

"Aw, I just found the cutest one too! It looks like a ball of cotton candy."

Somehow, he pictured her mentally pumping her fist and couldn't stand it. "Sorry, it's me or the hat."

"What if I counter?"

Joe groaned inwardly. It'd be about the mustache. He knew it. "What is it?"

"What if I say it's the hat or the mustache?"

"Then I guess I'll have to see the hat before I can answer it."

"Deal."

Joe stared at the dead phone in his hand, growing more nervous with each passing second.

Alexa flipped open her laptop and pulled up her email program. She began typing the name of her seamstress and hit enter as auto-fill did the work for her.

To: AdelaidePeters@letterbox.com
From: alexa@alexahartfield.com

Subject: Can you sew a hair dryer?

Laidie,
I need an enormous favor. Do you have time to make me the most hideous pink hat you can dream up? I'm talking tulle or stiff voile—anything that will stay poufed up in a muffin hat style. I want it to look like I have a pink hairdryer on my head. If you can do it (and it doesn't have to be well made—just put-on-able) and overnight it, I would really be obliged. Send me an invoice and I'll pay you immediately.

Fashionably in your debt,
Alexa

Chapter 2

On Friday afternoon, her hat and brother arrived simultaneously. Wes burst through the door carrying a big box and juggling his duffel bag and camera bag, calling, "Alexa! I have a monster-sized overnight box here. I didn't know people overnighted stuff this big."

Alexa rushed from the guest room, tossing a sheet she carried over the living room chair. "Oh! It's here! I can't believe she got it done!"

This side of Alexa—the whimsical side that became almost girlish over something that tickled her—appealed to Wes more than her serious side. As comforting as her placid and gracious demeanor was when their family stirred trouble, nothing beat the giddy silliness that made her look like a sweepstakes winner on random occasions.

He watched as she tore at the package, slicing the tape with a letter opener—who had those things anymore anyway?—and withdrew the most obscene-looking contraption he'd ever seen. "I'm almost afraid to ask."

Alexa grinned. "I convinced Joe to go to the high school's production of the *Music Man*. He said he'd do it if I promised not to wear Marian Paroo's enormous hat."

"So you bought the hat because you invited him but you don't want him to go after all? That makes no sense."

Shaking her head, Alexa fluffed the hat into a perfect imitation of a pile of cotton candy. "I counter-offered."

Wes roared. "You would." He'd missed this side of her over the past few months. The murders had taken a toll on her in ways even she didn't realize, but Alexa was back.

"What was the counter offer?"

Her cheeks grew slightly pink. This would be good. "It's silly, really. He shaved his mustache off for some kind of fundraiser."

"Why should you care? It'll grow back."

"I don't want it to. He looks better without it."

Wes gawked at her. "Um, Alexa…"

"Oh, don't be ridiculous," she snapped. That, too, interested him. "I can appreciate an attractive man without being infatuated. He's just even better looking than I realized, and I hate to see him hide it behind a mustache."

"Ooooh, my baby sister protesteth…"

She bopped him with the hat and began clearing away the packaging. "I wouldn't talk, Wes. How is Heather?"

"Hey, at least I don't pretend…"

"You think that if you like," she rejoined with a thick layer of condescension added. "It's good for you."

Wes carried his bags to Alexa's guest room and dumped them on the half-made bed. He'd have to remember that sheet. His stomach rumbled, sending him to the kitchen.

He found milk, cookies, and a frozen pizza—something he suspected she'd considered tossing while he was gone. "I like it," he argued as she glared at it on her way to finish making his bed. "Leave that. I'll do it. Don't you have a book to write?"

She nodded and tossed it on his bed before returning to the living room. "You're right. You're a big boy and I've been planning this chapter for an hour."

"I'll bet it's been a month."

"Okay," she amended, "I've been planning this section of the chapter for an hour. I think I know exactly how I want to word it."

While he ate, she powered up her laptop and got comfortable. It didn't take long for her to become engrossed in her work. He watched her type, her expression changing from concerned, happy, sad, to frightened as the story warranted. She didn't always act so animated, but he loved it when she did.

Wes glanced around, his eyes settling back on his sister. At home in this room, her dress complimented the subtle blues and greens of the walls and fabrics, and the breeze drifting through the window filled the room with the subtle fragrance of lilacs. She belonged in her little cottage at the end of Sycamore Court.

Would she be happy in another house? She'd lived in this one for over five years. Not much had changed in the house during that time. She purchased the new entertainment center and the new recliner in the office. The mudroom was also new. He winced at the thought of that mudroom and all it signified to his sister now. He was right to encourage her to buy the new house.

Her voice broke into his thoughts. "Oh, I forgot to tell you. I have a prospectus I need you to read."

"What?" Wes' mind struggled to switch gears. Jet lag would be a bear this trip.

"One of my favorite designers wants me to invest in a clothing line. The prospectus is on the desk in your room."

He nodded, smiling to himself as she went back to working on her novel. That kind of thoughtfulness always made him feel sorry for his parents. They didn't know the Alexa who would describe her guest room as "his room" simply because he slept there from time to time. They didn't know her because they refused to. The daughter they claimed to know was selfish—a sensationalist selling her talent for filthy lucre and, at best, backslidden from the Lord.

As much as he hated to do it, he pushed himself out of the chair and shuffled down the hall to the guest room—his room. There on the desk sat a stack of papers. That they were there, instead of her office, told him much—she wanted his input.

He sat on the bed, the papers in hand. The prospectus impressed him. Whoever sent it had done thorough research and had made careful calculations. As he read the amount requested, Wes forced himself not to whistle. Did Alexa have that much money to risk?

Even as he thought it, Wes knew the question was

unnecessary. Six books at over a million copies per book, another one hitting the shelves any week now, movie rights on two, no, three books. She could probably lose the money and not miss it. That he wasn't sure galled him as it always did. Alexa was too private for her own good sometimes.

A glance around him again made him question his assessment of her wealth. Was she as well off as he assumed? She lived simply enough. Houses weren't cheap in Fairbury, but hers was one of the smallest in town. She drove a modest car, and apart from her crazy wardrobe, she had few expenses. *Then again,* he thought to himself, *she can be generous — almost to a fault. That thing with Lori and the ball...*

As he realized that he'd turned to analyzing his sister and her finances, he meandered down the hall and leaned against the doorway to the living room, watching her as she worked. The incongruity of the picture struck him. With her hair piled high on her head, a few wispy tendrils around her face, she sat semi-reclined on her sofa. The dress she wore, white with tiny blue flowers scattered across it, had probably been recreated from some BBC period film. The room — one he always thought she should call a parlor instead of a living room — suited her ensemble, but the laptop her fingers danced across simply did not fit.

"Do you realize how ridiculous this picture is?"

Alexa glanced up at him, looking perplexed. "Which one?" Her eyes roamed the room, pausing at each of the few prints on her walls.

"No, Miss Hartfield. I mean the picture you make sitting on that couch — hmm, should that be davenport?" He shook his head. "Whatever — sitting there in your Victorian — "

"Edwardian, my dear brother."

Wes nodded solemnly, as if the era made a whit of difference to him. "Edwardian — got it. So you sit there on your davenport, in your Edwardian dress, your hair piled high up like..." His history failed him. "Like someone famous, during whatever century that was, with smelly flowers outside your window, and a laptop. It just doesn't work, Alexa."

"You did fine for a minute there, well, aside from your lack of basic historical time reference, you really did okay. However, once you called fragrant flowers 'smelly,' you ruined the effect."

A whiff of breeze sent a fresh burst of lilac through the room. Alexa rolled over, punching the pillow and trying desperately to quell the voices in her head. *That's the last time you're allowed to start asking your characters questions after ten o'clock,* she whined to herself as she pulled the blankets over her shoulder.

Every soporific inducement trick she'd ever tried failed. She "watched" her favorite romantic comedy in her mind, forcing herself to think of every scene in as much detail as possible. Why it usually worked, she couldn't say. It didn't work this time.

Prayer, a fail-safe she tried not to use, also failed. Frustrated, she threw back the covers, grabbed her summer robe, and slipped from her room. A glance down the hall showed Wes' door open. She tiptoed to the door and pulled it shut.

In the living room, she turned on the smaller lamp and pulled out her laptop. If she couldn't sleep, she'd work. Two seconds into the book, she decided she might as well grab something to munch on and some tea—she must have tea.

The kettle tried to whistle, but she snatched it from the stove at the first hint of one. Chamomile tea, a few cherry-almond cookies, and a napkin. Everything she needed to keep her going—or put her to sleep. Settled in her seat, laptop ready for her to work, she began.

The scene taunted her from several angles. Written from the viewpoint of the killer, it gave her the chance to build anticipation in ways a victim couldn't possibly know. However, that gave the reader too much insight into how the killer thought. She tried both. Deleted both. She tried the husband of the victim. Deleted that too.

Frustrated, she stood, pacing the room as she tried to recreate each one in her mind. Endless possibilities gave endless problems. She just had to find the right one. Somehow.

A new idea niggled at the back of her mind, pushing forward with the dogged determination of a toddler trying to reach his mother in a crowded room. Mother—no. Toddler—no. The woman's son—he was just old enough to understand and remember odd things that would both enlighten and confuse the reader.

The neighbor's cat screeched outside her door. Alexa jumped. Frustrated, she unlocked it and flipped on the porch light. "Scat!" Her hiss did little to scare off the animal, but one step outside sent the obnoxious creature racing across lawns.

The spring air, though cool, filled her lungs, making her want more. Alexa pulled open the door and grabbed the afghan from the back of her chair. Settling into her place on the couch, she tucked it around her and reached for her laptop again.

It took half a dozen—a dozen perhaps—tries before Alexa found a comfortable groove. Writing from the perspective of a boy of eight proved more challenging than she'd expected, but she was determined to master the boy's voice and the way he thought.

Lost in her new world, she never saw the lights that flashed through her living room window. She didn't hear the click of the latch on the gate or feel the slight whoosh of air as the screen opened. She did, however, hear Joe as he asked, "What do you think you're doing up at three o'clock in the morning?" Not only did she hear it, she jumped, her laptop flying from her and crashing against her coffee table.

"Aaak! Oh, no! Joe!" She pulled it gingerly from the floor, wincing at the damaged screen. "So help me, if you made me lose the scene I just did, I'll kill you." Her eyes rolled upward. "I can't believe I just threatened to kill a cop."

"I'd say I deserved it." He came around behind her and peered at the mess in her hands. "Is it ruined?"

"Screen is shot, but who cares? I finally got that scene

almost right." She punched control and 's,' hoping it would save the document if auto-save had somehow failed her. "I wonder..."

"I'm sorry. I just saw lights on and got concerned."

"Couldn't sleep." She chewed her lip. "Think I can close it? Think the wireless will do its thing if the screen doesn't work?"

"I don't know. I'll drive it to that guy in Rockland if you like—Nolan?"

"I can do it." It felt risky, but she tried closing the laptop. It wouldn't close. "Well, maybe that's for the best. I can't ruin it more by closing it if it won't close."

Joe examined the hinges, shrugging. "Don't know much about them. I'm still using my old desktop dinosaur—when I have to." He sighed. "Anyway, have Nolan send me the bill."

"I've got it, but thanks."

He shook his head. "No, really. How can I feel like I've done my penance if I don't pay for it?"

Alexa set the pile of twisted plastic and metal on the coffee table and pulled her knees to her chest. "Last I heard, you weren't Catholic." She frowned. "Have you eaten recently?"

"Chips half an hour ago."

She stood. "How about a sandwich?"

"You don't have—"

Ignoring him, she flung the afghan from her and hurried into the kitchen. As she pulled deli meat, cheese, lettuce, onion, and tomato from the fridge, she pretended to listen to him protest that it was unnecessary. The pretense lasted half a minute at best. "Hey, the drawer in my office—right-hand side. Can you get me the notebook in there and a pen?"

"Still on that scene?"

Alexa shrugged. "Don't want to forget the ideas I'm getting."

"Where's that recorder I gave you?"

Alexa swallowed hard, searching for an honest answer that wouldn't let him go searching and finding it amongst the other half dozen mini-recorders she had. "I need the hand-brain connection right now. If I can't type, I need to write." It wasn't a good answer, but it was honest.

He returned and set them in front of her. "Wes snores."

"Yep."

"How can you stand it?"

"I can't. I use earplugs—that's why I couldn't sleep. I forgot the earplugs!"

Joe took the sandwich from her. "I'll grill, you write."

She scrawled out a page or so of shorthand and closed the book. As he flipped the sandwich in the pan, Joe jerked his head at the notebook. "Was that shorthand?"

"Mmmhmm." The sandwich smelled amazing. Alexa pulled out the bread again and began layering meat and cheese on it. "Do mine while you're at it."

"Since when do people still learn shorthand?"

"Since you don't want them to know what you're writing." Even as she spoke it, Alexa winced. Telling a cop, even if he was becoming a good friend, that she didn't want him to read your writing just sounded guilty—of something.

"You know—"

"I know. That's not how I meant it." Alexa sliced the tomatoes thin and pulled the leaves from the lettuce. "Onion?"

"Sure, my hot date will probably be with a drunk and disorderly. I'll subdue him with one whiff."

"Bet that's one date you'd love to stand you up."

Joe grinned. "You betcha."

As she packed some cookies, his sandwich, and an orange in a plastic container, Alexa put on as casual an air as possible and said, "Oh, and my hat arrived."

"Should I be scared?"

She passed him the container and plopped a paper towel on top. "No, but you might want to invest in a better razor..."

24

Chapter 3

Joe's eyes bugged at the sight of Alexa's so-called hat. From the mischievous glint in her eye, he suspected he should be glad she hadn't worn it to church that morning—perhaps as a warning. "You win. I'll keep the mustache shaved for a year if you promise you won't wear that thing to the play."

"Deal." She winked. "Just think how much easier it'll be to run a razor all over your face instead of having to watch out for your mustache. I'm really doing you a favor."

Wes laughed. "I've never seen her like this. She likes mustaches on men."

Joe's eyebrows rose questioningly. Alexa tossed a pillow at her brother while giving Joe a "can you believe this guy" look. She rose to replenish their half-empty glasses of iced tea. "Ok, Wes. Tell me about the house. Joe's here now; he can be the voice of reason."

Wes launched into a description of the house's benefits and the great deal he'd convinced the current owners to give her. "They've been planning to sell and move a little closer to Lake Vienna. You gave them the incentive to do it a little sooner."

"Mmmhmm. I gave them," she muttered. "What about price?"

"Well, they didn't come a full five thousand under appraised, but they did go to thirty-five hundred. You've got to admit, that's pretty close."

Joe compared the pictures, the inspection reports, and the disclosure statement Wes handed him. "Um, are you sure this isn't undervalued? I've seen what homes over there go for, and this is about twenty thousand under what I would have expected."

"You were looking to buy over there?" Alexa cocked her head. "Why didn't you?"

"Can't afford it—not on a cop's salary. But, it never hurts to look."

"You should move over here," Wes commented. "Houses are smaller and cheaper."

"And aren't on the market long enough to have a chance to schedule a showing."

"Which," Wes added as if it decided the issue, "is why I want her to move. I'll rent this house, get a roommate, and then I've got a place near her without intruding on her privacy."

Joe shook his head. "Why would you rent a house? You're never home."

"Exactly why I am the perfect choice for a roommate. Anyone would love to have me." He pointed to the top of the three-story house in the photo. "She needs more space and look here." He tapped the picture. "This has a bedroom and a sitting room. The lighting in the sitting room is terrible, but I think it should be turned into her closet. Can you imagine from about there..." he pointed to a spot between windows, "to the other side all being one huge closet?"

Joe examined the pictures again, listening closely to Wes' ideas for Alexa's new home. In his mind, the deal only needed her signature to seal it. Before Wes had made his desire for her house so evident, he hadn't been sure Alexa would buy, but now he had no doubt.

"Okay, so Joe, you think this house is worth that much more?" Alexa asked. "Why would they sell it for less than they can get?"

Joe started to answer, but Wes preempted him. "I told them you were interested in the house—that you had decided you had a specific budget, and if they were interested in selling at that price, to please let me know. They took it with a small counter offer."

Alexa looked over the documents once more. With a bit of a sigh, she passed them to Wes. "Call them and see if they'll let me take a walk-through." She shook her head. "This is the oddest way to buy a house I've ever heard of."

Sensing that Alexa was done with the house discussion, Joe started to suggest a game of Malarkey, but Wes pulled out another manila folder and handed it to him. "What do you make of this?"

He took the folder, noting that Alexa looked both eager and nervous as he opened it. "What is it?"

Before Alexa could reply, the phone rang. She waved at Wes to start explaining and hurried into the dining room for quiet as she answered. Seconds later, Joe and Wes stood as they heard Alexa exclaim, "I'm on my way!"

She hurried through the living room, ignoring Wes and Joe, and almost ran down the hall. Two necks craned down the hall and watched as she flung open Wes' door. Thumps and bumps echoed back to them.

Joe glanced first at his watch and then at his cellphone as if it would tell him something more. "Wha—"

"I don't know."

Usually, Joe appreciated a quick and to-the-point answer, but this time it didn't satisfy. He followed Wes to the room and they found Alexa dragging suitcases from under the bed, packing them willy-nilly. Wes took a pile of random dresses from the suitcase and said, "Annie, what is it?"

Joe wondered, and not for the first time, why Wes called her "Annie" at tense or tender moments. He listened, concern growing as Alexa dissolved into tears. Her sobs prompted him to step back into the hall, but he watched as Wes stood in the middle of the room, his arms wrapped around her.

Wes turned his head as he deciphered the awkward mumbles she gave between bursts of emotion. "Lorie is back in the hospital and a liver is en route. They'll be doing surgery tonight."

Joe paused, watching Alexa's brother comfort her before he turned from the room and pulled out his phone again. If he knew Jeremy, he knew his brother was probably debating whether to call. He'd take away the debate. "Hey, Jeremy. Alexa just got the call. You okay?"

Wes watched as Alexa walked alone through security and toward the first-class lounge. Considering the increased notoriety surrounding her after the murders in Fairbury, he was as grateful as she was that the renovations in the lounge were complete. Not all authors have such national facial recognition, but with Alexa's unique style, people recognized her everywhere she went. The lounge made travel a little less difficult.

Alexa turned to take one last glance at her brother and watched as he shoved his hands in his pockets and shuffled off into the crowd. He'd wanted to go with her, but after ten minutes of arguing, Joe had sided with Alexa. He needed to be rested for his next assignment.

After an hour in the lounge, an hour on the plane, half an hour through Midway International Airport, and another half hour of weaving through the Chicago traffic, Alexa finally burst through the hospital doors and hurried to the information desk. "I'm here to be with a friend while his daughter is in surgery—transplant?"

The volunteer at the information desk showed her a map and explained how to get to the right floor. She took a wrong turn—twice—but finally found the correct waiting room. A volunteer asked her name and the patient's name. He assured her that if the doctor shared any news whenever she left the room for any reason, Alexa could get it from the volunteer desk in one corner.

Unfamiliar people filled the room. Families and friends congregated in small huddles as though ready to plan their next football play. Occasionally a child cried or a book dropped, but otherwise, the room remained relatively quiet.

Only the drone of a television in the corner kept it from feeling like a library.

Alexa sat in the corner nearest the door. She held a book in her hands, but the words swam in nonsensical sentences of unrelated ideas and actions. She eventually gave up the idea of ever reading it and put it away. Nervous, Alexa folded her hands in her lap, forcing them to lie still and she prayed.

An hour ticked past—two. She jumped at the sound of Darrin Thorne's voice beside her. "Alexa?"

She rose to hug him, and smiled through the glass door as she saw Joe standing there. "I think Jeremy called Joe. He's here."

Darrin turned and gave Joe a wan smile before taking the seat next to Alexa's and stretching out his legs. Alexa stepped through the door and into the hallway. "Hey, you didn't have to come. What about your shift?"

Joe shrugged. "Jeremy asked me to come. I took a few vacation days, but I have to be back by Thursday night."

"Where is he—Jeremy? Is he okay?"

"Getting drinks, ordering flowers, buying up all the stuffed animals, grabbing a deck of cards, and doing who knows what else." He frowned at her. "You been here long?"

"Forty minutes... I can't remember. Darrin says they just took her back. It's amazing how long it takes to get things prepped. I actually made it in time to see her, but I didn't know."

He nodded. "Hey, I got your bags at the airport too."

"Mine? How? I don't—I can't believe they let you do that."

"There was some mix-up with unclaimed baggage. They sent them through again with my flight—probably the Rockland connection—and when I saw yours, I just grabbed them."

She nodded slowly. "Where are they now?" The question annoyed her. Why did she ask? Why did she care?

"Rented a car—they're in the trunk." He looked at her closely. "Have you eaten?"

Alexa thought for a moment. She couldn't remember

when she'd eaten last. Just then, her stomach rumbled. "And some doubt the power of suggestion."

Joe nodded at Darrin. "Has he eaten?"

"Don't know."

"I'll see if he wants anything or if he wants to come with us. You need food. You won't be any good to him if your blood sugar crashes."

His last words drove away the argument she'd planned. "Okay... I could check into The Drake too, I suppose."

Joe squeezed her arm and went to talk to Darrin. She saw Darrin glance her way, concerned, and then nod at Joe. Everything had been too centered on her for too long. This should be about Lorie. Even as she thought it, she understood. They all wanted to *do* something. She needed to let these men *do*.

They rode to The Drake, talking about the clothing line prospectus and the pros and cons of investing. Joe's efforts to keep her mind off the surgery couldn't have been more obvious, but she appreciated it. As they pulled into the porte-cochère, Alexa kicked the floorboard, startling Joe.

"I'm doing it. This is ridiculous. My whole life is about 'playing it safe.' I live in a small house, have my little luxuries, and don't really do anything. What's the point of having this money if I can't enjoy doing something fun with it—something that helps more than just me?"

"Makes sense to me." He hurried around the other side of the car and opened her door. "If I was in your position, I would. It looks well planned, and you know fashion. I'd have a lawyer look it over, though."

"I know out-of-date fashion." She accepted the suitcase handle. "I don't know commercial fashion."

"You're known for yours, though. You can make it sell simply by your affiliation." Joe's voice held a twinge of pride that amused her. "Besides," he added, "your 'out-of-date fashion' was once commercial, right?"

"Let's get me checked in before you turn me into the next Coco Chanel."

Joe watched as Alexa systematically unpacked her suitcase. The concept was foreign to him. He'd never unpacked at a hotel in his life. She separated her clothing into two piles. One went into the closet—the other stayed on the bed. He started to ask what was wrong with the second pile when she picked up the room phone and dialed for laundry service.

Laundry service—to him it belonged in the fictional hotels of movies. He'd never known anyone who used it. "What's wrong with those?"

"They're a wrinkled mess."

"Don't they give you an iron in here? At these prices, you'd at least expect an iron."

Alexa's melodic laughter filled the room, warming his heart. The Alexa he knew had almost returned. "Joe, at these prices, most people don't wash their own clothes, much less iron them."

After twenty minutes of careful attention to the minutest details of her possessions and the room, Joe realized the problem. Procrastination. "Hey, Alexa. I'm really hungry. Do you think they'd have a table down at the restaurant?"

She reached for the phone. "I'll call for a table at the steakhouse. You'll like it there."

Having something to do seemed to settle her. She made reservations, handed her laundry to the attendant that arrived to pick it up, and then slipped into the bathroom. Joe shuffled his feet, waiting. Just as he was about to resort to pacing, she reemerged looking fresh and perfectly styled for the Roaring Twenties.

"I like that dress—reminds me of your soft one."

She frowned at him. "Soft one?"

"Yeah... last winter you had that pink one on your bed when I had to inspect your house. Man, whatever that skirt was made of was so soft that I would have had pajamas made out of it—even if they were pink too." He winked. "Not that I'd admit that, of course."

"Of course. I think I know which one you mean. Until Laidie made me that dress, I didn't know wool could be so snuggleable."

Joe's eyes widened in surprise. "That was wool? It felt like flannel that was super-infused with soft... um— somethings."

"Eloquent." She hooked her arm in Joe's and strolled through the doorway and into the hall with exaggerated movements. "I'm dressed twenty years too early, but I want to sing 'On the Town' and race all over New York right now."

"Um... no singing. Also, no racing anywhere. We're going to eat, you're going to change into something comfortable for the hospital, and we're to go back there and take Darrin some food."

"Agreed. Well, except I'm not changing. I chose this dress because it is cool and comfortable."

As they as the hostess seated them, Alexa stared at her menu. "I wonder if they serve prime rib on Sundays..." She smiled to herself in a way that left Joe wondering if she was thinking of her meal or something else.

"I don't know, but since it isn't Sunday, I don't think that's a relevant question," he teased.

The four of them sat uncomfortably slumped in the waiting room chairs. Jeremy and Joe half dozed fitfully as Darrin tried to relax. The minutes ticked by as though they were hours. Adrenaline fought against melatonin until their bodies screamed with their minds for relief. The surgery continued.

Periodically, someone stepped in the room with minor updates, but the news was minimal at best. Grateful for any news, Alexa clung to it with the hope that any word meant things were going well—that the doctors wouldn't say anything if things were bad. Joe insisted that it would be better to hear no news at all rather than the few words of "things are going as expected" every couple of hours. Darrin and Jeremy looked whipped as they spun on the emotional yo-yo that came with waiting, insufficient news, and the desire to know all was well with the girl they each loved in his own special way. Each time the door opened and a nurse or doctor looked their way, the hope intensified, crushing them as they realized that—again—the news belonged to someone else.

In the wee hours of the morning, just as Alexa began to lose the fight against sleep, the surgeon entered the room, beaming. "We got a slow start, but she did splendidly. She's in intensive care, and we'll have to watch her closely, of course, but I'm optimistic."

Once the doctor left, Darrin collapsed in wracking sobs of relief. Alexa turned to him, holding him until he regained some semblance of self-control. "I'm sorry. I just—"

"Shh. It's fine."

Darrin urged Alexa to get some sleep and went in search of the ICU to ask if he could see his daughter yet. Alexa returned to her seat as though prepared to make it her permanent Chicago residence, but Joe shook his head. "Oh, no."

Alexa stared at him. "What?"

"You are not going to settle in for a long winter's *or* spring's nap. She's out of surgery, the doctor is pleased, you're exhausted, and you're not going to be any help to them if you don't get some sleep. I'm taking you to the hotel."

"Excuse me?"

She started to complain, but Joe pulled out his cellphone. "Shall I call Wes and let him do the arguing?"

"That was low," she growled.

"Yeah, so was his threat to slug me and make me arrest him if I didn't." Joe grinned at her disbelief. "He said if I threatened to call him, you'd be reasonable."

Alexa's eyes flashed with partially repressed anger. "Oh, he did, did he? I'll take that up with him later."

Jeremy stood. "I have a paper due tomorrow, Joe. I've got to get back. I can come in the afternoon, but someone should be here in the morning." He glanced at Alexa. "Please get some sleep so you'll be rested. If you're rested, I think Darrin might consider leaving long enough so he can at least get a nap."

Knowing that protest was futile, Alexa picked up her purse and caplet and gave a slight grimace. "I know when I'm beaten. Let's go."

Chapter 4

Alexa stared at the text message, hesitating. She'd already been gone for nearly an hour. Maybe if she hadn't taken the time for a good meal…but a week of hospital food had eventually driven her to a restaurant with seasoned dishes that didn't taste institutionalized. Now the dilemma before her: stay or go?

She stepped into the elevator and rode it to Lorie's floor. Just outside Lorie's door, she hesitated. The girl still slept, but Darrin wouldn't be there for hours. If she left now, Lorie might wake up alone—and Alexa didn't have the heart to imagine that.

The nurse saw her deliberating in the doorway. "Something wrong?"

"How long do you think she'll be asleep?"

"She's tired—probably another hour at least. She's still weak after that rejection scare."

Nodding, Alexa glanced at the knobs and dials on Lorie's IV. "Her meds are straightened out though, right? She's still fine?"

"The doctor's confident that they've got the dosage correct now. Most patients need an adjustment or two."

Alexa chewed her lip. They didn't need her at the appointment, but she did want to see the property that Silva and Rhette had found for a storefront. Choosing Chicago had been a less expensive proposition than New York City.

The nurse touched her arm, smiling understandingly. "If you need to go have a quiet meal in a decent restaurant, take a nap, go shopping—even take in a movie, do it. You'll do her more good if you're refreshed and awake rather than exhausted."

"It's nothing like that. I have an opportunity to see some property a business partner is considering, and I can't—"

"Go, we'll be here with her. Her grandmother is coming this afternoon she said; remember? She might be here before Lorie wakes up, but even if she isn't, a few minutes alone won't hurt her."

"Still—"

"Go. We'll take good care of her."

Three women followed the realtor through the space, half-attending to the man's monologue on the virtues of each piece of the building. He punctuated nearly every sentence with "at the end of the Magnificent Mile." Alexa, desperate to silence him, lost all patience and finished his next statement before he had a chance. "And of course," she said, trying to keep her tone less snide than she felt, "it's nearly the 'Welcome to' sign of the Magnificent Mile."

To her relief, the man beamed. "Exactly—the perfect place for a boutique, and the workroom above is excellent for a design studio—so much light."

"We'd have to have someone come in to inspect the basement," Silva said, staring down the steps. "Any dampness down here at all would mean significant losses. We can't risk that."

"But is the space sufficient? It doesn't matter how great it is if there isn't enough." Alexa turned to the realtor. "Is the square footage the same on each floor?"

"Yes. Each floor is just under a thousand square feet."

"So…" Alexa walked eight feet from the back wall. "If we put dressing rooms on each side, we'd have plenty of space for two good-sized rooms. Can we get away with just two, or do we need three?"

Silva frowned. "What were you thinking about the space in the middle?"

"Oh, if the back wall was mirrors—a giant, framed one covering the door, and two padded seats along the dressing rooms, there'd be a place to change and step out to view with the mirrors..."

"Right." Relieved that Rhette caught her vision, Alexa turned to Silva. "Are we offering an alteration service? Will there be room upstairs to do that?"

"I don't see how we can avoid it."

"It'd be nice if we had sales staff who knew how to pin for alterations. That would prevent the hassle of having someone on staff fulltime." Alexa sighed. "This really isn't my decision. I'm just thinking aloud. I'm sure you'll come up with the perfect solution."

Something in Silva relaxed with those words. "Well, it is your money..."

"Not anymore. I turned it over to the corporation, so as far as I'm concerned, it's not mine. I chose to trust you both with it."

The realtor checked his watch—twice. "I do have another client who would like to see the building, so if you'd rather keep looking..."

Alexa laughed at the panicked glances between Rhette and Silva. "I don't doubt that this property is in high demand, but if he really had someone angling to move in that fast, he wouldn't be quite so eager to push you into a decision." As the man started to bluster, she added, "That said, I think it's perfect. If the decision was solely mine, I'd take it."

"It's not too expensive?" Rhette winced at the sharp look Silva sent her.

She ignored the silent chastisement and reassured Rhette. "If you're going to be taken seriously, you need a solid storefront in a good area."

"What kind of color scheme would we do?"

Silva stepped back. "I want art deco—everywhere. The architectural angles, the fonts—the works. It'll fit so well."

As Silva and Rhette debated gray or black as the dominant color, Alexa stood at the doorway, glancing up and down the street. If only the building was a block or two closer to the "mile." The cost would be enormous—too much for a new business. This would have the advantage of lower rent and spillover exposure.

Her mind tried to visualize window displays, mannequins, racks—customers shopping. The business would succeed; of that, she had no doubt. The sketches Rhette planned for the first season had impressed her.

Just as Alexa began to ask how long it would take for renovations, she overheard Rhette ask Silva, "Did you hire that accountant yet? Darrel?"

"Yep. Just this morning. I'll send the first receipts to him after we sign the lease."

Her mind raced at the idea. An accountant, a designer, a manager—they had it all. Once they hired pattern drafters, dressmakers, and did a launch for the line, the business would be on its way to success or failure. Alexa glanced at the eager women at the other end of the shop, chatting about renovations. *Lord, I sure hope for their sakes that it's a success. They've worked so hard.*

Lorie listened as Alexa tried to describe her favorite pieces of the line, excited about the possibilities. "I hope I'm well enough to come to the show," the girl said.

"You'd look fabulous in most of the ones I've seen. I'll have Rhette make up a couple of my favorites and see how you like the feel of them." At Lorie's protest, she added, "I am allowed to buy a friend a couple of dresses." She winked. "Besides, what's the point of having an in with the designer if I don't get to use it now and then?"

The girl—looking younger than usual—picked at the sheet. She started to speak, but a hospital volunteer stepped into the room carrying a narrow vase with a single red rose. "Lorie Thorne?"

The girl blushed, giving her the first real color Alexa had seen in a long time. "That's me."

"Got something for you. The girl who took the order is

totally jealous—says if you don't want him, she'll take him."

Lorie fumbled with the card, her blush deepening as she read it. She hesitated before slipping the card back into the envelope and passing it to Alexa. "I can't believe that without you, I wouldn't have met him."

The volunteer laughed. "Man, I love days like this. You have a good one."

As the door closed behind the woman, Alexa wiggled the tiny florist's card. "Are you sure you want me to read it?"

"If a stranger in the gift shop knows what he said, I think you should be able to."

Still uncertain, Alexa slid the card from the small envelope and turned it over. A smile crept over her lips as she read.

It's too soon to tell you how I feel & stupid to pretend you don't know. So glad you're better. I love you. Jeremy.

"The girl downstairs is right. He's a keeper."

"Dad says he'll consider letting me go to Wheaton for pre-law." Lorie's smile grew as she accepted the card back from Alexa and returned it to the pick in the vase.

"Where were you planning to go?"

"Northwestern—Dad's alma mater, of course. They have a good law school, but I can do pre-law at Wheaton and then transfer anywhere."

Alexa laughed. "If you want to follow Jeremy after he graduates, it'll have to be someplace like southern California, Arizona, or maybe Florida. Joe says Jeremy will leave the cold as soon as he can."

Darrin hurried into the room mid-apology. "I'm sorry it took so long. Has Dr.—" He stopped. "Oh, I thought you went home today."

"I can leave…" Alexa willed herself to look affronted and prayed she didn't appear ridiculous instead.

"Very funny." He nodded at the rose. "I suppose I can't thank you for that."

"Of course, you can, Daddy!" Lorie winked at Alexa. "She did introduce us, after all."

The two-second look of relief vanished. "Dare I ask to

read the card?"

Alexa spoke up before Lorie could give her father more risk factors for a heart attack. "I'd recommend that you don't."

"Do I need to call out my thugs to teach him a lesson?"

She shrugged. "Only if you don't value honesty and integrity."

"He'll live—for now." Darrin collapsed onto the end of Lorie's bed. "Did you answer about the doctor?"

"Hasn't been here yet."

"Whew. Traffic was the worst I've seen in a month—must have been at least two accidents."

The nurse arrived with evening medications. "Did Dr. Jansen tell you about the drains? He'll take them out tonight."

"I thought he said tomorrow?"

The nurse shook her head. "Nope. Your fluid output is low enough to get them out, so out they go." She recorded the medication on Lorie's chart and then added, "All the doctors are a little late today. Traffic must be a bear."

Once the nurse left the room, Alexa stood. "I should go. I haven't packed a thing, and I'm starving."

"I'll walk you out," Darrin offered.

"No, spend time with your daughter. You wouldn't want to miss the doctor either."

"That's okay. I'll be fine." Lorie fingered her cellphone. "I want to call Jeremy anyway."

"You heard the girl," Darrin agreed, rolling his eyes. "She wants to call Jeremy. We're third and fourth wheels."

"Three and four wheels are more stable than two..."

Darrin winked at his daughter. "She makes a point. Maybe we should stay."

"Get out of here! I want to talk to my boyfriend without eavesdroppers."

Alexa waited until they were in the elevator before snickering. "She is hysterical when it comes to that boy."

"And she's giving me gray hair."

An eyebrow rose just seconds before the other. She tried to resist teasing—for half a second. "How would you tell?"

Chapter 5

The stroll through Fairbury comforted her with its slow familiarity. After a week and a half in the hustle and bustle of Chicago, Alexa enjoyed walking along the tree-canopied streets and admiring the budding roses in yards as she passed. During the three weeks since Lorie's transplant, she had spent her time running errands, sitting at the girl's bedside, and discussing business plans. She longed for simple activities again—things like cooking and shopping.

She waved at Judith as the officer drove past, cruising up and down Fairbury's streets. To her surprise, the car whipped around and pulled up beside her. Judith jumped from the cruiser and strode around the front of the vehicle with the same deliberate swagger used by all of the town's cops.

Alexa couldn't help but note the contrast between herself and Fairbury's only female police officer. Judith wore the dark pants and shirt of the Fairbury police force and boasted a fine assortment of accessories—gun belt, holster, flashlight, and the policeman's cap perched on cropped hair almost the exact shade of Alexa's. Her radio occasionally bleeped static as if to show it was still worked. On the other hand, Alexa looked as if she stepped from the pages of a Gatsby novel.

"You're back."

"Just got in yesterday."

"Two trips in three weeks. Good thing we caught our serial killer, or the chief would have had a coronary." The officer blushed. "Please tell me that girl didn't have a heart transplant."

"Nope, liver."

"Whew. I'm not known for my delicacy, but that would have been cold—even for me."

Alexa adjusted her hat to see Judith's face better. "You want something. What is it?"

"I never was very good at small talk," Judith laughed. "I need a favor."

Wary, Alexa searched the other woman's face for some clue as to what the officer wanted. "What…"

"It's this stupid fundraiser for the prom. At the end of the mustache vote-off, we always do that stupid bake sale. We get a hairy winner, a sugar-coma, and the kids get to have a night of decadence before graduation."

"Ok…" Alexa's confusion mounted. "What's the problem?"

"Look at me! I'm not old enough to grow a mustache, and even if I was, I can't compete with Martinez and Joe." Judith winked. "Even the chief is playing this year. He gave me the stupid job of organizing the stupid bake sale. I'm the stupid girl, you know."

"I'd hardly call you stupid…"

"I got roped into this, didn't I?"

Alexa had the crazy feeling she should say something like "touché" but couldn't imagine why. "Okay, so you want me to organize a bake sale?" She didn't understand what the big deal was. "I can do that."

Judith beamed. "Great. With you helping, it'll be a success, if only because people will want to see you—no offense."

"None taken, but what will you do?"

"Work. I'm better at that than hawking cupcakes at fifty cents a pop."

"If you only charge fifty cents, those kids will be holding their prom in someone's basement and using crickets for a live band."

Judith shrugged. "Good enough for me. Thanks. I'll see you around."

Alexa took three steps before she called back, "Hey,

Judith!"

"Yeah?"

"Is the goal to have a bake sale, or is the goal to make money?"

"To make money, of course. Why?"

"Am I allowed to do whatever I like to raise it, or do I have to do the bake sale?" Other ideas, most much more interesting than selling brownies and cookies, swirled in her mind.

"You'd have to get the mayor's approval first. Never know when zoning issues or whatever comes into play, but Tim is good about that. He just wants the kids to have a good prom."

Alexa nodded. "Good."

Joe listened, munching on a plate of eggplant parmesan as Alexa explained her idea. "So, the officers, and all other male citizens who want to, make the lunchboxes and those are auctioned off. Then, after they judge the contest and we eat the lunches, we'll have the dance. I mean, come on. We should have a dance if we're doing this for prom."

"Sadie Hawkins?"

"Oh!" Alexa brightened even more. "That's a great idea! It can be Sadie Hawkins Day—perfect with the guys making the lunches and everything."

Joe took another bite of his food as he shook his head. "The poor women will starve." His finger toyed with his fork. "Will you be bidding on a lunch?"

"If I see one that looks interesting..."

Joe stood and refilled his glass with more grape juice. "Okay, I'll participate under one condition, and remember, you owe me for that 'Music Man' thing. I'm still getting digs over Shannon's hat."

"Our agreement was that I would not wear it."

Joe glowered at her. "Alexa..."

"What's the condition?"

"You make my lunch and then be sure to win it."

She counter-offered. "Then you have to take me to the dance, which means you'll have to work to get the night off."

"Deal."

He stood once more and rinsed his plate. After draining his glass, he rinsed it as well. Alexa slipped on an apron and filled the sink with hot water, washing and rinsing plates and glasses as it filled. Something about the scene gripped him— so familiar now. As much as he hated to admit it, he enjoyed it. Joe grabbed a towel and dried each dish as she finished rinsing.

They talked about the clothing line, the work being done on her new house, and plans for the newly named Sadie Hawkins Day. As they worked and chatted, Joe noticed her glance surreptitiously at his upper lip a few times and chuckled. "It really drives you crazy, doesn't it?"

"What does?" Her feigned ignorance didn't fool him.

"You're a lousy actress. The mustache. You really don't like it, do you?"

"I can't say that. You look nice with it, but—"

He nodded. "But you think I look better without it."

"That's the understatement of the age," she muttered under her breath.

Joe barely heard it and snapped the damp towel at her. "You just want to doom me to a life of extra shaving." He leaned a bit closer and added, "You know, men are much more vain than we're given credit for." He snapped the towel again.

Alexa squealed and snatched another towel from the counter. Her first flick was pathetic. He snapped his towel again, making her jump. To dampen the towel, Alexa plunged her hands in the water and then dried them on the towel, all while trying to dodge Joe's strikes. "Impressive."

"You are so dead," she warned.

They dueled out the back door, into the mudroom, and onto the back lawn. They spun in circles around the lawn, dodging and striking with the towels until Joe grabbed Alexa's in midair. She took one look at his expression and raced for the house.

"That's not fair, Jordan Freidan," she cried, but her protest proved useless.

Joe, two steps behind her as she raced through the mudroom and into the kitchen for another towel, sent several stinging pops to her backside. She reached for another towel and found the basket empty. Her eyes darted around the room. Working quickly, she pulled at her apron strings as she dodged new snaps from Joe's towels.

Joe realized her intent almost too late. He dropped the towels in surrender, pinning her arms to the pantry door behind her. "Don't take it off."

"That's not fair! You stole my towel, and now you want to forbid me a simple weapon of self-defense?"

He jerked his head toward the towels he'd dropped. "I laid down my weapons. I am unarmed. Just—"

"Just what?"

He stood back. "Leave the apron on—it's cute." Joe grabbed his hat, keys, and the thermos of iced tea she'd made for him when he arrived. "I'm on duty in fifteen. Thanks for lunch—delicious as always."

"Sure—"

"Hey, I get an hour for dinner around seven. I'll bring steaks if you like."

Alexa nodded, following him to the door. "Bring three just in case. I think Wes gets back tonight. Doubt he'll be here anyway. I imagine he'll want to see Heather, but—"

"Gotcha. Three steaks."

Joe jogged down the walk, out the gate, and hopped into his Jeep. She waved once as he drove away before turning back to the kitchen and punching her iPod dock. Music filled the kitchen while she finished cleaning. Half an hour later, Alexa removed her apron. She stared at it, remembering. *An apron is cute?* she mused as she tossed it through the kitchen door and onto the washing machine.

Alexa sat at her desk, the office door open, with a notebook lying open before her. As she listened to the principal of Fairbury High School talk about raffles and such, she scribbled ideas on the page. She could add one of her Christmas tree sets, but would anyone buy a Christmas tree in May?

"That should work just fine. I'll go around and see what people will donate and we can decide between a raffle and a silent auction once we have that information." She listened, tapping her pen against the paper until she had the opportunity to cut her off. "Okay, I'll get back to you as soon as I can. Thanks. Bye." She hung up the phone before Principal Alderman could continue.

She flipped the page and reached for the phone again just as it rang. She stared at the screen and sighed—relief. "Hello, Silva. Good to see your name."

"Is there a problem?"

"Not at all. I've been stuck on the phone with the local high school principal and was sure she was calling back to suggest that we do a bake sale in addition to everything else we're doing."

"Small town life, I suppose. Look," Silva added, "I just thought I should update you with where things are. I have a few minutes so if you can spare the time…"

"Absolutely! You're all so good to keep me updated."

"You're taking such a big chance on us. We appreciate it."

"So what's happening? How are renovations?"

Silva described the work going on in the storefront, excited about the finished work. "Cabinetry, counters, shelving, and slat boards are up in the workroom. Rhette is in heaven."

"Have the machines arrived? How is the hiring going?"

"Great! I hired two shop assistants, and we're working on finding a manager for the year for The Cutting Room Floor. That way, I can stay in Chicago and help get this one going."

"Great idea!" The excitement building with the business

made her wish she were closer to watch it all. "So what about the patternmaker—did you find one?"

"Patterns are finished, prototypes made, and Rhette has several dressmakers working on the samples."

"Already?" They hadn't expected to reach that point for weeks.

Silva explained the sacrifices Rhette had made to create the patterns and prototypes. "She's been a machine. We're at least two weeks ahead of the game. If we keep going the way we are, we'll be able to move the launch up—which is part of why I'm calling. What do you think? Is it worth the financial risk to move everything up?"

Alexa's excitement grew. "I don't know for sure, but what are the pros and cons? Why wouldn't we?"

"It'd be better for the sales season to do things three weeks earlier, but to do that means if anything goes wrong, it'll cost a fortune to get stuff done in time."

"If you think it's reasonable to try, go for it. If the accounts take too hard of a hit, I'll see what my lawyer and financial manager say to another deposit."

"Really? I mean, it would be months down the road if it was that bad, and even then, if we get big orders, it won't be a problem, but..."

"I love it. I can't wait to see everything."

"Oh! That's the other thing I wanted to tell you. I sent an email with pictures."

At the words "sent an email," Alexa opened her new laptop and called up her email program. "Junk mail, junk mail, ooohhh—something is downloading slowly. Must be it."

The first pictures excited her. The workroom looked bright and clean, and the storeroom below had been completely revamped with better lighting and plenty of shelving. The first picture of a dress on a mannequin brought an exclamation of surprise. "Oh! Silva, the red polka dots—amazing!"

"Right? I tell you, Rhette is a genius. I've never seen anyone with such a consistent design aesthetic. People will recognize it anywhere but it's not repetitive."

"Where did you find that clear mannequin? Is it acrylic?"

"Yes—and we have a few Lucite forms too."

"I can't wait to see it all finished. It's going to be amazing—oh, these white Hollywood pants! I love them. They look perfect with that sweater."

"Did you see the evening dress?"

"Edwardian with beads?" Alexa nearly salivated as it loaded in her photo viewer. "I have to have one."

"She's made one for you that's a bit more authentic—same style but—"

Alexa interrupted as another dress appeared. "Oh, no. This midnight charmeuse. Is it thirties?"

"Yep. You know your decades. Awesome."

Alexa looked up and saw Wes leaning against the doorjamb, fighting to control his laughter. "Look, Silva, my brother is here and he's making fun of me for my clothing obsession. I have to go torture him. If you need anything, let me know."

As she disconnected, Alexa leaned back in the chair. "You know I'm going to have to tease you about Heather for that."

"How do you propose to do that?"

Her laughter filled the room. "How about we start with the fact that I mention Heather and you mention propose. Freud would have a heyday."

"Thankfully, I know you don't care for his opinions." Wes winked. "I thought maybe I could take you out to dinner. I want to hear about Marielle's work on your house."

Alexa closed her notebook, shaking her head. "You couldn't care less about what my interior designer is doing. You just want to know how soon I'll be out of here."

"Well..."

"Joe's bringing steaks soon. Talk to me while I make a pasta salad." As they stepped from the room, Alexa asked, "Heard from Mom or Jeanne lately?" The discouraged slump of his shoulders told her what he hadn't been willing to say.

Things between her brother and their parents weren't any better—maybe worse.

"Wes?"

"Hmm?" He didn't turn around.

"You can't make anyone be reasonable. How many times have you told me that?"

"I know."

She turned and followed him into his room, pulling him into a hug. "You're good to me. Thank you."

Chapter 6

The plans for Fairbury's big event slowly fell into place. As the day approached, Alexa grew a little nervous about her status as Joe's date. It was one thing to be eccentric—another to drag him into it and put him on display. Could he stand an entire day of it? Maybe she should be merciful and wear something "normal."

Frustrated, her fingers hovered over her cellphone keypad as she tried to choose the right words. All she had to do was ask—just ask. He'd be honest.

The door creaked and Joe's voice called out to her. "You got a minute?"

Just ask him, she ordered herself. *Just ask.* "I'm here. You hungry?"

"Nope, had a burger at the diner. I just brought the fliers from Tim. He said you wanted them?" Joe held out two small boxes. "Where should I put them?"

She led him to the office and pointed to the desk. "There's good." The opportunity waited.

All she had to do is ask. "You know, I thought I'd wear jeans and a t-shirt to the picnic, but I can't decide between two different dresses for the dance. Wanna give me your input?"

"Wanna?"

Alexa laughed, pulling Joe into Wes' room. "I was going for the fifties teen vernacular."

"Don't. It just doesn't work. In the fifties, you would have had a few fifty dollar words."

She pulled out the two dresses in question. "Which one?"

Joe leaned against the foot of the bed and crossed his

arms over his chest. "I didn't know you owned anything so... so... *boring.*"

"Boring?" She hadn't expected him to rave, but boring?

"I've never seen you wear anything remotely like those." He rifled through the closet, pulling dress after dress from the rod. "What about this?" He grabbed another. "This is nice." Another he shook in a seesaw fashion. "Hey, I really like this one."

After several dresses covered the two new dresses she'd purchased from Rhette—specifically to wear to the dance, no less—she took the hint. "You want me to be me."

"Would you want to be anyone else?"

As she rehung the dresses he'd piled on the bed, Alexa tried to explain. "I just thought it might be uncomfortable for you to be so—conspicuous."

"Where did you get the idea that I cared about—I didn't make you—"

"No! Never. I thought it just might get old or be different when it was something so big—tourists—friends."

Joe helped rehang the dresses, flipping through them as he did. When they finished, to her surprise, he moved to her room and looked through the dresses and gowns in that closet. When he didn't find what he wanted, he moved toward the office. "Does the one in there have dresses too?"

Suddenly she felt more extravagant than she ever had before. The closet was packed—with only spring clothing. The winter clothes were in storage. "Yep. Mostly dressier things—formals and semi-formals."

"Good. Exactly what I wanted."

Hangers slid across the closet rod before he pulled one from the rack. He laid it on the guest bed and pulled another dress from the closet. Her row of hats didn't seem to satisfy him, so he left the room again. Alexa snickered.

In her room, Joe found the perfect hat—the one she would have chosen to wear had she been looking—and removed it from the wall of hats by her door. He compared it with the dress in his hand and nodded. "There. Will you do me a favor?"

"Wear that dress and the one in the other room? What about my jeans idea?"

"Would you normally wear jeans to something like this?"

She returned to the guest room, picked up the dress, and held it up to herself, catching a glimpse of it in the mirror. Another favorite. "I'll wear this. You have good taste."

Joe nodded his approval. "Don't you forget it."

"I'm surprised. Why do you care what I wear?"

He pulled her from the room and led her down the steps. "Walk me to work."

"But your Jeep is here!"

"That'll give me an excuse to come back and get it and give you an excuse to bake a pie or something for me to enjoy after I get off work."

Laughing, she punched his arm. "Subtle. Answer the question. Why do you care what I wear?"

"More than anything, I just want you to be comfortable. You'll be most comfortable if you look like Alexa Hartfield, not Heather or Shannon or Judith or Lee…"

"I get it."

"Well," he added after they had passed a couple of houses, "I also have to admit that this is going to be a big tourist thing. You're a draw, Alexa. We'll do better and people will spend more if you look like the famous eccentric author, rather than everyone else."

From Heather's picture window, she and Wes watched them stroll past, laughing and talking earnestly. "Why doesn't he hold her hand or something?"

Wes shook his head and took Heather's. "Maybe no one ever told him how great it is."

Wes' eyes grew wide as Joe did grab Alexa's hand. He pulled Heather onto the porch and watched, laughing as Joe and Alexa wig-walked down the sidewalk and disappeared around the corner. Wes released Heather's hand and dropped his arm around her shoulder. "Just when I think there's hope for her..."

"Can't get models anywhere! We've sent out calls to all the agencies, but they don't have anyone available on the right date, they're the wrong look—I don't know what to do!"

"Did you call modeling schools?"

The silence almost sizzled between Fairbury and Chicago as Alexa waited for Silva to process her question. At last, the other woman said, "I could do that."

Something in Silva's tone bothered Alexa. Why would she call and ask for help if suggestions offended her? "I'm sure you'll figure it out. If you want me to do anything—make calls, start emailing, talk to local agencies here and see if they have anyone who can fly out that weekend—just tell me."

"Are you wearing one of the dresses to your little thing?"

The way Silva said "little thing" bothered her. It felt snide—almost snarky. She couldn't imagine what she could have said to offend the woman. "I was, but my date requested specific dresses, so I'll be wearing them some other time."

Silva's voice grew a little cold. "It's too bad we'll lose the opportunity for exposure. I wouldn't have pegged you for the kind of woman who lets a man dictate her wardrobe."

Stunned, Alexa couldn't speak. The awkwardness grew as she tried to formulate some kind of response. Before she found her voice, Silva announced that she had to go. "I just wanted to talk about the models. We'll figure it out."

"If you need me to do anything, let me know."

Again, silence hovered, but this time Silva's voice softened. "I'm sorry. I'm really under a lot of stress. I didn't mean to be rude."

"It's fine. I appreciate the call and I meant it. If you need anything, just let me know. If I can help, I will."

For some time after the call ended, Alexa's mind mulled

the situation. It seemed strange that there would be such a dearth of qualified models. Were they trying to cut too many costs? Was her initial investment too low?

Before she could call Wes for his input, her phone rang. The screen flashed her interior designer's name. Suddenly, all the changes of the past few months seemed ridiculous. *I just want my quiet life back, Lord!* she wailed inwardly. Alexa stared at the phone until it stopped ringing. Voicemail—savior of sanity in the modern age.

She listened to the message and ground her teeth as the woman prattled on about things they'd already agreed to do. Something sounded off. There it was. The couches she had chosen wouldn't fit in the room the way Marielle had planned to arrange them.

Everything crashed over her at once. The fundraiser, the new business, her new book, and now the new house. Alexa plugged her phone into its charger and strode away down the hallway. She stepped into the bathroom, plugged the tub, turned the water on to the hottest setting, and hurried to grab clean clothes. She needed a bath, dinner, and a movie—in that order.

Sadie Hawkins Day boasted perfect weather. As she stepped out her back door and felt the warm late spring breeze, Alexa breathed in the heady scent of blooming flowers. With such fine weather, the turnout should be amazing.

The clock warned her that time would slip past if she didn't hurry with Joe's lunch. She slowly filled the basket with sandwiches, grapes, potato salad in frozen bottomed bowls, crackers and cheese, and a chocolate cake. That left no room for drinks. After several attempts to rearrange the basket, Alexa gave up and decided to bring a separate cooler for their drinks.

As she tied a gingham tablecloth around the top, Alexa stood back and admired the effect. Somehow, it looked like a large hobo sack that belonged at the end of an enormous stick. That thought gave her a ridiculous idea. She rushed to her room, pulling dresses from the closet as quickly as possible. One glance at the clock told her Joe would arrive any moment to pick up the basket, and she was still in her summer pajamas and robe.

She raced back to the kitchen with her closet pole and slipped it under the knot. A giggle escaped as she tried to imagine how funny someone would look trying to carry anything like that. Though tempted to try it, she knew there just wasn't time. She had to get dressed!

Too late! As she flew into the living room, she saw Joe standing just inside the door, hands on hips, shaking his head. "I'm pretty sure that's not the dress we agreed on."

She wrapped her robe around her a little tighter. "I was just on my way to change."

"Mmm hmm. The amazing Alexa is late. That's interesting."

She dragged him into the kitchen and showed him the basket. "I just thought it looked like a hobo sack, so then I had to unload my closet to get the pole and—"

Joe smiled and moved to get the basket. "Do I take the pole?"

"Sure! I think it'll be funny." She grinned. "Just make sure I get it back. My dresses are all over my bed."

He grabbed the basket and pole, tugged her hair as he walked past, and headed to the front door. "Bidding starts in an hour. Don't be late. I don't want to get stuck eating with some crazy stranger."

"You pull my hair again and I'll let Nina Hostetler win you—I'll pay for it too."

He set the basket by the door and walked back, standing before her. "You wouldn't dare."

"Try me."

He eyed her hair and then gazed into her eyes. Reaching up, he gave a curl near her temple a gentle tug. Of course, he managed to choose the most sensitive place on her head. Alexa's eyes smarted. Joe's eyes widened as she blinked a way a couple of tears while attempting to glare at him.

"Did that hurt? I—"

"Not really. Just one of those tender spots that overreacts. Happens when I brush a snarl there too, but I'll get you for that." Alexa had never hated her sensitive temples more.

In a move that caught her breath and held it, Joe brushed a stray tear away with his knuckle. "Still—I didn't know. I'm sorry."

"You're making me feel ridiculous. My temples are touchy. No big deal!"

Joe grinned and tugged a lock near the back of her head. "I'll just have to pull back here."

"And I'll let Nina have you," she snapped.

"No, you won't."

Alexa's eyes widened. "And what makes you think that?"

"You like good food, and you know that if the other guys made their own lunches, the pickings won't be slim, they'll be disgusting."

"Okay, okay, you win. Now get out of here so I can get dressed. I'll see you in an hour."

She hurried into the bathroom to change. The dress, a new one she'd ordered after her last trip to New York, slipped over her head, hardly mussing her hair at all. She stared at her reflection in the mirror. It had been a good choice. While the bateau neckline always flattered her, something about the sleeveless bodice seemed extra chic. Yards of chiffon circled from the waist, creating a very full but gather-less skirt. With her white belt and the robin egg blue dress, Alexa felt a bit like a walking Tiffany box.

In her room, she hesitated between a large white wide-brimmed hat and a pillbox. The larger hat won as Alexa imagined being in the sun all afternoon. Besides, Joe had chosen it—reason enough to wear it. She grabbed sunscreen and rubbed it into her arms before pulling on her gloves and stepping into her shoes. One last glance at herself in the mirror sent her back into the bathroom. She'd forgotten her makeup—just a light, natural look with a hint of pink on her lips.

Ready to go at last, she locked the door behind her and stepped onto her porch feeling absolutely wonderful. She made a mental note: *Thank Joe for reminding me to be myself—always.*

Chapter 7

People swarmed Fairbury. As usual, tourists gawked and pointed at her, but rather than ignoring it as usual, she smiled, hoping to add to their visitors' enjoyment. Happy tourists meant more money for the prom. Mayor Tim, acting as auctioneer and emcee, announced the beginning of the mustache judging as she approached the crowd around the gazebo in the center of the square.

She took one look at Joe and giggled. How he'd managed to make such a drastic change in the space of an hour, she didn't know, but he'd gone all out for the event. Wearing ecru trousers, suspenders, a white shirt, and a bowtie, he looked as if he belonged at the turn of the twentieth century. Somewhere, he had even found spats. A straw boater sat perched on his head, complete with a string tied to his collar button—as if Fairbury's gentle breeze would come near blowing off his hat.

However, nothing beat his mustache. Somehow, he'd managed to make each end curl—not noticeably, but it gave the illusion of length. He'd win. From the way the crowd responded to his style, she was sure of it.

A volunteer pressed a ballot into her hand as she filed past the contestants with the rest of the crowd. A few women shamelessly stroked some of the mustaches as they passed, claiming to need more evidence before they could vote. Alexa hardly contained her laugher when Mrs. Varney "accidently" stumbled into a woman just seconds before the stranger reached up to touch the chief's mustache.

As she stood in front of Joe, she grinned. "Should I examine it closer? Pet it like you're a puppy?"

He winked at her as he groaned loudly for the benefit of

any listeners. "You'll mess up my miniature handlebars, and I'll lose."

She moved along, observing each mustache and teasing each contestant as she passed. She'd been wrong. Joe's mustache was by far the shortest. He didn't have a chance, and as she glanced back at him, she realized that he knew it. Only something for the kids could have induced him to join a contest he was sure to lose. For the first time in six weeks, she was glad she had let him see her appreciation for his shaved face. Perhaps it had helped take the sting away from certain loss.

Mayor Tim crowned Officer Martinez, who won by a landslide. Amazed how swiftly the crowd had shifted from rooting for Joe to voting for Martinez, she gave him an encouraging smile and found a comfortable place to wait for the auction.

Alexa had expected a break between mustache judging and the auction, but the sight of dozens of boxes, baskets, and bags explained the push to start the auction itself. If they didn't start immediately, it would be dinnertime before they finished.

The crowd became animated again, cheering and clapping as Mayor Tim began auctioning off the first lunch with rapid-fire speech. He sounded remarkably authentic. Alexa bid on each meal as it came to the auction block and stopped her bidding just before it closed. She watched each bidder carefully, trying to judge just how high she could drive the price. She somehow managed to avoid purchasing an unwanted meal.

At first, Joe looked distressed. She could see his panic and enjoyed keeping him nervous. It served him right after pulling her hair. She ignored several pleading glances, trying to focus on watching the other bidders. He'd figure it out soon enough. If she bid only on one, some of the others might guess it was his. Bidding on all kept people guessing—exactly as she hoped.

The basket that came before Joe's nearly wrecked her plan. She made a bid of a hundred thirty-two dollars. Silence hovered over the crowd. No response. Tim rattled for a hundred thirty-three. No takers. "Going once..." Alexa prayed. "Going twice..." She begged the Lord. "S—"

"One thirty-three!"

Tim repeated his call for final bidders and pronounced it sold to a tourist. She nearly sagged in relief. That had been too close.

Joe's basket rose to forty-five dollars quickly. Alexa and one of the junior high teachers battled it out in five-dollar increments to ninety-five. Alexa raised it to ninety-six. Her opponent bid ninety-seven. At ninety-eight dollars, Jacklyn Whethers quit bidding, and Alexa stepped forward to claim her basket.

Joe jumped from the gazebo and took the basket from her, sending Tim into a speech about the fine officer she'd managed to snag for a lunch date. "But Alexa," Tim warned, "everyone knows Joe can't cook."

Alexa turned and grinned up at their mayor. "No, but I can."

The crowd cheered.

Joe managed to find a tree with shade and a little privacy near the corner of the square. Alexa untied the tablecloth from the basket and spread it out for them to sit on. Joe whistled low. "I was just about to comment that you'd ruin your dress and I'd get grass stains, but you're all prepared—as usual."

"Speaking of grass stains, why didn't you tell me about your clothes? I have the perfect dress to go with those."

He shook his head as he doled out sandwiches, opened containers, and found flatware for each of them. "Isn't the point of your style to wear what you like without rhyme or reason?"

Alexa looked for the cooler and realized she had left it on the dining room table. "I forgot our cooler."

Joe stood, "Be right back. What do you want?"

Before she could answer, Hunter Badgerton pulled a wheeled trashcan toward them. "Need drinks?"

Alexa reached into her purse and pulled out a cordless

razor instead.

Laughing, Joe dug into his pockets for change and paid Hunter. "You bought a cordless razor."

She wiggled it. "Charged it too. Put it in here last night so I wouldn't forget."

Joe took the razor and strolled across the grass to the public restrooms, waving and calling out jokes as he passed friends. A few minutes later, he returned looking more debonair than he'd ever looked before.

"Joe?"

"Is that better?"

She reached over and brushed a little bit of fuzz from his bowtie. "Better than better."

They strolled away from the picnic arm in arm, looking as if they belonged in a black and white movie. Joe stared at her white glove on his arm, her purse swinging at her side. It explained a lot of things.

"I think I know why you pull off that look."

"What look?"

"Your 'any era as long as I like it' look."

"I can just see a fashion magazine defining it like that." She shook her head. "Okay, I'll play along. Why does it work?"

"Details. It's part of why you're such a good writer. I've heard people talk about it often. You care about the details—make sure they're correct."

"I suppose that makes sense with writing, but—"

Joe interrupted. "No, really, that dress is amazing. You look stunning in it, but it's the gloves, the hat, that purse—everything. You never leave those things out."

"Which explains how I almost left the house without my makeup today, I suppose."

"You wear makeup?" He knew it was a risk, but he tried to manufacture an expression of bewildered surprise. Her eyes told him she'd bought it, and his demeanor swiftly changed to amusement.

"Nice try. You watched me put it on in Chicago, and you've seen me without it often enough."

At her door, Joe gave her dress another glance. "I almost wish you didn't have to change."

"I don't. I can wear whatever I want. I have permission from one of the cops in town, in fact."

He grinned. For a moment, he almost urged her not to change. It was the most flattering thing he'd ever seen on her. However, as he met her gaze, he shook his head. "Fairbury has few opportunities to dress up. You should wear the other one. I'll probably take one look at it and say you should have worn it all day."

Alexa hesitated. "Are you changing?"

"I have another surprise for you."

As she stepped into her house, she glanced over her shoulder. "I'll pick you up at six forty-five. Be ready."

That sassy self-confidence—it was good to have the real Alexa Hartfield back. Very good indeed. "Yes, Miss Hart—" he stopped himself and winked. "Hawkins. I'll be ready."

Wes found Alexa curled up on her couch, surrounded by fabric swatches, paint cards, furniture catalogs, and decorating magazines. "What are you doing?"

"Finishing decorating the mausoleum I purchased."

"Isn't that why you hired Marielle?"

She rolled her eyes. "Yes, and that's why I only have these," her hands swept over the small pile of choices, "rather than warehouses full."

"You always say that you leave it to the professionals, but that looks like a lot of decisions to me."

Alexa slid the swatch book across the coffee table. "Look at that. You tell me the difference between khaki and army sand."

Wes stared at the colors. "This one has a bit more yellow, but not enough to care about."

"Close your eyes and feel them."

The second Wes touched the fabrics his eyes flew open. "I see."

"She picks the styles and colors and I approve. Then I tell her what I want it to feel like. Whatever floats her boat. I just want to finish this stuff. Every time I think we're done, she brings me more. That house is ridiculously large for one person."

"You can afford it."

"That wasn't what I said."

"I know, but it's true. You can." Wes glanced around him. "Any reason you aren't getting ready? There's a dance tonight."

"You don't say!" She glanced at the clock. "I still have two and a half—okay, two and a quarter hours. I have to pick up Joe at a quarter till."

"Why are you picking him up?"

She shoved the books aside and stood. "C'mon, I'll make us dinner." As she pulled out leftover pasta, she chattered about the evening. "I have to pick him up. It's Sadie Hawkins. I take him, remember?"

Wes pulled the apron from her hands. "I'll get this. You go change. That dress is great, but you have a closet full of gorgeous clothes. Go put on something spectacular."

"Got one ready to go and hanging in the bathroom."

She reached for the bread and buttered it. As Wes went to check out her planned outfit, Alexa sautéed garlic in the pan and spread the cloves over the bread, sprinkling it with a liberal coat of parmesan cheese. His wolf whistle told her he approved. He leaned against the peninsula and grinned. "Good choice, Annie. He's gonna love it."

"He'd better; he picked it out."

"Um, do you think all that garlic is a good idea?"

She shrugged. "Why not? I love garlic bread."

His sigh made no sense to her at all. The only sounds in the room as they ate were the crunch of Alexa's teeth in her garlic toast and the occasional clink of a fork on a plate. Wes' toast sat untouched, although he inhaled a heaping plate of pasta. As he pushed his plate aside with only the toast remaining, Alexa grabbed it and ate the garlicky morsel, carrying their plates to the sink.

"Now will you get ready?" Wes almost glowered at her.

"It's only going to take me a few minutes to freshen my makeup and twist up my hair. I have at least an hour and a half." Alexa shook her head at him. "You're worse than a fussy old woman."

Wes followed her to her favorite chair where she reclined, propping her feet on the ottoman and wriggling her toes in anticipation of tired feet later. He hunkered down on his heels and smiled into her eyes. "He likes you, Annie. He's going to be the envy of every man there. That dress is going to be stunning — particularly on you —"

Alexa interrupted, protesting. "Honestly, Wes! You're my brother. It's your job to tell me that I'm bucktoothed and have no sense of style."

Wes growled, shaking his head. "Annie, you'd be the death of any man. Sheesh! Get in there and do whatever you do when you go all out. I've seen it. You go from being attractive to a knockout!" She started to protest again, but he added, "Knock his socks off. I have a feeling he'd like it."

The idea grew on her. Wes was right. Joe had never seen her at her absolute best — not even at the Policeman's Ball. She glanced at the clock. She could do it in time and without rushing. Absently, she ticked through the things she'd have to do. "With that red dress, I could dust me with talcum powder, add red lipstick..."

"Don't forget your nails. Put your hair up in one of those twisty things you do."

Listening to Wes talk about clothes and hair nearly sent her into a fit of giggles. "Hey, do you think Heather would have time to come hold my hair? I could put it up so much faster if she'd hold sections out of the way for me."

Wes was out the door before she finished speaking. Infatuation had already grown to something more meaningful. When he pulled out his phone, she giggled. Walking the half dozen houses to Heather's while calling her in the process... her big brother would be head over heels in no time.

As he stepped onto the sidewalk, Wes pulled out his phone. Impatiently, he waited for Joe to answer. Just before Wes expected it to switch to voicemail, Joe answered. "'llo..."

"Joe?"

"Hey, what's wrong? Is Alexa—"

"Whoa! Slow down. Remember, you caught the murderer. Alexa isn't in danger anymore."

"Right. Sorry. You sounded a bit panicked."

Wes tried again. "Look, you need to be here by six-forty. I can't keep her here past that."

"No, no. She's picking me up—Sadie Hawkins."

Great, he'd have to let Joe in on it. Oh well, he'd still be surprised, Wes mused before saying, "Look, Joe. I talked her into pulling out all the stops. She's not going to be able to drive and keep that dress looking as good as it should. Be here. You won't regret it."

He and Heather returned to Alexa's house to find her dressed in a summer robe. For the next twenty minutes, Alexa brushed and handed hair to Heather as she twisted small portions, pinning them to her head.

Heather held her hair and watched with interest as the style formed. "I love this—looks great—but isn't there an easier way to do it?"

Alexa laughed as she pinned her final coil, leaving a few tendrils for her curling iron. "There's a much easier way to do it, but I can't do it on myself. I could do yours. Wouldn't take but ten minutes or so."

Wes frantically signaled to Heather, telling her to decline, but she ignored him. "Do you know how to do a French twist?"

Another five minutes passed as Alexa turned Heather's hair into a perfect French coil. Her neighbor beamed. "It's going to look perfect with that dress you sent over. I just love that—from your new line, right? I really appreciate it."

Wes sent Heather home with a quick kiss and a promise to be there soon. Alexa meticulously applied her cosmetics and then carried her shoes and a bottle of nail polish into the living room. Wes followed. "That poor man."

"It was your idea. You can't take it back now."

"Why are you putting on your shoes? It's early yet."

She waved a hand at him and continued buckling her ankle straps. "If I paint my nails after my shoes are on, I won't mess up my nail polish. Murphy's Law dictates that my nail polish will never dry if I paint them first."

"Only you, Annie," Wes muttered, pulling on his socks. "Only you."

At six-thirty, Alexa still sat with eyes closed and her fingers hanging—supposedly "curing." She'd pronounced them dry five minutes earlier, but to Wes' consternation, she insisted on allowing them to sit for another five or ten minutes to harden. The next time he glanced out the window, she kicked him.

"Get out of here. Go get her. I'll make it. I'm going to sit here until six thirty-five, put on my dress, grab my bag and gloves, and be in my car and on my way by six-forty. I'm fine."

Wes' protest died before he voiced it. It was the perfect opportunity to catch Joe before he knocked on the door. He didn't want to miss Joe's reaction if he could help it. Grabbing his jacket, he flung it over his shoulder, picked up his camera bag, kissed the top of Alexa's head, and hurried out the door. The jacket was a token to formality; he'd never put it on in this heat.

As he stepped out the door, Joe's Jeep rounded the corner. "Just in time," he mumbled to himself. A movement in the window told him that Alexa had gotten up to put on her dress. *Man, this'll be great.*

"Joe!" Wes' stage whisper would have alerted Alexa had she not been locked in her home with the air conditioner blasting.

Joe jogged to the porch wearing a black pinstriped Zoot

suit and carrying a red silk tie. His watch chain jingled with every step. "It's your fault that I can't tie this thing. You'll have to do it. I'm too nervous."

Wes backed away, hands in the air. "No way. There's a reason I don't wear ties. Leave it for Alexa. I'm just going to grab a few pictures and be out of your hair." He pulled his camera from the bag. "While we wait, let me get a few of just you."

"Really, Wes?"

"Be a good example to the kids, Joe. You know the moms want pictures of their little pimple-faced boys and those boys don't want pictures."

"They'll never see it! You're nuts."

"Just do it."

It took a few wasted shots for Joe to relax, but eventually Wes got a few shots by the porch railing that satisfied him. Alexa dashed out on the porch, pulling her skirts free of the screen. "Wes! You're still here—good. I can't get this thing zipped that last inch—something's stuck."

Joe turned and saw Alexa as she stood with her back facing Wes, waiting for him to zip her. "Whoa."

"Joe!" She turned, glancing over her shoulder as Wes tugged the zipper pull to the top. "What are you doing here?"

Wes stepped in, not allowing Joe to answer. "Let me get a few pictures. I'll send one to Mom. That'll confuse her!" Once done, he hustled down the street to Heather's house before Alexa realized his part in the change of plans. If there was one thing Alexa hated, it was having her life readjusted without her consent.

Joe and Alexa stared after him for a moment before Alexa shook her head. "Wait—I thought I was picking you up."

"Wes called and said your dress shouldn't be in the driver's seat and suggested I come." He waved his tie. "And I can't get the dumb thing to tie. It's like it's not cut right or something. I asked Wes, but—"

"Wes can't tie one to save his life. Here, let me have it."

She turned up his collar and positioned the tie. Joe

found her close proximity disarming. Her cosmetics—a masterpiece of retro style. "You look incredible—really, I—"

"Thank you."

Joe almost sighed in relief. He hadn't known how she would respond. His last attempts at paying her compliments hadn't gone well.

"There." Alexa stood back, examining her work.

He felt the knot, impressed. She hadn't tied it tight enough to choke him, but it lay nicely against his shirt. "Thanks." He glanced at her skirt. "Is it too far to walk? Even in the passenger seat, that thing is going to get crushed. Now I get why people rent limos to these things."

"A walk sounds nice. I think we're going to get rain tonight. It sure cooled off unexpectedly." Alexa draped her skirts over one arm, allowing them to come up to her knees as she strolled down the sidewalk. As they rounded the corner, they talked about the success of the mustache contest and auction, about her ensemble, and about Joe's suit.

"If you hadn't hired the Zoots to play, I'd never have thought of it."

She laughed. "Like I'd even consider planning any kind of dance without seeing you swing."

Lights filled the town square and Alexa beamed. "She did it."

"Who did what and why?"

"Listen, Friday, this isn't an interrogation." After a wink, she added, "Judith got all the white lights put up. I think we borrowed about five hundred from the town Christmas bin."

"Makes sense to me."

Joe nearly lost it when Alexa snorted. "I had to promise to replace them myself if anything happened to them. You'd think they were the lights of Bethlehem the way Tim acted."

The band's first notes played as Alexa and Joe claimed a table at the back corner of the square. An enormous rented dance floor covered the parking lot and half the street. Joe whistled low. "How and why did you manage that?"

"I've got connections... and I wanted to be comfortable while dancing. Asphalt is rough on shoes, feet, ankles, knees—"

"I get it."

His fingers tapped the tablecloth until she tapped the back of his hand. "Are you going to ask me to dance, or do I need to go stand with the wallflowers and hope someone takes pity?"

Glenn Miller's "One O'clock Jump" burst forth from the gazebo seconds later. Joe led Alexa to the dance floor, starting her with simple steps until she grew confident. They looked out of sync with the modern disjointed jerking motions of dancers around them, but Joe didn't care and he couldn't imagine that she did.

Two bands alternated in thirty-minute sets. The mixture of modern and retro music was intended to give the most pleasure to the largest number of people, but Alexa realized too late that she'd never get a break. The mayor, Chief Varney, her brother, their friends—nearly everyone--asked and waited to dance with Fairbury's eccentric author.

By eight o'clock, she'd kicked off her shoes in utter disregard for the condition of her stockings. By eight thirty, her gloves followed. By nine, Joe realized he'd have to be more assertive in claiming his position as her date, or he'd never have another dance with her.

Strains of "The Way You Look Tonight" slowly swelled from the gazebo and over the dance floor. Alexa sat massaging her feet after a particularly difficult time with a salsa number moments before. Joe stood behind her— hesitating. She must have sensed his presence, because she glanced up at him, smiling. From the corner of his eye, he saw Wes spin Heather into the arms of Martinez and slide his camera around to capture the picture.

How Wes did it, Joe couldn't tell, but seconds later, he had her back in his arms, dancing and laughing. Alexa, unaware of the attention she'd garnered, just smiled at Joe. He glanced at her feet and raised his eyebrows in question.

She stood. "Can you foxtrot?"

He took her hand and led her to an empty spot on the floor. "You can ask that question..." The memory of her massaging her feet prompted him to ask, "Are you sure your feet can take it?"

"You're already trying to get out of it?"

Laughing, Joe led her in the long, gliding steps of the foxtrot. "I'm just making sure. The song fits, the night is young, but your shoes—I thought shoes were supposed to protect your feet!"

"I'll put them back on around ten, take them off at eleven, and walk home in them at midnight—maybe just before. I think I'm going to be a pumpkin. That's the secret of keeping your feet fresh—alternating."

They danced around the perimeter of the floor while a hesitant singer attempted to sing the words to the song. Disappointed, Joe almost complained about the ruined song, but Alexa sighed, preempting him. "I wish I could sing like he can."

"He can't. That's the trouble."

"Oh, no. Can't you tell? That kid can sing. He's just nervous."

"Nuh, uh." Joe listened for another minute and shook his head again. "No way."

"I'm serious. He's nervous—probably never done anything like this before. He's not letting himself go. I always sound a little better when I sing at the top of my lungs. I get off key less that way."

As he listened, Joe realized she was right. Regardless, he hated to hear the song cheapened by a nervous singer. "I just wish he did it justice. The song suits you."

As the crowd gave unenthusiastic applause, Alexa left Joe and wove through the dancers, across the grass, and to the microphone where an embarrassed college student argued with the bandleader about the next song. "I can't do it, Steve. I just can—"

"Excuse me."

The men turned to her, the bandleader smiling as he said, "Oh, Ms. Hartfield. How are you? My wife is so excited to see you out and in one of your dresses."

"Thank you." Alexa turned to the younger man. "And

who is your excellent singer?"

"I gave Dylan a chance tonight, but he wants to quit. Some of these songs need vocals—"

"Oh, Dylan, don't quit. I know you were nervous, but I can tell you're good—really good. I'll double whatever he's paying you if you'll keep going. Try something peppier next time and let your voice go. Have fun."

She teased, joked, and then threatened to sing herself. Dylan insisted it would be an improvement, until she tried singing with him. Steve begged her to stop. Before she left to rejoin Joe, she whispered a request for the last song. Dylan smiled. "That's one of my grandma's favorites—sing it to her all the time. I could do that one in my sleep."

As the night wore on, with Dylan's voice crooning half the songs as Alexa knew he could, she skipped every other dance, trying to save her feet. She chatted with tourists, signed scraps of paper, and mentally kicked herself for not including dance cards as a souvenir of the evening. Too soon, the band began playing the song she had been waiting to hear.

She glanced around her, beckoning Joe with one finger. As he reached her side, she grinned. "It is Sadie Hawkins, after all."

All formal dancing, ballroom, swing—anything with steps—disappeared. Being close to midnight, only a smattering of party stragglers shuffled around the dance floor. Joe's voice joined Dylan's as he sang Alexa's request for "On the Street Where You Live," changing a few words to suit the occasion. "...lilac trees at the Hartfield house? Can you have a lark at any other house in town? Does enchantment pour out of every pore? No, it's just on the street where she lives..."

Alexa's laughter and a thumbs-up behind Joe's back seemed to give Dylan the courage for a final flourish. Gripping the mic, he removed it from the stand and stepped forward. "Thank you, Ms. Hartfield for such a lovely evening. The band and I wish you well and hope we get a chance to work with you again soon."

Chapter 8

The moon shone bright and full overhead as Joe and Alexa walked home. Wes and Heather drove past, offering rides, but Alexa waved them on. "You don't mind, do you? I'm having too much fun; I don't want it to end."

"Not if your feet can stand it."

"Feet are fine." With a sassy grin and a blatant disregard for her hemline, Alexa dropped her skirts. Inspired by the last song, she began singing Eliza Doolittle's "I Could Have Danced All Night" at the top of her lungs.

"You're acting punch drunk. Shh!" Joe grabbed her waist, spinning her around in an attempt to hush her. "You'll wake your neighbors."

"I've never been in a fistfight in my life, I'll have you know."

Joe grinned, taking her hand and walking slowly down Elm Street. "You'd better not, either. I don't think you head could stand any blows, and I don't want to have to arrest you for assault and battery."

"Never knew what good salt would do for batteries anyway."

"Ha-ha," he muttered.

Their repartee on the walk home made her wish for a recorder. As fodder for writing material, she couldn't ask for better. "Joe, don't forget this."

"I couldn't." His tone hinted of more than their conversation.

"No, silly. This is good stuff we've got going here. I could use this banter in a novel. Don't forget it. I have a feeling I might."

"You won't," he assured her with confidence Alexa wished she felt. "But I'll write down key words when we get to your house."

As they climbed her steps, Alexa passed Joe her keys and dropped into her porch swing, moaning. "Forget my feet, my legs are killing me. Would you please bring me a glass of tea?"

When he returned, Joe passed her cellphone to her. "I saw the light flashing—figured you had a message."

Alexa accepted the glass and took a sip. "Mmm... What did—oh, pineapple. That's good. I wouldn't have thought of it in tea."

"Mom did it once when we ran out of sugar."

They sat in opposite corners of the little porch swing with Alexa's legs stretched across the seat and her feet resting in Joe's lap. He rocked the swing gently with one foot, balancing his glass on the opposite knee. "Thanks for inviting me. I had fun."

"Well, you don't have to make it sound like I did you a favor. Who else would I go with?" He shook his head and bit into a cookie. She truly didn't realize that any available man would have accepted an invitation from her. She wasn't naïve enough not to know it, but she was humble enough not to think of it.

After a moment's hesitation, he reached for her hand—just as she began pulling pins from her hair, piling them in her lap. He watched, fascinated, as sections of her hair slowly tumbled around her shoulders, and the pile of bobby pins grew to mountainous proportions. As she freed the last locks of her hair, she ran her fingers through it, pulling stray pins as she came across them.

Semi-satisfied, she swung her legs to the ground and turned, presenting the back of her head to Joe. "Do you see any more pins? I think I got them, but one or two always hide from me until I roll over in the middle of the night and jab them into my skull."

Joe picked at her hair, uncertain of how to find pins in a "hairstack." Alexa misunderstood and chided him. "Friday, you're not going to hurt my head. Just dig for 'em, will you? I want to scratch my head."

Eventually, Joe found three. To his surprise, she stood, carrying the pins in an upper layer of her skirt to the wastebasket near the front door and dumped them in. "You're just going to throw them away?"

"I don't feel like washing them. It's worth the loss of a couple of dollars to save the trouble."

"I never thought about needing to wash hair pins."

"Well, I don't always, but I used a lot of hairspray on my hair, so I imagine they're probably coated." She ran her fingers through her hair again and sighed. "I need to wash it. It's disgusting. I'm starving too. Are you hungry, or should I kick you out so I can take a shower?"

Joe's laugh rang out across lawns and into the windows of sleeping neighbors. He sent her to shower, promising to make sandwiches and a salad. Although woefully inferior to what he considered Alexa's culinary perfection, Joe's sandwiches made up for lack of originality with quantity and speed. By the time she emerged from her shower, Joe had a feast set out for them at the dining room table.

He watched, amused as she inhaled her food, holding a sandwich or piece of fruit with one hand and tossing her wet hair with the other. "Why do you keep flipping your hair around like that?"

"I have to get it to dry or it'll be a mess by morning."

He took her empty plate and refilled her tea glass, adding more pineapple juice to it. "Let's go outside then. We can sit on the swing, listen to the silence of the night, and dry your hair in the breeze."

"In my robe?" Alexa's attempt at a protest failed.

"You're covered. Put your back to the street and no one would ever know."

Half an hour later, she pronounced her hair almost dried. Joe nudged her phone toward her. "Did you ever check your messages?"

She shook her head and scrolled through a list before punching one and listening. Her face grew concerned and confused as she disconnected. Curious, Joe asked, "Something wrong?"

"There's been some vandalism at the shop in Chicago."

"Did you get in an iffy area?"

She shook her head. "Um, not hardly. We're on Michigan Avenue, steps away from the best boutiques and chain stores you can imagine. Audrey Hepburn might not have eaten breakfast there, but man she'd stop in for a snack."

Joe threw up his hands in mock surrender. "Ok, so you're hob-knobbing with the posh crowd. Got it." He winked to ensure she didn't assume offense on his part.

"Yeah, and now we've lost all of our prototypes and the samples. The gal who created them is already on another project, so we have to find someone else to do it."

As she described the damage to the clothing, fixtures, and large display window, they tallied the approximate costs in damages. Frustrated with losses at such an early juncture in her investment, Alexa used Joe as a sounding board. She shifted in the swing, laying her head on his leg as she rambled about the financial ramifications of a failed business venture. In time, she talked herself to sleep. Joe continued to rock the swing, lost in thought.

Wes jogged up the steps half an hour later. "What are you still doing—" The sight of Alexa asleep, her head in his lap, changed his question. "What happened?"

"She got bad news. Something happened at the store in Chicago."

"That's open already?"

Joe shook his head, absently brushing Alexa's hair away from her face. "No—something about vandalism to fixtures and the windows—oh and clothes destroyed. We guesstimated somewhere around ten thousand in damages."

"That sounds bad but not devastating."

As he gave Wes more particulars, Joe watched Alexa sleep and smiled as she twitched, her nose wrinkling. "Man, I hate to wake her up. She was really upset."

"You strong enough to carry her?"

"She'll wake up anyway."

Wes shook his head. "Bet she won't. Not unless you force her on her feet. When she's out like that, Alexa is a very sound sleeper."

Alexa awoke, disoriented as sunlight streamed into her room. The clock, blurry through sleepy eyes, said it was nearly ten o'clock. How had she gotten to bed? She didn't remember leaving the swing. In fact, the last thing she remembered was trying to work out ideas for fixing the problems at the shop.

Her heart sank. The shop. She had to call Silva about the shop—see if they had called the insurance company. She reached for her phone and found it missing.

As she stood, Alexa stared at her robe, confused again. Why had she worn her robe to bed? It didn't make sense.

She stumbled into the living room and out onto the porch. The swing swayed lightly in the breeze—no phone in sight. She checked the porch floor and even the ground surrounding the porch. It was gone. Why had she decided to get rid of her landline?

A new idea occurred to her, and sent Alexa flying down her hall, stopping short at her guestroom door. Wes snored loudly. She crept inside, smiling at the sight of his phone on the end table. After a second glance at him, she snatched it and hurried from the room, closing the door silently behind her.

Four missed calls and two texts—all with Heather's name on them—flashed on the screen. Never had she been so tempted to snoop into her brother's life. Instead, she scrolled through his contacts and punched her number. The "Pink Panther Theme" rang out from her kitchen. Her confusion compounded. She had not plugged it into her charger, but there it was—three messages blinking.

The first, from James, told her he needed to talk to her— yesterday, if his tone was any indication. The second made her laugh as she listened to Joe telling her he'd connected her phone to the charger and then realized that she'd know that if she heard his message. She'd have to tease him about that. Rhette's message sounded unnecessarily panicked as she called, asking for help in how to solve their supply woes.

She slid her finger over the screen to previous calls and punched Rhette's number. As she waited, she filled the coffee maker and switched it on. A glance in the fridge showed little that tempted her—except for a few early strawberries she'd gotten from the market. Belgian waffles sounded good.

"Hey, Rhette. Sorry I missed your call. What can I do to help?"

"Silva is driving me crazy. She's so focused on fixtures and materials that she's losing sight of the big picture. We won't have anything to fill the shop!"

"Ok, so did anyone call the insurance company?" Silence hung between them. Her heart sank into her stomach at what it likely meant. "Did she get the policy yet?"

"No."

"Ok. Do me a favor. Call her and tell her that I said the first thing she needs to do, after getting that window fixed, is to call the insurance company. Oh, and make sure that the window isn't covered under the leaseholder's policy."

"What about the prototypes. We have nothing!"

"Patterns?"

Again, silence. Alexa wanted to cry but before she could say anything, Rhette squealed. "I was right. They are here at my house. I forgot that I brought them home. Silva told me to take them to the draft printers on Monday." Relief filled Rhette's voice as she spoke.

"Ok, give me until Monday. I'll have a solution by then if you don't. Keep doing whatever you were going to be doing. Don't get behind on your work." Wes stumbled into the kitchen with a questioning look in his eye. She shook her head and pointed to the coffeemaker. "And tell Silva I said insurance immediately. We can't afford losses like this."

Wes groaned as she hung up the phone. "No coffee?"

"Nope." She slid his phone to him. "And I couldn't find my phone. Had to use yours to call it."

"What's up with the shop?"

"Well, it's both worse and not as bad as I thought. Silva never got the insurance, so this is out of pocket, but Rhette had the patterns at home. That would have been harder to swallow. We know the patterns are good, so we can skip prototypes and order samples."

"Is what you just said intelligible to you?"

Alexa laughed. "It's expensive but not devastating."

Wes nodded. "Good. Are you sure this is worth it?"

The question niggled at her as she mixed waffle batter. Waiting for the first waffle to cook, she sighed. "I guess we'll see."

"Hmm?"

She glanced at Wes nursing his first cup of "mocha flavored milk." "Never mind."

Chapter 9

On Monday morning, Alexa packed quickly as she talked with her seamstress. "Oh, thank you, Laidie. I knew you could help us. I'll have Rhette overnight the drawings, the patterns, and the fabrics. What would we do without you?"

Sounding pleased, Adelaide Peters chatted about the weather and asked about Alexa's fall wardrobe. "Have you sent me anything yet? I want to be sure to keep plenty of room in my schedule for you."

"Do you have a busy summer planned?"

"Three weddings this summer—brides abound here. I'm drowning in tulle, white satin, and chiffon."

Lost in thought over whether to pack a swimsuit or not, Alexa made a non-committal answer. Unaware that she left several questions unanswered, she thanked Laidie for her time and disconnected the call. Seconds later, the phone rang again.

"Hello?"

"Miss Hartfield?"

"Laidie?" Alexa tried to remember if she had said goodbye or if they had gotten disconnected without her realizing it.

"Yes, sorry for bothering you again, but have I offended you?"

"Not at all, why?"

"You seemed… unlike yourself. I just wanted to be sure. I'll get right to work on those samples. You just take your trip and don't worry about a thing." Before Alexa could say anything, Laidie disconnected the call.

She stared at the phone for a moment before pulling out

her second suitcase and placing her piled clothes inside it.

Wes interrupted her work, waving a pile of lists in her face. "Tell me about these again."

"That's a list of what you have them pack..." she flipped to the next section, "those are the change of address forms, those are—"

"Wait, that's all they pack? That's not very much stuff. Won't you need more furniture? A bed? Sheets?"

"And what will you sleep on or make the bed with? What will you use for linens and dishes? Are you really going to go home and cart your stuff back to Fairbury now?"

Wes muttered something unintelligible as she dragged her suitcase from the bed. She adjusted the handle and smiled at him. "Marielle will have everything set up for me in the new house. Don't worry about it."

Wes glanced around him and back at the lists. Alexa wasn't taking much of anything to the new house. Her clothes, her books, a few personal items—that was it. "I didn't expect this to be such an expensive thing. I thought you'd just move your stuff over there, buy a few pieces of furniture now and then to fill up the empty rooms, and—"

Alexa dismissed his ideas with a hug. "Just take care of," she pointed to the lists, "those and don't worry about me." She dragged her suitcase down the hall and to the front door. "Oh!" she called back, "don't forget to hang my clothes in the new closet. You'll make a mess of them if you leave them lying on the bed." She glanced at her watch. "Oops! I'm going to be late."

Her car whizzed around the corner, making Wes wish that Joe were nearby to order her to slow it down. He stared down the empty street, his eyes roaming over fenced yards, flowers in bloom—home. His eyes took in the yard, the shrubs, and bushes. Those would be his responsibility. He'd have to hire a kid to mow and trim for him when he went on assignments.

He stepped inside again, glancing around the living room with a new eye. It would be a bit feminine for a man—or two if he got a roommate—but remove the flowers and knickknacks and things wouldn't be too ridiculous. The dining room looked fine as it was. Curious, he stepped into the kitchen and glanced around it, looking for telltale signs that said "feminine domain."

"Dump the jars maybe—or maybe not. It's not bad."

Alexa's room would need denim or something to adapt from the white and ivory ethereal theme. Just moving the hats from the wall—hats. Wes shuffled through papers and saw nothing regarding her hats. Had she mentioned them and he forgot? How did he pack hats? He started to whip out his phone to call but realized that she'd have to pull over to answer, and then she'd worry about them until she saw that he did whatever she wanted done—right. He'd figure it out.

A step into her room confirmed his concerns. The canopy over the bed would have to go. The white bedspread—gone. But with those out, her hats gone, and a less feminine lamp, it would be okay—for someone else. He stepped into "his room" and glanced around. The sleigh bed was a bit feminine but he loved it. Change out the bedspread here and he was good to go. It could work.

A slow smile spread over his face. He was six houses down from Heather. He could stomach a pink room with fluffy bunnies while he slept for all he cared. Almost.

Joe pulled into Sycamore Court and smiled at the sight of Wes tossing a football back and forth with Zach. The way Wes charged the boy, swinging him around and ruffling his hair before sending him into the house—presumably for the night—told Joe that Alexa would need another renter sooner rather than later. Wes wouldn't live there long.

As he pulled into Alexa's driveway, he suddenly realized what a ridiculous move it had been. She wasn't there. She wouldn't offer him lunch, and Wes had seen him. He couldn't just back out and leave again without opening himself up for some serious ribbing.

Facts. What were truthful facts he could focus on to keep

Wes' mind from going places Joe wasn't ready to go—yet? House. Zach. Heather. Kids. Empty house. Yep. That'd work.

"What are you doing here, Joe? Alexa isn't due back for a week yet."

"Have a question for you. I figure, you make me a sandwich and we'll talk."

Wes laughed. "You don't want my sandwiches. Help yourself, though. Her food is going to go bad at this rate."

Once in the kitchen, Joe knew his idea would work. He also realized, just as he layered the last thin slice of turkey on his half-stale bread, that the idea bordered on genius. "So, I have a proposition for you."

"I'm not accustomed to being propositioned by guys, Joe."

"Not funny." Joe watched Wes salivate over the sandwich and decided to ensure he had the best chance of success. "Here. I'll make me another one."

"You sure?" The words were mere formality. Wes bit into the sandwich seconds after he asked. "Womph foo ooh womph?"

Joe pulled out the remaining ham and sniffed a dubious looking piece of roast beef. "Eh?"

After a swig from a Dr. Pepper can that Joe passed him, Wes repeated himself. "What do you want?"

"You have a house with two—technically three—rooms and you're almost never home."

"Yeah... gonna have to get me a roommate. Houses shouldn't be empty all the time. Don't want Alexa to regret—"

"Who do I give my application to—you or Alexa?"

Wes removed the sandwich from his mouth without taking a bite. "You want to be my roommate? You have an apartment."

It took a few minutes to convince Wes that he was serious. At the dubious look on Wes' face, Joe expected him to say no. Instead, he asked, "Why do you want to move in here?"

"I've wanted to live in this neighborhood since I moved

to Fairbury. Houses sell before I even hear they're up for grabs—and I drive the streets almost every day. You won't live here long, so—"

"What, you kicking me out already?"

Joe glared at Wes until he had the decency to look reasonably chagrined. "I give you six months tops before you ask Heather to marry you. Another six months for planning a wedding..." Wes started to protest, but Joe continued. "Heather's house is larger, so you'll move in there, leaving this one for me. At that point, I intend to try and convince Alexa to sell it to me."

"You don't think you and she—"

"No."

"I thought things were looking a little interesting in that direction," Wes persisted.

"I walked through her house today when I dropped off the last of those hats. Have you seen it?"

"What?"

"Her house?"

"Not yet. Marielle said she'd call when I could bring the dresses—something about the room still smelling like paint and it getting into the fabrics."

"When you do, you'll know what I mean. Here—in this little house—it was easy to forget who she is sometimes."

"Alexa's not like that, Joe. She—"

"It's not just that, Wes. To be honest, it's just a good excuse. I'm not interested in marriage, and anything less would just be using her."

"But—"

He didn't care to discuss it. "Do you want a roommate or not? I have to give notice before I pay the rent."

Alexa's brain nearly fried with the discussions between her lawyer and the financial advisor. They examined police reports, checked the books, and discussed revenue projections. In short, she wanted out of the clothing business—yesterday. Had it been Silva's project alone, she would have written off the initial investment, told Silva to find a new backer, and walked from the project. Only Rhette's enthusiasm and excitement stopped her.

"Okay, what are you saying? Forget the vandalism and the hiccoughs. Look at where the business needs to go and the projected income." Alexa waited for the others to find the information they needed. "Is it a reasonable investment?"

"Sure—if it's not run by incompetents." Rich didn't hesitate.

She ignored the jab and continued her questions. "Then what do they need to ensure success?"

The list of items grew—a better insurance policy, a CPA instead of Silva's cost-saving bookkeeper, a lawyer, and someone to handle advertising and marketing. Rich frowned and turned to her lawyer. "Do you have an attorney you can recommend?"

Their server brought the lunch check, and Alexa slipped her credit card in the folder before gathering her notes into her briefcase. "If there is anything else you think of that I need to address, I'll go talk to Silva and Rhette. That said, if you think the business idea by itself is too risky to invest in, I need to know now before I release additional funds."

"It's a sound idea; they just don't seem to know what they're doing," Rich admitted.

"Well, who of us knew what we were doing when we first started our chosen professions. Did you never make a mistake?" She glanced around her, waiting impatiently for the server to return. Losing money on a foolish investment was one thing, but she could live with a few expensive lessons if it meant that the venture made a profit in a reasonable amount of time.

From the restaurant, she rode through the streets to Michigan Avenue and directed her cab driver to the building undergoing window repairs. She might not have noticed the curious looks people gave her had a little girl not asked her mother, "Why is that lady wearing that funny hat?"

She smiled at the girl and stepped around the workmen

at the window. Her reflection in the glass door amused her. The child had a point. Her hat was nearly as broad as her shoulders, and with such a large feather drooping over one side, it probably looked strange to the child's modern sense of style.

Rhette met her at the door, unlocking it for her. "Silva had to step out. She hired someone to do advertising and Darrel wants him to help with nitpicky things. She's out putting Adam on the accounts so he can do payroll."

"Excellent. So how goes the window work?"

"They said they'd be done in about another hour. They had trouble getting out some of the old glass."

"And have you spoken to Lai—Adelaide?"

"Yes! That woman is a wonder. She overnighted the first three samples, and they are perfect. Would you like to see?"

Though Alexa showed eagerness to see the dresses, she knew the woman's work. She happened to be wearing one of Ladie's masterpieces at that moment. The workroom looked as though it hadn't been touched. The damage she'd seen in pictures and on her first visit had already been repaired, and work had already resumed. Only the lack of prototypes and samples on the mannequins hinted at the prior destruction.

"—then Silva said that maybe someone like that guy from your town was trying to do the same thing but on a smaller scale."

Alexa blinked. "She said what?" The words made no sense—obviously a case of lack of inattention on her part.

"Oh, she wasn't blaming you," Rhette assured her. "She just wondered if that guy who was killing the people in your town didn't give someone else an idea to try to stop you. I think she was just trying to make sense of it," the designer hastened to add.

"I doubt it, but who would have thought a man would start killing people to stop me from writing about murder? I obviously do not know the depths of depravity that the human mind can conceive."

"Maybe better than most," Rhette agreed, "but that wasn't just depraved. That was stupid and illogical."

"I don't think insanity keeps company with logic, Rhette." Silva's voice startled them from the doorway.

"I was just telling her your joke about how someone was using the dresses to stop her writing."

Rhette's nervousness bothered Alexa. Had it been an employer/employee situation, it might have made sense, but Rhette was an equal partner in the venture. She had no reason to cower under Silva's tongue, no matter how sharp it appeared.

"So, my advisors suggested a few things..."

Chapter 10

Joe jogged up the steps of Alexa's new home. As he knocked, he tried the door and found it open. Stepping inside, he reflected on how quickly a person adapts to changes in life. Just a year earlier, he'd hardly known Alexa Hartfield, apart from a nodding acquaintance at church or on the street, and now he entered her home without waiting for her to answer his knock—he even had his own key!

His shoes squeaked across the marble floors as he started toward the kitchen. The sound of Alexa's television sent him upstairs to the large sitting area on the landing. He placed his hand on her shoulder just as Jack Nicholson's voice crowed, "Heeerrre's Johnny!"

Flying popcorn hit him in the face, followed by Alexa's piercing scream. "Joe! What—how could—"

He sat on his heels, making his head even with hers, and reached over the couch for the remote. As he hit the pause button, he asked, "What *are* you watching—well, I know what, but *why* are you watching it?"

She sat in the middle of the couch, papers surrounding her and a stack of DVDs tumbled over the coffee table. Setting aside her notebook, Alexa closed her laptop and stood. "I'll get the mini-vac." A glance at the clock made her eyes widen. "Oh! I worked through lunch. Are you hungry?"

As they went downstairs to the kitchen, Alexa described her research for an upcoming manuscript. "I needed something fresh, so I started with this."

"Premise?"

She grinned. "I love how you've learned terminology just to amuse me. Okay, I originally planned to have a screenwriter creating murder scenes as a way to ensure a realistic manuscript—kind of a twist on Ray Connor's thing."

"Well, he might not have a poker fall off before he can kill his victim..."

She slugged him as she reached for an avocado and a paring knife. "Very funny. Anyway, the more I studied about screenwriting, the more the plot changed. Right now, I have a movie buff that goes from watching murder to creating it."

"But that sounds a lot like what Ray did. You called it cliché, and I know how much it annoyed you."

"It's the why," she explained, visibly exasperated. "The killer wants the variety. No M.O. However, if he doesn't find a way to make sure that the details are all different—tape or pen or knife style or whatever, the police will be able to connect the murders."

Joe took the knife from her when she sliced through the avocado and into her hand. He flipped on her faucet and handed her a paper towel, ordering her to put pressure on the wound. "But Alexa, eventually something will point to him. They'll connect it all from there. Video rentals or purchases, downloads—even if he does it in other cities on business travel, they'll find him that way."

Alexa bandaged her hand and continued assembling avocado, tomato, and turkey sandwiches. He salivated as she put them on plates with pasta salad and watermelon slices. A new thought occurred to him.

"Okay, off topic, but how on earth do you not weigh five hundred pounds? You eat such great food, every meal, don't skimp on calories, and I've never seen you exercise."

Laughing, Alexa handed him a glass of mint iced tea and followed him to the table. "Well, that was one advantage to this house—stairs. That and it's even farther from town." She hurried back to the drawer for forks as she added, "Everyone tells me that once I hit forty, my metabolism will slow down, and I'll start to gain. I figure burning more calories can't hurt."

"Hmm... hadn't thought about a high metabolism. Bet it's genetic."

He accepted the fork, spent several seconds in rushed

thanks for his food, and stabbed the first piece of pasta as his stomach rumbled in anticipation. "Okay, so tell me about this character."

"Well, one thing you have to remember is that we do want him caught. I mean, I'm not trying to create the perfect, unsolvable crime. If a book ended with the killer never getting justice, my purpose in writing it all would be gone."

"Right. You write to 'give people justice in a world where we don't always see it.'"

"You've been reading an interview."

"That was in the Gazette after the Connors arrest," Joe admitted. "It's a good description, though."

"And it explains my point in writing. I have to make sure he can get caught eventually."

Joe shook his head. "Alexa, the minute there was any connection to him, they'd have a paper trail so clear it'd be glaringly obvious."

"I've got my ways around that. Want a cookie?"

She pulled a fresh box of mint chocolate wafers from the freezer and tossed it to him. "I've got popcorn to clean and a movie to finish." She rinsed her dishes, popped them in the dishwasher, and grabbed her mini-vac.

Joe stared at the box of cookies, debating. He didn't really want to spend his day off watching horror films. The temptation to harass the swim team guys at the pool was strong, but he hadn't had a free day just to hang out with Alexa since she'd moved into her new house. Resigned, he sorted his own dishes into the dishwasher, poured a glass of milk, grabbed the cookies, and followed her upstairs.

She'd left room for him on the oversized loveseat. From the chair, he wouldn't have to see as much of the screen, but she'd tried to be thoughtful. With a sigh, he seated himself beside her and opened the box.

"You okay?" Alexa glanced at him curiously.

"I have the cookies. I'm good."

Halfway through the third movie, Alexa punched the stop button on the remote. "I can't take anymore. If one more person gets murdered, hacked, or otherwise has a bad day, I'm going to need Nurse Ratched myself." She stretched. "How do you feel about a drive? We could go around the lake, past Brunswick, and be back in time to grill steaks."

"Or, I could take you out to dinner—maybe go to New Cheltenham. That restaurant out by the hunting club has amazing steaks and seafood."

Her laptop mocked her from the coffee table. She didn't really have time for jaunts about the countryside. She couldn't plan her outline without knowing the basic facts of the murders—what they had to have, where they had to be, what might make it fail. A glance at the stack of DVDs next to her laptop sealed the deal. She simply could not endure another minute of blood, gore, and vice.

"It's a deal—if I can change."

Joe waved in the direction of her room as he picked up her notes. "Mind if I read them?"

Alexa shook her head as she hurried upstairs, her cropped sailor trousers and middy blouse looking about six decades out of place. As Joe read the notes, he saw where Alexa would take the story. She wrote mostly one-word descriptions of what would happen and when. It read like a telegram.

From the classic Psycho shower killing to the most recent blockbuster films, she had enough fodder for several books. Certain crimes stood out to him as excellent choices, while others seemed too far-fetched. Why had she chosen the ones she had? Had she weeded out any of…

He laughed as he realized the method to her murder madness. She had gathered her movies and was watching them in alphabetical order.

As he heard her coming down the stairs, Joe made a decision. He would discover her favorite period movie—no matter how nauseating it might be to him—and he'd suggest they watch it when they returned from dinner. It would be a sacrifice, but she needed an alternate diet of viewing material, and he seriously doubted she had the mental stamina left for a game or a puzzle.

At the sight of Alexa's dress, he knew he'd made the right decision. Her sky blue dress, several sheer layers of Regency beauty, softened the weariness that he had seen in her expression. She looked cool and crisp—even with skirts hanging to the floor. A capote hung from one arm and a reticule from the other. He almost winced as he realized that he not only had identified the era of her dress, he knew what the words "capote" and "reticule" meant.

She smiled. "Ready?"

In her garage, she passed him her keys and climbed into the passenger seat of her Mini Cooper. Minutes later, the car whizzed around the lake and onto the highway. After a period of relaxing silence, Joe nudged her and said, "Have you decided on a title for the book?"

"Oh! Definitely. It's what inspired me to write it."

Relieved that he no longer heard the strain in her voice, Joe asked, "Well, are you going to share?"

Eyes closed, she nodded. "I decided on a play on words—*Scriptease*. Catchy, don't you think?"

"Scriptease. Well, it has shock factor going for it."

Alexa nodded. "That's what I thought. People will feel compelled to see what a title like that has to do with murder. It's perfect."

The miles flew past, and as they did, he could feel her relax. Joe, on the other hand, fell deeper into turmoil as he fought to find a way he could convince her to reconsider her title. Hers were usually simple but powerful. The sensationalized name sounded more suited to an overly romantic and dramatic eighth grader's home video—or something worse.

By New Cheltenham, he'd rejected half a dozen attempts to suggest other names. They wandered through the streets, stopping to peruse little shops. Alexa carried a shopping basket she'd pulled from her car, and tucked her purchased trinkets into it.

Street vendors strolled the sidewalks, carrying trays

similar to those of the cigarette girls in the nightclubs of days past. Some held candies, others flowers or paper bonnets and top hats. Joe stopped a teenager selling flowers and bought Alexa a small bunch of violets.

Alexa sniffed them. "Didn't Peter Marshall describe violets as having a 'haunting, wistful fragrance?'"

She smiled at the vendor and turned, but the girl asked, "I thought we weren't supposed—I mean, are you working today?"

Joe laughed. "There you have it, Alexa. If you ever get tired of writing murders, you can always come here, wear your extensive wardrobe, and sell flowers and candy."

The longer they explored the little town, the more interest they drew. In an attempt to keep the awkwardness at bay, Joe made jokes about the names of various establishments. "Wool Gathering sounds delightful after a day of 'shear violence.'"

"Joe!"

Before she could continue, he pointed to a pub. "We could skip the restaurant and eat here at the Hog's Head. I'd rather eat tenderloin or chops, but no. They only serve the head, it seems. Do you think it comes with an apple, or is that extra?"

"You are ridiculous," she laughed. Pointing to a tearoom she asked, "So what do you say to Tea Thyme?"

"I say they need to rethink their menu. Mint, not thyme in tea."

By dinnertime, not thyme, as Joe insisted on spelling—twice—Alexa seemed utterly relaxed and her usual carefree self. Joe drove them to Briarly House, where they enjoyed the most succulent prime rib and Yorkshire pudding either had ever tasted. Too stuffed for dessert, they returned to her car and Joe started toward home.

As they climbed from the car, Alexa glanced at her phone and smiled at the time. "I even have time for another movie or two before bedtime."

"I'll make you a deal."

Curious, she stopped mid-turn on the front lock. "What

would that be?"

"I'll watch any period movie you like—any—under two conditions."

She unlocked the door and pushed it open. "What are they?"

"First, you have to watch your movie, go to bed, and before you even think about popping another one of your horror movies into the DVD player, you have to look at your notes and see if you have enough material to write already. I suspect you do."

She shook her head and poked him as she carried her basket to the kitchen. "That's only one condition."

Joe smiled and reached for the canister of popcorn on the shelf above the kitchen window. "You make popcorn halfway through."

She unloaded her basket, put away her purchases, and set the wilted violets in a small, squatty vase. Slipping off her shoes, she brushed them briskly with a shoe brush outside the back door before carrying them and her flowers up to her nook on the second floor. She settled her flowers near her favorite corner of the couch, selected a movie, slipped it into the DVD player, and told Joe to make himself comfortable.

While Joe watched the promos and credits, Alexa slipped upstairs, presumably to put away her hat and shoes. She returned with her brush and a favorite headband just as the woman he assumed would be the heroine appeared. Alas, previews for other movies continued to slide across the screen.

"I'm going to grab me a glass of tea. Do you want anything? I might have one of your energy drinks in the fridge."

Joe nodded and followed her downstairs, kicking off his shoes by the front door. He tried to remember to remove his shoes before entering her house, but once he sat on her furniture, the desire to put his feet on the ottoman usually reminded him on days he forgot. Alexa found him amusing—he knew that—but her furniture was too nice to prop up his dirty shoes. He just couldn't do it.

By the time the heroine arrived at her destination, Joe and Alexa had settled into their places on the couch. He could see that she was already engrossed in the movie. "She's a lot like you," he remarked as the main character spoke her opinion with frankness.

She smiled, nodding slightly. "I think that's why I like her so much. Gaskell's heroines often feel like friends — strong personalities without losing their femininity."

Twenty minutes more into the movie, Alexa fell fast asleep. She looked uncomfortable all twisted on the couch as she was, but Joe knew he'd never manage to carry her up the stairs. The open door of one of the guest rooms gave him an idea. He paused the movie long enough to turn down the bed and fluff the pillow a bit.

Though he tried to lift her, he realized that he'd wake her either way, so Joe nudged a half-awake Alexa off the couch and into the guest room. Pulling the sheet over her, Joe snapped off the light. As a last minute thought, he took the spare pillow with him. He shuffled the cushions, afghan, ottoman, and pillow into the most comfortable arrangement possible and flipped the movie on again.

Three hours later, Alexa stumbled out of the guest room, confused. The small bed and the sound of the movie credits repeating incessantly had finally awakened her. She pulled the DVD from the player and discovered that Joe had watched both disks.

She gazed down at the sleeping man. It seemed a shame to wake him. She glanced at the clock — too late to send him home. Resigned, she climbed the stairs and closed the door behind her. It might be inappropriate for his car to be there all night, but it would just have to look bad. He looked comfortable and driving while tired was nearly as dangerous as driving while intoxicated.

Chapter 11

The tantalizing scent of muffins and omelets eventually reached the second floor. Joe cocked one eye open cautiously as he heard the distinct sound of Teresa Brewer's "Music, Music, Music" accompanied by Alexa's not-so-musical voice. The sight of Alexa's TV under the large picture window made him groan aloud. "She's going to kill me," he muttered.

"No, but if you let your omelet get cold, I might. Breakfast's done. Get in the kitchen and eat it while it's hot."

Alexa's voice startled him but receded as she returned to the kitchen. He hurried to the bathroom, groaning again at the sight of his hair curling around his head. He didn't have time to wash and blow it dry and straight before he sat down to breakfast. Knowing that getting it wet would only make it worse, he ran his comb through it, rubbed his scruffy chin absently, washed his hands, and hurried to the table before Alexa became genuinely irritated.

"Mornin', Lex. Sorry about that. I—"

"It's fine."

He shook his head as he grabbed a muffin from the basket she passed him. "No, it's not. I can't be careless with your reputation like that."

"Don't be ridiculous. You're not going to move in tomorrow, and we're not going to get careless about you falling asleep on my couch every night, but if this one move ruins my reputation, it wasn't worth it to begin with. It'll be fine."

Joe stabbed his omelet. "This is amazing. I always eat better at your house. Wes and I seem to live on frozen boxes and the occasional grilled meat. Once in a while, one of us remembers to bring a bag of salad, but I never remember to buy fruit. This pineapple is delicious."

She nodded absently as she chewed her own piece. "I used to hate fruit."

"Really? You always have the best—"

"That's just it. Most fruit isn't the best, so I have it shipped to me—a box a month."

Joe's low whistle told her that he not only was impressed, he also liked it more than she had realized. She made a quick note in her organizer to have shipments sent monthly to the cottage. Without another word, she passed the plate of pineapple slices to Joe and speared another bite of omelet.

Her cellphone rang. Alexa grabbed her planner and answered it. "Good morning, Elise. What do you have for me?"

She listened as Elise explained that the release of her next book had been rescheduled for the end of summer—two months early. Book signings, television appearances, writers' conferences, articles—Elise pushed for all. If Alexa followed Elise's plans, between appearances, the clothing line, and trying to see Lorie before she started her last semester of high school, she would be gone from Fairbury for most of summer and part of fall as well—particularly since this was her year to travel to California.

As Elise started in on other options, Alexa interrupted. "Elise, I've got to run this past James. He always helps me narrow things down to the most impor—" Her face twisted into an annoyed expression. "Elise—Elise, listen. I know your job is my publicity, but the books are doing great. You do a marvelous job—" She took a deep breath, rolled her eyes at Joe, and tried again. "We've been over this. I work with James. He has my personal interests as his primary responsibility, and we both know that you have to split your loyalty between me and the publisher. I'm not going to spend my time on something unnecessary."

Elise rattled on for a few minutes, but Alexa hardly listened. She made a few notes in her planner, rolled her eyes at Joe again, and then interrupted. "I'm sorry, Elise. I need to go. I'll get back to you by Friday with a tentative itinerary based on the dates you gave me. Bye."

"How do you do that?" Joe waved his fork at the phone. "I mean, you didn't let her push you around, but she does represent the publisher…"

"I understand her point of view and I respect it. I just don't have to make mine agree if it isn't what is best for me and for my career. James has worked hard to make a part of my persona a little unreachable. He didn't want me to be a recluse or anything that extreme, but he knew that with my style and genre, we could get more impact from fewer appearances.

Joe started to ask a question but hesitated. She nudged his elbow and motioned for him to continue as she took a bite of her muffin. He shrugged. "It's just that I wonder about James. I mean, do all agents get so involved?"

"No. From what I understand, James is one of the few who does what he does, and I pay him well for it. My percentage is higher, but he provides a level of service that almost guarantees success—far above contract negotiations and submissions. Many agents will advise, but James actually shows up and watches for himself to see how people respond and where we need to make changes. He's a genius."

"Why do you need a publicist, then?"

Alexa refilled her cup of coffee as she answered. "Well, the publisher recommended Elise's services. She does a lot of the groundwork for James but doesn't seem to realize that—no matter how blunt I am."

"James does what, then?"

"He just takes her suggestions and tells me what signings are overkill, which TV shows get maximum exposure, and he almost always rejects writing conferences."

"Does it ever feel like too much?"

The question was one she had pondered often. She sighed. "Sometimes—particularly after the thing with Ray Connors. There are times I'm tempted to take a sabbatical, but as long as I can write, I will."

"But why? I mean, if you want to take a couple of years

off, why don't you?"

She shook her head. "I can't. It would be selfish. I can write and I do enjoy it. James doesn't get paid as well if I don't work, and readers can be fickle. If you disappear for a few years, it is possible someone else will take your place in the public's heart. If I want to keep my career—and I do—then as long as I *can* write, I will."

The question hovered in his eyes. Alexa saw him struggle against asking it. Taking pity on him, she nodded. "Yes, Joe. I can afford to stop writing at any time."

"Even after buying this house, and investing in—"

"The house and renovations are paid for, and Rhette and Silva have the money I invested. I don't miss it."

"I suppose with your success—the movies and all—you probably don't have to worry about where your next meal comes from."

She coughed. *What an understatement!* "You could say that."

His eyes were on her as she ate, cleaned the kitchen, and put away the food. Did he think it strange that she scrubbed the sink and hung her apron to dry? His voice interrupted her thoughts. "I suppose you can write off your airfare and hotels and such."

"Most of it. I mean, if I stay over—like a few days after a meeting or something so I can visit Darrin and Lorie—I can't deduct those days, but the rest I can." She grabbed her planner and motioned to her deck. "I'm going to call James and run these by him. Come on out when you're done. Oh, and if you'd like a shower, I have those shorts and that t-shirt you left here when you went swimming last week. They're in the laundry room, in the cupboard to the left of the dryer."

Music filled the second floor. Alexa sat in her nook, her fingers flying over the keys as she typed up her notes. A list of scenes appeared as she typed out her plans. Occasionally, she switched the order of things and inserted new scenes. A smile grew. Several scenes practically begged her to write them, but she continued typing. Organization first. Every time she deviated from her writing plan, she regretted it. Work before play—the motto was a good one.

Wes and Joe found her there. "Annie, where is the volleyball set you bought?"

"Garage, why?"

Wes was already scrambling back down the stairs. Alexa laughed and winked at Joe. Her phone rang. He smiled at the familiar tune of her ringtone before turning and slowly descending the stairs—no reason to wear himself out before the game. Alexa's panicked tone once she answered sent him back up again—faster this time.

"Wait—what happened?"

Joe listened as her initial panic turned to the deliberately calm tone she used to steady herself when something went wrong. He leaned over her shoulder, reading as she penned the words "*The shop had a fire last night*" on a sticky note. Her laptop teetered on her knees as she fumbled to turn the page in her notebook. He grabbed it, carrying it around the couch and setting it on the table.

"Okay, so the new clothes weren't there? I thought they were delivered yesterday. You called when—oh, I see. Okay, that's a relief. So what did the fire marshal recommend?"

The longer he listened, the more unglued he became. It seemed like every time they climbed the next rung of the business ladder, a great hand came along and knocked them off with the flick of a finger. His radar pulsated with warning signals.

By the time she disconnected the call, Joe almost burst with frustration. "What is going on with those people and at that place? Are you sure this is a good idea?"

She rubbed her temples as she tried to explain. "Apparently while the building was empty, rats moved in and they chewed through some exposed electrical wires. Rhette left lights on to discourage more vandalism, and the stupid wires caught fire."

"Shouldn't there have been some signs of rats before

now? Why didn't they get an exterminator out there?"

"I don't know. At least the clothes Laidie remade weren't there, so the money for the fashion show isn't lost."

Everything sounded more and more suspicious to him, but the words "fashion show" distracted him. "Wait, what? What fashion show? I didn't know about that."

Alexa launched into an animated description of the launch they had planned for the first week in July. "It's a bit late, but it'll have the winter lines, and we'll get a jump into things. Silva has a manufacturer lined up to send out boutique stock by that date, and it'll be ready to ship to stores by mid-August.

"Why should people come to your store instead of one of the others—or vice versa?"

"Rhette's of Chicago will sell the high-end versions of the line—kind of the difference between what you see at Fashion Week and what ends up in places like Neiman-Marcus or Bergdorf's."

"You know," Joe said, laughing, "that I have no clue what you just said."

"It's the difference between..." she chewed her lip as she tried to find an analogy. "Oh, it's the difference between ordering a custom Mustang with everything you could possibly want and buying one off the lot."

"Gotcha. Kind of like legitimate knock-offs?"

"Joe?" Alexa waited for him to meet her eyes. "Don't use the word 'knock-off' around Rhette, okay? I don't want to have to rescue you from Miss Goth herself."

Chapter 12

Exhausted from the drive, Joe stepped into the large room at the convention center and glanced around him. From the look of the number of people, it seemed like a good turnout, but what did he know about fashion shows? Forget that. What did he know about fashion, period?

As he started to take a seat at one side, a young man touched his arm. "Sir? Mr. Freidan? If you will come with me please, Ms. Hartfield would appreciate your assistance."

Joe followed the young man to the side of the room and backstage. He wondered—again—why he had decided to attend a fashion show at all. However, three days after Alexa had boarded a plane for the Windy City, he'd jumped in his Jeep and made the six-hour drive to attend. *Sucker.*

Pandemonium reigned behind the curtains. Alexa stood perfectly still as a hairstylist wrapped her hair into a Gibson Girl pompadour. She wore an updated outfit that even he recognized as Gibson-inspired. If her dress was indicative of the line, it'd be a success. After all the setbacks, that thought relieved him.

However, Joe was confused. She hadn't mentioned being one of the models. As he glanced around the room, he recognized Rhette, Silva, and his sister, Jocelyn all wearing the clothing.

"Joe! Come here! I need you." Alexa sounded panicked.

He tried to get closer, but the hairstylist kept him a few feet back as she worked. "What's up? Why is Jocie wearing—going out on the runway? In that—"

"Our models didn't show."

"Models—what? How many?"

"None of them! Silva came in an hour ago and

announced that she had half a dozen voice messages and texts saying they'd gotten better offers and aren't coming in!"

"What?" The idea was ridiculous. Models wouldn't risk their reputations like that—and all six? "You have no models."

"No! Here; come here."

Alexa waved off the hairstylist and pulled him closer. She slipped Joe's sport jacket from his shoulders and gestured for him to kick off his shoes. Jeremy burst through the door carrying two tuxedos and shoes in sacks.

Joe realized she had tricked him when Jeremy thrust a tuxedo at him, and she pointed to a makeshift curtain. "Get into that as quickly as possible. I need you now!"

He'd never seen her like this—demanding. So out of character, and yet he still felt the undercurrent of her in it. The full impact of what would happen to the business if the fashion show failed hit him as he tore off his clothes and put on the tuxedo.

Stepping from the inadequate dressing corner, Joe tried to ignore half-dressed girls rushing past, begging the closest person to them to zip this or hook that. Alexa met him near the back of the main curtain and pointed to the catwalk. "You look perfect. They're playing Strauss for this one. Just ham it up a bit."

He'd never heard of a runway show like it. Joe stepped from behind the curtain with her on his arm, fighting to ignore the blast of lights. Unlike the pulsing beat and the long model stride expected, they strolled up the narrow walk, arm in arm, pointing to non-existent things along the way. She stopped at the end of the runway, sat on a double-sided bench, and smiled up at him before she stood, spun slowly, and took his arm again.

The moment they stepped behind the curtain, Rhette skipped out on the runway wearing something from the sixties with natural makeup and a hair flip with headband. He tried to compare it to Alexa's outfit—understand how they could look so perfect next to each other—but Alexa dragged him to where her next outfit waited.

"Take off the jacket and put on the suspenders—wherever they are. I'll be right back."

How it worked, he didn't know. When she wore a flapper-inspired dress, she minced her way down the runway and kicked up one heel at the end. Wearing a suit that looked designed for Nancy Reagan, she walked with quiet confidence—serious but approachable. As she stepped out from behind the curtains that he suspected wouldn't have been there if they had had "real" models, an idea hit him. He rushed to the sound tech and begged for Glenn Miller's "In the Mood" before racing back to her. "Okay, let's do a modified Lindy Hop on the way down."

"I can do that."

Aside from a couple of stumbles the audience likely didn't notice, it worked well. He expected to be shoved off for some other shirt or jacket change, but as they stepped behind the curtain again, Alexa collapsed in a chair, exhausted. He watched Jeremy and Jocie attempt a "peace-era" dance through imaginary daisy fields, wondering if the audience thought they were supposed to be high on marijuana or if it was just him.

Once the show ended and Silva took the microphone to explain their aesthetic, he turned to Alexa, who guzzled water and still looked drained. "Why didn't you just walk? You—"

"I knew I'd never be able to do it if I was trying to 'be a model.' I needed to be me, or I'd never get through it."

"Well, it worked," he admitted. "That was amazing. I just wish I could have seen it from the audience's vantage point—for more reasons than one," he added with a wink.

Alexa grinned. "You can. We had a videographer out there so we could decide where we needed to improve, the models we liked—stuff like that. I'll get you a copy."

"No hurry. I can catch it at your house sometime."

As Silva stepped through the curtain again, Alexa sighed. "I have to get changed into my dress for the opening."

"What's wrong with that?"

She glanced down at her dress. "Nothing, I suppose, but Rhette designed a dress especially for me. She took one of the formals—that one Jocie wore—and made it a little more historically accurate. I'll be back in a few minutes."

"Should I change or stay in this?"

"Why don't you put the tuxedo back on?" She winked. "And thanks for texting Jeremy that you were coming. Gave us time to get you a tux."

"Yeah, won't be doing that next time," he joked. Seeing the concern cross her face, he added, "Really, I didn't mind. I wouldn't have done it if you had asked, but now that it's over—it was fun."

Alexa stopped him, untying his bowtie. "This thing is a mess. Let me fix it for you." She smoothed the wrinkles with her thumb and retied it into a perfect dress bow.

Joe stood awkwardly, waiting for her to finish. "You were great tonight, Alexa—really. I think you've made waves in the fashion world with your unconventional show. Rhette's collection is going to be a hit and all because somehow all of—" He frowned.

She cocked her head. "What?"

"Don't you think it's odd that every single one of your models got better offers at the very last second possible?" He thought for another moment and added, "Actually, don't you find it interesting that your store was vandalized, caught fire, and you lost all your models within a two month period?"

Alexa spun and caught his eye. "I never—I'll be right back."

Alexa stepped into Rhette's of Chicago and smiled up at Joe. "Isn't it amazing?"

"Looks incredible. When do they open?"

She gazed around her. "Tomorrow. They did a great job of giving it all the appeal of a full service boutique with the possibility of an independent shopping experience for those who prefer to shop unassisted."

"I shop in the Levi's store. I walk in, find my numbers, grab a few, pay, and walk out. I have no idea what 'full-service boutique' means, and I'm pretty sure I don't want to."

He led her through the store, awkwardly trying to steer her around the crowd without touching her back. The gown Rhette had made was truly gorgeous. From the moment she'd stepped from the dressing area, he'd been impressed by the midnight charmeuse dress. However, when she had turned to grab her purse, he had swallowed hard. The gown—a replica of something from the thirties, she said—had the deepest plunging back he had ever seen. The gentle cowl covered her backside and not much more. Though exquisite, the gown showed a little—no, a lot—too much bare skin for his comfort.

While he sat in the corner, nursing a glass of some kind of fruit drink, Alexa welcomed their guests, explained the design concept numerous times, and signed several books—completely in her element. It was a side of her he hadn't seen, though. For someone as private and alone as she chose to be, Alexa managed to make each person feel as though he or she was present as her personal guest.

Eventually, Joe slipped out the back door and climbed the stairs to the loft. Industrial sewing machines lined one wall and bolts of fabrics lined another. Patterns hung from clips at one end of a large cutting table, and beneath it, he found drawers. A glance around him showed no one had followed, so he pulled a few open. Most of the contents were foreign to him. He recognized thread, elastic, and buttons. Zippers on spools, paper-like fabric—all odd but somewhat familiar. The rest could have been auto parts for all he knew.

A strange dripping sound broke through his thoughts. He followed the noise from the main loft to a small washroom next to the stairs. Water covered the floor. The sink remained empty, but the trap continually dripped water onto the floor. In the bad light, it took a moment to see the clear plastic tubing that ran from the faucet down the drain.

His mind whirled. Without thinking twice about the possible destruction of evidence, Joe shut off the tap. Uncertain if it would be enough to prevent any real damage, Joe turned off the water at the base of the sink as well.

"Joe? Are you up here?" Alexa's shoes tapped the steps up to the loft.

"Yeah! In the washroom. You've got a leak—"

"What?"

Alexa's voice so close to him startled Joe. He jumped, whirled, and slipped in one swift, smooth movement. Sitting on the soaked tile floor, Joe crossed his arms and jerked his thumb at the sink. "Check out the faucet. Someone turned the tap on, unscrewed the trap, and then left it. If it had been left on all night, you would have had a soaked second floor—serious damage most likely."

Alexa braced one foot against the doorjamb and held out her hand for Joe. The movement slammed him into her as his feet slid across the slippery floor. "Sorry, I'm—"

"No worries. Are you okay?" Alexa grabbed a roll of paper towels and tried to mop up the floor, but her dress refused to cooperate—and gave Joe mental hives as the cowl back slid at provocative angles in the process.

He took the roll from her. "Here, let me do that. If you keep it up you're going to destroy that dress. I'm already soaked."

While Joe dried the floor, Alexa called a local taxi service and requested a cab. She led him down the stairs and along a sidewall, said goodnight to Rhette and the others, and left the building. As they waited for the cab, Silva came out to talk to them and Alexa told her about the sink episode. Distraught, the woman rushed inside to tell the other partners of the averted damage.

Across town, through the lobby, and into the elevator, Joe and Alexa discussed the ramifications of what they now realized was sabotage on the business. As she slipped her card key into the door, she said, "You know, we haven't discussed motive. Perhaps if we focused on that—"

"Jealousy and money are the top two that I can think of." Joe hurried into the room and grabbed the phone, dialing room service as he pulled off his tie and unbuttoned his shirt. "Steak or burger?"

"Steak—you know me well. Gotta have food after an

event."

After he ordered, Joe washed his hands, spending as much time in the bathroom as he could. When the time that had passed became as embarrassing as his attempts at mental self-preservation, Joe stepped into the room, examining the furniture as if he had never seen one of her rooms at The Drake.

Slowly, he became aware of her movements. She slipped off her shoes and put them into the closet. Bobby pins dropped into the wastebasket as she pulled them from her hair. A small wave of relief washed over him as her hair covered her upper back, but it didn't last long. She twisted and his eyes sought the ceiling. The Drake had lovely ceilings—perfectly painted and...overhead, too.

Joe groaned inwardly, wondering if he should say something about her dress. He wasn't in the habit of telling women, no matter how good of a friend they might be, that their clothing was more provocative than he could stand. Perhaps he should leave. Or, maybe once she sat—yes. She'd sit down soon and he wouldn't have any more trouble.

At that moment, she turned, pulling her hair over her shoulder to brush it. The movement showed much more of her body than he could imagine her wanting to reveal. The sight of her bare back—and more—made his decision for him.

"Alexa?"

"Hmm?" She didn't give him a chance to answer before she murmured, "Maybe one of Silva's other designers is jealous of Rhette..."

"Would you do something for me?" Joe prayed that appealing to her as doing him a favor would show her he didn't mean to criticize.

"If I can—hey, will you pull a tip out of my purse for me?"

Joe opened his wallet, retrieved a ten-dollar bill, and laid it on the nearby table. As he tried to find a way to return to the conversation, Alexa spoke again. "What was the favor?"

She gave her hair one last stroke of the brush and set it on the dresser. Impatiently, she pulled the skirt up past her calves and sank into the corner of the couch. With her hair hanging down and her back hidden by the couch, Joe decided not to say anything. Why make her feel uncomfortable for something he doubted would ever be an issue again. She was covered, and his mind would quit replaying the vision of it — eventually. There was no reason to step into awkward territory.

"Joe?"

"It's nothing." Honesty forced him to add, "Anymore." He hated that part of him that occasionally ignored the basics of discretion.

"That's not true. I've never seen 'just-the-facts-ma'am' Friday be so evasive. If you think you know who did it, I want to know."

"It isn't that." He hated that he'd even spoke.

"C'mon. Spit it out."

Before he lost his nerve, Joe swallowed hard and said, "I just wondered — that dress."

Her forehead wrinkled. "You want a favor about my dress?" Before he could speak, she added, "Is something wrong with it? A rip? Did I embarrass — "

"No!" Joe cleared his throat and tried again — more quietly. "No, the dress is stunning, and you never embarrass me. You know that. It's just — "

A knock prevented an answer. Joe bolted to the door and flung it open, eager for the diversion. The attendant pushed the cart through the door, and everything spiraled from there.

Alexa untangled herself from the couch and strolled across the room to tip the attendant and sign for their food. As she turned to inspect the plates, she caught the appraising eye of attendant and frowned. Joe sent the young man an understanding but firm glance and closed the door behind him, hoping that awkward moment would distract her from their unfinished conversation.

"Thank you, Joe."

Frustrated at the failed attempt to drop the subject, he played innocent. "What for?"

"I don't know what that boy thought he was doing with his inappropriate gawking. I've never—"

"I do."

"What? You think that kind of behavior is okay?" The incredulity in her tone sent warning bells off in his mind, but it was too late.

"He tried to be respectful, but—"

"All right, Friday, spit it out. I don't know what you're talking about. The guy was inappropriate."

"I didn't say he wasn't," Joe corrected. "I said he tried. It's just hard—that dress."

"You don't like my dress?" Leaving her plate on the cart, she returned to her corner of the little couch and drew her knees up to her chest—almost protectively.

Joe suddenly realized why he had felt so reticent about saying anything. Had it been Shannon, he would have been forthright—gentle, but honest. Alexa was accustomed to having the people she trusted be cruel about her choices and decisions.

He gathered flatware, her plate of food, and a towel from the bathroom. Hunkering down on his heels, he handed her the plate and spread the towel across her lap. With the most reassuring smile he could muster, Joe said, "On the contrary, Lex, I like the dress very much—too much."

The guarded look in her eyes vanished, and in its place, a question formed. "Too much?"

Begging the Lord for a complimentary way of telling her the kind of effect her dress had on him, Joe shook his head. "Well, you could say that the front of your dress is exquisite and..."

"And?"

His ears burned as Joe added, "And the back shows just how exquisite you are."

She stared at him for a moment, allowing the words to sink in. He knew the moment she understood. "Is it really that bad? I mean, I knew it showed more skin than any gown I've ever owned. I certainly wouldn't request it, but I thought since it's the back..."

The quiet of the room grew awkward as Joe tried to formulate an inoffensive response—again. Hoping he wouldn't make a miserable situation worse, Joe covered her hand with his and said, "I don't know that every man would find that dress as provocative as I—well, and obviously Mr. Gawker—did. Some guys have problems with short skirts, and they never faze me. But when a dress is bare past the waist—"

"Is it really that low?"

He grinned. "Forgive me if I don't check the accuracy of my facts—this time."

She slipped her hand behind her back and blushed. "Oh, ugh. That's what I get for not trying it on at home where I could see—I'm so sorry." Alexa's eyes closed as she fought her own embarrassment over the situation. "Joe, thank you."

"For telling you that your dress is indecent? Gee, what a pal I am."

"Thank you for being firm about the effect it can have, but gentle with *me*. My mother would have raked me over the coals and—" Her blush deepened to an unattractive hue. "I am ashamed to admit that I probably would have worn it again—often—just to spite her." She sighed. "I'm still trying to 'get back at my mom.' How pathetic."

"No, you're honest about the fact that you might have that temptation."

"Forgive me?"

He nodded. "Only if you forgive my interference. I feel like a jerk for saying anything."

Alexa set her plate aside and backed toward her closet, winking at him as she fumbled for something to wear and then backed into the bathroom. Minutes later, as she exited, she dumped the dress in the wastepaper basket.

Joe stood and retrieved the gown. "Don't throw it away. It's too nice. Maybe your sewing lady can fill in the back or something."

She shook her head. "I don't know if I could bring myself to wear it again, Joe. I'd be too embarrassed."

He dropped the dress into one of the laundry service

bags. "You have the wrong idea. Wear it with the back covered and your head high. It's a great dress. I hate that I said anything now."

They ate their meal, neither speaking. As minutes passed, the comfortable camaraderie settled between them again until Joe stood to leave. "Great show, Alexa. You guys did a smashing job."

She walked him to the door and as he reached for the handle, Alexa hugged him. "Thanks again, Joe—for being a true friend."

Chapter 13

Rich's voice echoed in Alexa's mind as she flipped through dozens of receipts, reviewing the expenses of the business to date. *They are wise to have your signature required. It keeps them from being accused of misappropriation of funds. If you don't want to sign yourself, have them sent to me.*

Maybe she should have had them sent to Rich. She could still do it. It would take hours—she stopped at another exorbitant bill and receipt for repairs. Initial purchases and renovations had seemed reasonable, but the repair bills were astronomical. Joe's questions about money and jealousy swam through her mind, making her rethink the idea.

She punched Joe's number, shuffling receipts as she waited for him to answer. "Hey, do you have time to look at a few things? I brought home copies of the bills and receipts from Rhette. They cover everything from the initial costs of the prospectus to the rental agent and lease. Those and the fabrics, payroll, and rental of the room at the convention center all seem fine, but the repairs—they're awfully steep."

"I'll stop by on my lunch—about an hour and a half?"

"Thanks. I was thinking about grilled salmon; what do you think?"

"Sounds great. See you soon. We'll sort this."

Her conscience nudged her for her semi-deceptive words. She had been thinking about grilled salmon—for dinner. However, she also knew that Wes and Joe practically lived out of frozen and boxed foods when they didn't skip cooking and eat at The Diner. Feeding either of them something "real" had become a hobby for her.

By the time Joe arrived, salad, salmon, and her herbed rice pilaf waited for him. "Wash up. It's going to get cold!"

He stepped up to the sink as she carried their plates to the breakfast nook. "Looks great. Thanks. I really appreciate it." As Joe seated himself, he glanced around him. "Where are the receipts?"

"Eat first. It's not so urgent that you can't have a decent meal before you read about rats and flooding washrooms."

"Good point. Thank you for that lovely mental picture."

She grinned. "You're welcome."

"And a piece of spinach has taken up residence again."

She prodded it with her tongue and gave up. "I'll get it when I'm done eating. If it's not one piece, it'll be another. Stupid tooth."

As Joe took a bite of salmon, he moaned. "Oh, man, this is good."

Those words made the loss of her dinner plans worth it. She'd have to go over to The Coventry or maybe The Deli for dinner, but at least he'd have a good meal. "I've been craving it for days."

It took longer for him to eat than she had expected. He polished off all of the salmon, most of the salad, and quite a bit of the rice. As an afterthought, she jumped up and cut open the watermelon that Jill at The Market had assured her would be perfect. The scent and the juices as she drove her knife into the rind told her it was sweet, and the crunch of the rind and flesh assured her it wasn't yet mealy.

"Okay, you eat watermelon and I'll show you these receipts."

She read each one, what it was for, and the amount paid, stacking them in piles. At last, she reached the repairs. After the first numbers, Joe dropped his fork. "What?"

"That was my exact response. Doesn't it seem a bit excessive?"

The tallies rose as they went through replacing damaged counters, drawers, floors, mirrors, and electrical. "I don't understand why the repair of the renovation was more than the renovation."

Alexa nodded, relieved. "Again, my thoughts exactly. I mean, maybe it's because they had to remove things and there were disposal fees?"

"Probably grasping at straws, but we're talking about Chicago. Things can be way high there. Dad has friends in construction. Want me to call and ask him what he thinks?" Alexa answered by handing Joe her phone. He pushed it away and grabbed his. "Call now. Got it."

She carried their dirty dishes from the table as Joe called his father and explained the problem. She loaded the dishwasher, listening intently for any hint of John Freidan's opinion, but Joe was his usual interrogating self—asking the questions while his father apparently answered them.

Joe disconnected the call and smiled. "Dad says he'll get back to us."

Something in his expression made her curious. "What else did he say?"

"He said to tell 'my girlfriend' that she's invited for Labor Day weekend—whether or not I get it off."

Alexa laughed.

"Yeah. Funny for you. I told you letting them think what they want to is dangerous."

Alexa worked in her old kitchen. As the sandwiches grilled, she pulled inedible food from the fridge. She dumped the produce in a bucket, ordering Wes to bury it by the lilac bushes. She dumped containers, dropping them in a sink of sudsy water, and then flipped the sandwiches just as they started to get too dark for her preference. Wes watched with dutiful protests erupting at semi-regular intervals.

She slid the sandwiches onto plates, dumped chips next to them, and quartered a couple of Granny Smith apples. "Eat up."

Wes shook his head. "Not until you sit."

"I'm not sitting until I get us something to drink. Iced tea or soda?"

"Which are you having?"

She filled a glass with ice and flipped on the water.

"H20."

"That's good for me." He took a bite and muttered, "I could have gotten drinks."

"But I did so you don't have to. Stop whining and eat."

Three bites into his sandwich, Wes suddenly asked, "What effect would my job have on a family?"

The question spun seemingly out of thin air and hovered as he waited for her response. "I'm not sure I understand the question," she replied at last. "Are you asking for a simple positive or negative answer or for actual examples of the impact it could make?"

"Yes."

Chuckling, Alexa shook her head. "It doesn't work that way, Wes. What would be devastating to one family is perfect for another."

"You know what I mean, Annie—"

"You're asking me if I think your job is a bad fit with Heather's children."

Wes nodded miserably. "It just doesn't seem fair to those kids to let them get attached to me if I'm not willing to give up my job—"

She interrupted again. "Wes, those children *have* a father. Granted, he doesn't live in the same house with them, but they do have one."

The sounds of chips crunching echoed around her breakfast nook. "What if we had a child together? I'd be the only dad…"

Unsure how to answer that question, she tried a new idea. "Would your job have to stay exactly the same? Could you change where you go or how often?" Seeing the dubious expression on his face, Alexa lost her temper. "Wesley Harper Hartfield! I'm ashamed of you. This isn't an either/or proposition. You can choose to adjust your work schedule to make this happen. If you don't want to, that's fine, but don't use your job as a cop-out if you decide you just don't want a family."

A derisive snort escaped with little attempt to hide it. "Pot? Kettle?"

Furious, Alexa's eyes narrowed. "Just what are you alluding to, Wes?"

"For someone so high and mighty about cop-outs, you sure feel free to indulge in them yourself."

"Again I ask, what do you mean?"

She saw him waver—hesitate. He'd drop it and save them both an argument. She felt her expression change to a challenge and wanted to kick herself. The moment he opened his mouth, she wished she had more facial self-control.

"You look me in the eye and tell me that you don't use your lack of uterine capabilities as an excuse to push men away."

"I do no such—"

"Uh, yeah. Ya do." Wes left no room for argument.

"For someone who hates confrontation, you're awfully good at it."

Wes smiled again at his sister. "Annie, you're doing it again. I saw it with Clay and Tom. With guys like Nolan, you rejected them before you even met them. You've got to stop it."

"And I'm doing what again?"

"Pushing away a good man."

"I'm not pushing away anyone. How did this turn from a conversation about you and Heather and parenthood to me and my lack of a love life."

Wes' hand crept across the table and covered hers. "I don't know, but it's something we should discuss. You're going to let another good one go—probably the best for you—all because you're afraid to trust a man when he says he'll survive missing out on the opportunity to pass along his genetic material."

"Not this time," she argued. "This time it's because I'm too independent to give up the life to which I've become accustomed, and Darrin didn't want that—not now anyway."

"I wasn't talking about Darrin. We both know that you like and respect him, but he isn't who you're attracted to."

Indignant, her head snapped up. "That's not true! He's an attractive, thoughtful—"

"Friend. And as much as you like him, you'd never care one way or another if he grew or shaved a mustache. You'd never go shopping with his favorite foods in mind—"

"Of course I would! And I have!"

"Not if he lived here and dropped in every day or two." Wes' voice developed a teasing lilt.

"We're supposed to be discussing the feasibility of fatherhood with your job."

"I'd rather discuss my sister's budding relationship with a fascinating man named Joe."

She took a sip of water, wiped her mouth with a napkin, and stood to gather their plates. "There isn't one, Wes. Not like you're thinking. Joe's a friend—a good friend, actually—and I'm not about to risk that friendship by complicating it."

"Why would—"

"Because, Wes, Joe isn't looking for a girlfriend or a wife. I'm convenient because I'm safe. I don't want a family. I'm not going to demand commitment. With me, he can be just a friend. I don't want to ruin that."

Wes took the plates from her hands and set them next to the sink. He kneaded her shoulders for a moment before asking, "Even if you'd like more?"

She swallowed hard, not allowing her thoughts to follow Wes' direction. "Greed is an excellent way to destroy a beautiful friendship. I'm not willing to risk that." Her voice dropped to a whisper, "I enjoy having a friend here, Wes. I haven't had that until now. I want to make sure I keep it."

Alexa's phone rang as she and Wes entered her house. She pointed to the back deck where she wanted him to look at a loose railing and listened as Silva described a man seen going up the stairs of the workroom just an hour before the show had started. "Should I call the police?"

"The mustache will make it hard to place…" She thought for a moment. "Still, they should know."

Silva seemed hesitant but added, "Alexa, Diana said that

there was a man at the party later that looked exactly like the man except—"

"Except what?"

"His mustache was gone."

"That would be smart," she agreed.

"Alexa, she swears it was the guy you were with—Joe."

Fury filled Alexa. "Who is this Diana? That sounds like the exact kind of scheme someone who is guilty would use. She obviously didn't know he's a cop."

"Diana has been a friend ever since I was a kid. She offered every penny in her savings when she heard I was looking for an investor."

"So why didn't you accept her offer?"

Silva didn't answer for the better part of a minute. "She doesn't have the money for it, and she doesn't have the recognition you do. Call me mercenary, but I wanted that recognition. With your style…"

"That makes sense to me." What didn't make sense were Silva's friend's assertions. "I wonder if whoever did it knew enough about my life to know about Joe. He was in that paper. Maybe he looked enough like Joe to try—or found someone who did just for that reason."

"Oh, that makes sense. Maybe it's not worth telling the police then."

Alexa sank into her couch and propped her feet up on the coffee table. "No, call them. It can't hurt."

Just as she hung up, Joe's voice startled her. Embarrassed to be overheard talking about him, she flushed. "Joe!"

"Sorry, thought you heard me." He dropped into the chair beside the couch. "Dad called—said his friend thinks the prices are high, but more from the standpoint of the contractors are milking you. It's padded—definitely."

"So what do we do? I mean—"

"Dad thinks he can get the restaurant down the street to agree to ask for some estimates. Do a kind of consumer watchdog thing and see what turns up."

Alexa closed her eyes in relief. She hadn't wanted to

think of Rhette, Silva, Adam, or the new girl Lisa embezzling from corporate funds. "I'm glad to hear that. So now what?"

"Now I have bad news."

"What?" Alexa rubbed her temples and tried not to assume the worst.

"Rhette called me, and—"

"Why would she call you? I don't—"

Joe interrupted her. "She called to see if I'd seen two large boxes on the cutting table when we were there." He sighed. "There were no boxes."

"What was in those boxes, and why didn't Rhette call me about it?"

"I told her I'd tell you since I'd see you anyway." The frustration and apology in his eyes answered her question before he did. "It was some kind of stock for the boutique. She'd gotten two huge boxes of things from your seamstress up in Wisconsin."

"And it's gone?"

"It's not there anyway. She has people working 'round the clock, trying to recreate this stuff, but she's overworked. I think you need to get a dedicated business manager. Silva doesn't know how to handle product on this scale."

Alexa's fingers flew over the laptop keys, searching for a Chicago employment agency. Once she found one that looked reputable, she called and discussed the need for a general business manager with fashion industry experience. The woman she spoke to assured Alexa that they would get back to her as soon as they could. "I'm sure we have someone perfect for the position."

The doorbell rang as she called the next on the list. Joe jogged down the stairs to answer it and watched as a UPS driver began unloading four oversized boxes. Alexa skipped down as he called for her, asking if he should sign.

She spun in circles for a moment, groaned, and started toward her office. "What is it, Lex?"

"I don't have scissors here. Remind me to buy a table with a drawer and put it next to the door. I need it for scissors."

As she took another step toward the office, Joe called to her again, "Hey, will this work?" Joe flipped open the largest pocketknife she'd ever seen.

"Yippee!" Alexa raced back to the boxes and pointed to the first one. She stepped closer, waving him back again. Confusion filled her eyes as she read the shipping labels. "This one belongs at the boutique! Wait—both of these were the ones that Rhette asked you about. I'll call and let her know they're here. Can you try to see if the UPS truck is still on the street?"

While Joe jumped in his Jeep to track down the UPS driver, Alexa pulled out her phone and called Rhette. It took a full half hour before they managed to get the extra boxes back on their way to Chicago and Alexa back to the business of opening her boxes. From the moment she pulled back the flaps, her excitement bubbled over. "Oh, look, Joe! Look at this one!" She held up a pink-white afternoon dress in the style of the World War I era.

"Are these all dresses?"

She laughed and tossed the dress to him, pulling out a new one. Dress after dress, skirt after skirt, the clothing piled in, on, and around the boxes. She tossed a new coat and a short cape over Joe. "Oh, I love this day. It's my favorite day of the year!"

Alexa hurried upstairs, her arms loaded with clothing, beckoning Joe to follow. "Can you grab those boxes? I have clothes to pack away."

For the next few hours, Alexa packed the boxes full of clothing that she no longer enjoyed or was fading or worn. Joe watched for a while and then left, promising to return with Chinese at dinnertime. He tried to encourage her to attend a game night at church, but she laughed, waved him off, and went back to sorting her clothes.

"Joe?"

Buttoning his uniform shirt as he left his bedroom, Joe

looked up to find Wes leaning against the dining room doorjamb. "What is it?"

"Alexa."

Joe's expression changed instantly from nonchalance to concern—the recent murders in Fairbury and the threat to Alexa still too fresh in his mind. "What is it? Is she all right?"

"She's fine. I just want to know when you're going to quit pretending that you—"

"It's none of your business," Joe growled.

"She's my sister."

Joe tied his shoes, strapped on his gun belt, and grabbed his hat. "Then maybe *she* will feel obligated to tell you what you want to know. I don't."

Chapter 14

Adelaide Peters read Alexa's glowing email and smiled. The only thing that delighted her more than making the garments Alexa dreamed up each year was the email that inevitably followed. Alexa's thank-you notes filled a spot in her heart that nothing else could.

To: AdelaidePeters@letterbox.com
From: alexa@alexahartfield.com

Subject: Guess What Arrived?

My Laidie,

What can I say? You've outdone yourself. As I opened the first box this afternoon, I realized how blessed I am to have found such a jewel as you are. To have managed to get these things finished in record time, while helping Rhette with her clothing samples… All I can say is that you are even more amazing than I ever knew or imagined.

The three dresses you surprised me with are delightful, and that walking suit is the most amazing thing I've ever owned. I'm going to be wishing away the months so that I can wear it. Do send me an invoice, though, or I'll be afraid of underpaying and insulting you.

And, on the off chance that you try to be

stubborn *cough*, I have to add that if I do not receive an invoice in two weeks' time, I will assume that you no longer wish to sew for me, and I will be forced to find another—and obviously inferior—dressmaker to work with. Please don't break my heart.

Thank you again, and I hope you have plenty of time to work on your Christmas presents. I know I've commandeered too much of your time as it is. So, until next January, I'll try to leave you alone.
Thank you again. You can't possibly know how I love the work you do for me.

The best dressed woman in town (probably the world, thanks to you),

Alexa Hartfield.

P.S. You'll never believe what happened. Somehow, the boxes of dresses you shipped to Rhette were shipped to me from Rhette's. We've been trying to discover what happened, but no one knows. With so many things going wrong with the business, I am beginning to think it has to be genuine sabotage. I know that you are a great prayer warrior. Please remember us when you pray. Poor Rhette is killing herself to ensure the business is a success. As for me, I'm afraid that you're stuck sewing for me, because as much as I like Rhette's work, yours suits me better!

Adelaide leaned back in her office chair and allowed herself to reread the note once more. Although she had other clients, Alexa did provide the bulk of her sewing income, and sewing for the author was more interesting work and paid better than the occasional wedding or alterations she did. Most people hoped she could save them money—never Alexa. And the variety...

Nearly everything Alexa Hartfield wore emerged from her farmhouse attic studio. While her husband worked with the animals or in the fields, she created clam diggers, swimsuits, lingerie, suits, coats, and ball gowns. If Alexa wanted it, Laidie made it and occasionally in record time. No one but her family knew how many hours a day she cut, measured, cut, pressed, cut, and then sewed the beautiful fabrics together to create the masterpieces that helped make Alexa famous.

She stood and strolled from the office upstairs to her studio. Sunbeams shone into the room. Behind the wardrobe doors at the end of the room—nothing. The fabrics she had purchased during her two-week stint to New York in January—gone. They now hung as garments in Alexa's new "closet." She couldn't wait to see a picture of that.

Her eyes roamed to her project board, resting on the photos Alexa had sent when she first moved into her new house. That closet was amazing—almost exclusively filled with her creations. She peered closer and saw one pair of jeans hanging with trousers of every kind and era. That one piece of incongruity kept Laidie's job interesting.

Scraps from the work for Rhette's boutique still carpeted the floor. The moment she had finished boxing up the garments, she had closed the door, desperate for a break. She had resented every stitch of those outfits as taking time away from the work she'd rather do. She hadn't tended her garden, and most of it had withered, died, or become overgrown with weeds. Her chickens had been neglected in favor of chic garments that, though attractive, did not hold the same appeal as Alexa's.

Housework suffered, meals suffered, even her relationship with her husband suffered. Tim understood, but she had resented that he had to. Her perennial flower garden had suffered the most. Weeds choked the flowers there, but they still couldn't smother her growing sense of satisfaction.

Alexa appreciated her sacrifice. Miss Hartfield appreciated *her*.

Something niggled at the back of her mind. She hurried

downstairs and into the office. Her finger swirled around the touch pad of her laptop and she reread the postscript. So many strange things had happened at Rhette's. Adelaide ticked off each event that she knew of, weighing each one against the others.

Her eyes widened. Hesitation held her hand over the phone as she tried to decide if calling was too presumptuous. Her fingers closed around the handset and she punched pound and a single number. "Tim?"

"Hey, hon. Have you gotten any rest today?"

"Woke up feeling wonderful. I might clean the attic. Listen—"

"Save it for the weekend. I'll help."

"That's okay, Tim. Really. I'm feeling better. It was just a lot of work and that cold..." She took a deep breath and spoke again before he could derail her. "I got an email from Miss Hartfield."

"Did she like this year's wardrobe?"

"Yes. I think she forgot until it arrived that we had planned so many extra outfits. She's feeling bad that she asked me to do the Rhette thing."

"Well, you send her a nice note back and assure her it was your pleasure. You saved her a bunch of money."

"That's why I'm calling."

"Want to take a trip to Fairbury or Chicago?"

Adelaide laughed. "Not on your life. But she said something strange in the email."

"Oh, yeah?"

"You know the boxes we shipped to the shop?"

"The ones that went out a week or so before hers?"

"Right," Adelaide hesitated before plunging ahead. "Well, they were shipped to the shop—and then to Miss Hartfield's."

"Really? How?" Tim coughed, the wheeze of his lungs making her heart ache. He really needed to stop smoking on the sly when he was out in the fields. "That just doesn't make sense. You can't 'accidentally' ship something to another state."

"My thoughts exactly. And it got me thinking…"

"Uh oh…"

Adelaide laughed. "You behave, old man. Listen. Every single one of the things that have happened has been something that wouldn't hurt the business—not in the public eye. It's almost as if whoever is doing this wants to cost the business money, but not truly damage it."

"That is an excellent point, hon. Did you call Miss Hartfield and see if she has noticed that?"

"I wasn't sure if I should." She sighed. "It's really none of my business, but…"

"You said she sent an email? Just reply, comment on how strange the box thing was, and maybe put a hint in there about how it's a good thing that none of the pranks would really hurt the business. She writes mysteries. Her brain can connect it all."

Adelaide brightened. "You're right! I can do that. I kept thinking I had to call and it seemed so presumptuous. I'm a seamstress. I'm not a business partner or a detective."

Unaware that she disconnected without another word, Adelaide hit reply on the email and began typing.

To: alexa@alexahartfield.com
From: AdelaidePeters@letterbox.com

Subject: Re: Guess What Arrived?

Dear Miss Hartfield,

I am pleased that you enjoyed your box of clothing. I will send an invoice for the three extras I sent if you insist, but I would prefer at least one be my gift. You brought me much extra business this year. I appreciate it. If I do not receive an "acceptance" of that gift by the end of the week, I'll send an invoice for all.

I was astonished to read about the mix-up with the boxes. I cannot imagine how anyone could accidentally mail two huge boxes labeled for Rhette's to you after they'd already arrived at the shop. It just makes no sense. I keep thinking about all these little pranks and the vandalism and I cannot help but be thankful that none of it will actually hurt the business. It's expensive, but at least everything could be put right before your public and customers were affected. I just hope it doesn't escalate. Meanwhile, as requested, I will be praying (and I have been for weeks) that whoever is doing this will get tired of it and go away—if not repent.

Affectionately,
Laidie

Alexa read the email, unnerved by Laidie's innocent remarks. Had the woman found the true problem? Her hand rolled her cellphone over and over as if a stone tumbling in water while she thought. Frustrated, she punched Joe's number.

"Joe? Laidie just sent me an email and I think you should see it. We need to talk."

Joe's eyes traveled over the screen—twice. Two things bothered him about the email. His eyes traveled to Alexa's anxious face. "What did you see in it?"

"Well, she makes a valid point—even though I don't think she realizes it."

"I think she does."

Alexa's eyebrows drew together as she stared at him. "What do you mean?"

"I see two things here. One, she does make an excellent point. I've often thought similar things, just not quite so succinctly."

"And two?"

Joe sighed, hating how suspicious he would sound. "She knows exactly what she's doing. That email was a way to make you think in a certain direction. The question I have is: why?"

"You think she deliberately wanted me to get suspicious after reading her email, but didn't want to tell me her own suspicions? That is absolutely—" She faltered.

"I'm sorry, Alexa, but yes, I think she wanted to make you suspicious. I just don't know why she wouldn't say, 'I just realized something.'"

Alexa leaned back in the chair, thinking. A few seconds later, she grinned. "I feel so silly. I know exactly why she didn't say that."

Joe waited, watching emotions and thoughts flicker through eyes that he'd never realized were so green. *Snap out of it, idiot.* "Well?"

"Laidie is a very private person—even more than I am. She respects privacy and would consider it none of her business, but she is loyal too. She'd want me to think of it myself. That would appease her conscience while still helping. It's so *her*."

Those eyes, twinkling up at him—her lips smiling at the thought of her friend—Joe almost groaned as Wes' words came back to him. *When are you going to quit pretending...*

Chapter 15

When are you going to quit pretending... Wes' words echoed through Joe's mind—again. Each day that passed, they grew louder—stronger. He'd been rude, and he really didn't care. It *was* none of Wes' business. But the words, once spoken, had taken root in some place in his heart that he had intended to keep barren. Since then, every time he stopped in—to talk, to help, to eat—they taunted him, refusing to leave his thoughts.

Alexa set a plate of steaming food in front of him, her hand resting on his shoulder. Joe nearly salivated at the scent of her homemade cream cheese and crab ravioli. "Mmm..." He glanced up at her and her smile nearly killed him.

"I thought that after that fight at the school, you might need a pick-me-up."

Before he stopped to consider the ramifications of his actions, he slipped an arm around her waist and pulled her onto his lap. Alexa's eyes clouded with confusion as he searched her face for something he couldn't have identified if he had tried. To his astonishment, she returned his gaze, obviously searching as well.

His kiss, if her response—or initial lack thereof—was any indication, surprised them both. Tentative, almost searching, he held her close and tried to block out the mockery he could almost hear from Wes. Just as Alexa relaxed and responded, Joe jumped to his feet, pushing her away from him. "I—I'm sorry, Alexa. That was so inapp—"

"Don't, Joe. Don't insult me too."

She turned and strode from the kitchen. Seconds later, he heard the staccato tap of her heels on the stairs—swift, but not running. Did that mean she was hurt or offended? Both?

Joe muttered half a dozen expletives under his breath before he caught himself. He stared at the still piping-hot ravioli. Would he irritate her more if he left it uneaten or if he ate it? Would eating it be another sign of his insensitivity and tactlessness? As if all he cared about was her cooking after he'd obviously offended her in some way? Then again, she had made it expressly for him. Not eating it would also be a slap in the face.

He found a disposable plastic container and poured the food into it. He grabbed a plastic fork that she kept just for him—the thought kicked him in the gut—for those times he was called back from his lunch break early. Her plate sat beside his on the table. He wrapped it, setting it in the fridge. Step by step, he cleaned the kitchen, all while trying to decide if he should find her upstairs and apologize or leave a note.

The sight of her shopping list on the fridge answered the question for him. He tore a sheet from it and grabbed a pen from the drawer. How to write the note, though… Everything he said sounded like she had ruined the lunch. At last, he scribbled the only thing he could think of, praying she would understand: *Thank you for taking the time to make my favorite meal. I'm sorry for ruining it. Can we talk later?*

He slipped the note under a tacky plastic flower magnet that looked ridiculously out of place in her kitchen, and left. Joe drove to the town square, parked near the gazebo, and ate his lunch. Though not as hot, it was still delicious, and each bite made him feel sicker than the last.

Alexa's phone went straight to voicemail—again. Joe shoved his cellphone in his pocket and climbed from the cruiser. Wes should be home. Maybe he knew where Alexa was and why she wasn't returning his calls. He couldn't believe one awkward kiss would make her so angry that she'd never speak to him again. Alexa just wouldn't—couldn't—be that petty.

As he opened the gate, Zach's screams pierced the air.

Joe whirled, ready to race to help, when he saw Wes tickling the boy on Heather's lawn. Despite his deep love for children, Joe despised their ability to mix squeals of joy and screams of terror and agony into one horrifying sound.

He half-jogged to the scene of "Chinese torture" and gently kicked Wes, who rolled on the ground with Zach. "Know where your sister is? I can't get a hold of her."

"She took off for a week or so. She does that now and then." Wes sat up, eying him. "She didn't tell you?"

Joe knew his face answered Wes. As he stared down at Alexa's brother, understanding dawned. "Dang it, Wes, you talked to her about me, didn't you?"

"What do you mean, 'talked to her about you?' We always talk about you. It's almost all we ever talk about! You two—"

"No, you idiot, you pulled the same—" Several choice expletives ran through his mind, but he clenched his teeth and swallowed them. "Wes, in the future, I'll thank you to worry about your own relationships and leave others'—or at least mine—alone." He glared at Wes. "You—"

Furious, he turned and stormed back to his cruiser, unable to speak without saying something nasty to someone. Joe saw Wes' astonished face as he whizzed past, but he chose to ignore it. Why couldn't people leave others alone?

Wes gaped in disbelief as Joe pealed out of the cul-de-sac with little regard for speed or safety. Zach stared at the scene, awestruck. "Man, he should write himself a ticket!"

"I don't get it, Lexi. What's the big deal? So he kissed you. Friends cross those lines sometimes."

Alexa, disgusted with it all, didn't falter. "We don't."

"It's a different line, Alexa, and you know it. Don't compare apples to oranges and men to women." Suzy sat on the foot of the bed in Alexa's suite, her fingers following the waffle weave pattern of the coverlet.

Leaning against the headboard, her knees drawn up to

her chin protectively, Alexa wiped away tears of frustration with the back of her hand. "Wes talked to him—put crazy ideas in his head, and now a perfect friendship is ruined."

"Thanks a lot."

Suzy's droll tones brought a smile to Alexa's face. "You know what I mean—guy friendship. I feel like I've lost my best friend while sitting on a bed with my best friend. How sick is that?"

Alexa knew she had responded with hurt, anger, and a little irrationality, but it didn't matter. She felt all of those and more. Suzy hesitated and then prayed in her charming, yet often irritating, way. "Lord, give me the ability to accept that I may hurt a friend, the courage to inflict that 'faithful wound,' and the wisdom of knowing when to strike."

"Cute." Despite her best efforts, Alexa snickered.

Suzy swirled her Sonic cup in her hand, took a drink, and cleared her throat. "Start over. Go back to whenever things were great, and tell me everything that has happened since then. Even irrelevant stuff that makes no sense, like Wes being home from an assignment or a run in with your chief—I want to hear it all."

"I know what it is. It's Wes. He talked to me the other day—saying stuff about how I care about Joe and—"

"You must. You are positively inarticulate. Did you just hear yourself? Saying 'stuff?' Really? You? Are you nuts?"

Alexa flushed, her face probably the color and consistency of borscht with sour cream. "I—"

"Alexa, don't you realize that you just gave credence to everything that Wes must have said by running off like this? Since when do you run away from an uncomfortable situation? Last year people were dying because of stuff you wrote. You didn't run away then; you stood there and fought back—even when the police chief's wife practically ordered you out of town."

After an unladylike emptying of her nose, Alexa sighed. "But with that, fighting back was the only way to stop it."

"And you think running away now is going to help this situation? What else has happened recently?"

Her mind blank, Alexa fumbled over jumbled and unrelated incidents. At last, she started sharing everything she could think of—starting with Lorie's transplant. She told Suzy everything from what she did, what she wore, things she wrote, and problems with the business. Suzy laughed at her mustache eradication fixation, sighed over the Sadie Hawkins dance, and became enraged at the non-appearance of the models at the show.

"Then there was my dress—ugh." The moment she spoke, Alexa regretted sharing it. Suzy's radar was too keen to let it slip past. She saw Suzy start to ask about it when Alexa's phone rang. Again.

This time, Suzy snatched it, read the caller ID, and punched the button. "Hey, Joe." Alexa lunged for the phone, but failed—as she knew she would. "No, this is Alexa's friend, Suzy—yeah, that would explain the accent. Look, she's here in Arkansas... nice little B&B down the road from my house. Right—quieter than my bomb shelter. I think I like you."

Alexa stood and disappeared into the bathroom. Suzy took the opportunity to pounce. "So what's going on, Joe. Alexa is here, angry, hurt, and confused, and from what I can tell, she doesn't really know why."

Joe demanded to speak to Alexa, but Suzy shook her head as she said, "Nope. Not going to happen. She's not going to talk to you." Taking a deep breath, she added, "Tell me something. She was just about to tell me something about a dress. Her exact words were, 'Then there was my dress—ugh.' Know what that means?"

His groan enlightened her, but she refused again when he asked once more to speak to Alexa. "Sorry, Joe. She won't talk. She's not even in the room right now." Suzy did not feel the need to share that Alexa was on the other side of the door, probably listening—the shower came on. Okay, not listening to the conversation. "So tell me about this dress."

Joe tried to explain and failed. With an apology for interrupting their visit and a request for Alexa to return his call, Joe hung up, leaving Suzy staring at Alexa's phone with a silly grin on her face. "Well," she muttered under her breath, "it's about time."

Joe threw his cellphone across the room, denting his wall and bringing Wes down the hallway to pound on his door. He glared at the knob. "Go away, Wes."

"Let's go shoot some hoops. You can get your angst out on a ball and net instead of Alexa's walls."

Now aware that he had just damaged Alexa's property, Joe sighed, running his hand over the odd dent in the wall near his closet. "Be right out."

Thirty minutes later, Joe and Wes dripped with sweat and Joe's basketball was definitely worse for the wear. They hadn't spoken a word on the way to the court or while playing. A couple of the junior high boys had joined them for a few minutes, but as the intensity of the game became too much, had slunk off to the bleachers to observe.

"Wes?"

Panting, Wes managed a "huh?" before he made another dive under Joe's arm. The ball missed the basket.

"You tried talking to me the other night—about Alexa."

"Yeah," West gasped, "so what?"

Joe, though his shirt was soaked, was hardly winded. He played hard and often with the guys from the varsity team— something he now appreciated. It felt good to have an edge over the man he wanted to pummel. "Did you talk to Alexa about us too?"

"Yeah. We talked about her chronic habit of pushing away good men."

"Why? Why would you do that to her. You interfered, she left town, and I may have lost a dea—reat friend." Joe pivoted on his right foot as Wes snatched at the ball. "All because you want to try your hand at wedding photography." His attempt to turn his tirade into a joke flopped.

Wes stood still, ignoring the ball. "Oh, man! I hadn't

thought of that. She'd be stunning. Can you imagine the dress—whoa."

"Don't I know it?" Joe muttered under his breath.

"I don't get it, Joe. You like her. If you're not in love with her yet, you soon will be. So what is the problem with you guys?"

Joe lobbed the ball gracefully into the net with a final swish. "The problem is that your sister is the best friend I've had in a long time—"

"'Friend' that you're seriously attracted to—"

Joe collapsed on the nearby grass. "Come on, Wes! Who wouldn't be? You would be if she wasn't your sister."

"If she wasn't my sister, she'd be my wife if I could make it happen. I certainly wouldn't wait around for some other guy—Darrin, for example—to swoop in and cart her off. That's the great thing about being best friends with a woman, you idiot. You can make sure no one else wrecks it."

They lay on the grass for some time, each with one arm covering his eyes, Wes panting, Joe thinking. Aloud, Joe murmured, "It's not like she doesn't know I think she's amazing…"

"Women don't know half what we think they do, but they do know more than they think they do." Wes sat up, hanging his arms over his knees. "Wow. That sounded profound. I wonder if it makes sense."

"Well, it doesn't matter, because neither of us want to mess up a good thing. I don't need to marry her to be content in this relationship—"

"Uh, yeah, ya do." Wes frowned. "I seem to be saying that a lot lately." Standing, Wes added, "I'm going to get a bottle of water. Want one?"

Joe nodded and jerked his thumb at his wallet by the basketball pole. While Wes jogged to the convenience store, Joe sat up and thought about the ramifications of allowing himself to explore a relationship with Alexa. He remembered the kiss—brief as it was—and wondered for the trillionth time what had possessed him. That thought kicked him in the gut. He knew what had possessed him; he didn't know why he hadn't resisted.

Minutes later, Wes tossed a bottle in Joe's lap and dropped to the ground next to him. "Solved the world's problems—or at least Joe's?"

"Nope, and I don't know how to get her to talk to me so we can get back to where we were."

"Why go back? Just drive down to Arkansas and tell her—or better yet, just kiss her. That should—"

"No!"

Joe stood, retrieved his keys and wallet, and walked toward his Jeep. Wes stared after him before jogging to his side. "What is your problem, Joe? I don't get it!"

Once in his Jeep, Joe rolled down his window, hung one hand over the steering wheel, and stared out over the empty road ahead of him. "Because we are better as friends. I'm Joe, the cop who spends most of his free time with the kids around town-the cop who has made it clear to every woman he's ever met that he's not looking for a serious relationship." Joe closed his eyes for a moment before continuing. "And she's Alexa the author. She's worth millions, and I can't afford the gas to drive twelve hours to apologize for hurting her."

"Joe, she doesn't care about money. We're from an average middle-class family—just like you. She's not a snob!"

"No, but she's from a different… sphere. You know how in those old movies—the ones she looks like she just stepped out of—you know how they say things like you don't mix beer and fine wine? Yeah. That's us. It won't work." He interrupted Wes' protest as he added, "Even if I *wanted* that kind of relationship, it wouldn't work."

Joe turned the key in the ignition and put the car in gear. Wes stared after the vehicle as it drove down the street. He had never heard Joe talk about anything so personal—ever. He pulled out his phone and punched his sister's number. Time to play the brother card.

"Annie, he's hurting."

"Good." Her voice didn't sound nearly as self-satisfied as she had intended.

"He doesn't think he's 'good enough' for you."

"He's not." *He's too good for me,* she thought to herself.

"Annie..." Wes' tone warned her she had stepped over the line.

"I'm sorry. I just—"

"What happened?"

Something I hope to forget but never will, she wailed inwardly. Aloud she said, "Some things are just too private, Wes. I'll be home in a few days."

"Call him. The last thing you want to do is throw away a good friendship because you overreacted to whatever you overreacted to."

The phone went dead. She sat near the downtown fountains of Siloam Springs and listened to the splash of water in the pool. Staring at the phone in her hand, she wondered. Should she call? Would it begin erasing her ridiculous reaction or would it make things worse?

Joe's phone rang once. "Alexa? Where are you?"

"Siloam Springs."

"I want to say I'm sorry, but—" Joe stammering was nearly as embarrassing as the topic.

"Don't. It's insulting when a guy kisses you and then apologizes for it. Why did you call?"

He didn't answer for several seconds, making her wish she hadn't called at all. Just as she started to close the phone and turn it off, he said, "It's just that I *am* sorry, Lex. Not sorry I kissed you, exactly—that's not something to be sorry about. I'm just sorry that I overreacted to it."

"That's it!"

"What?"

She sat up straighter, swinging her legs over the ledge. "I've been trying to figure out why I was so furious."

"You lost me."

Alexa stood and began walking back to her bed and breakfast. "I—" She sighed. "Joe, this isn't a comfortable thing to talk about."

"Well, if we don't, we'll have something awkward hovering over us until it smothers our friendship."

"That was good—sounds like something I could use in a book."

Joe's rumbling chuckle sent lovely but unwelcome shivers through her. "You're avoiding the subject, Lex."

She knew he was right. She hated that he was right. "It wasn't the kiss I minded, Joe. That was—well, I wasn't sorry about that. But one second you were kissing me and the next you practically flung me across the room. I've never felt more rejected in my life."

"Oh, Lex... it wasn't you! I—"

Taking a deep breath, Alexa interrupted. "How about we just agree to forget about it. We can pretend it didn't happen and work our way back to how things were."

As Joe and Alexa pocketed their respective phones, they both said, "Like that'll ever work."

Chapter 16

As he turned over the steaks, Joe glanced at his watch. He hoped Alexa hadn't taken a side trip on her way home. She said she'd be home by half past six at the latest. He glanced at his watch—six twenty-five. In less than five minutes, the steaks would be done. He had cleaned her kitchen and filled her favorite salad bowl with a bag of salad. It wasn't perfect, but it was there. Baked potatoes rolled over on the grill as he pushed them with the long tongs.

The neighbor's obnoxious dog began yapping like crazy. Barking as if a platoon of soldiers invaded, the dog raced up and down the long side yard that separated Alexa's house from her neighbor's. "She's back," he whispered to himself. "Time to get this over with."

Joe turned the grill down to low and moved the steaks away from the heat. At the door, he took a deep breath and opened it. He smiled down at her as she climbed the steps, "Hey..." Time to clear the air. He took the overnight bag from her shoulder and dropped it inside the entryway. As the door shut behind him, he hugged Alexa fiercely. "I'm really glad you're home. I've got steaks cooking and a salad—nothing like yours, of course—on the table."

The air between them felt different, and it was plain that she felt it as much as he did. Could they return to their casual friendship?

She sighed. "Can you bring it up to the nook? I'm exhausted."

Joe whistled as he filled a plate of salad for her. He doused it with Italian dressing and parmesan cheese, grabbed a bottle of her favorite root beer, and carried it up to her. "Here's your salad. I'll bring steaks up in a few minutes."

"Going to eat your salad up here?" Her eyes met his, questioning.

Already their relational rhythm had begun resynchronizing. "Nah, I'll eat while I watch the grill. Go ahead."

Minutes later, Joe found her in her usual corner of the couch. He'd wondered about that. If she had been sitting in the chair, he would have suspected things were still awkward. Her salad lay half-finished in her lap. Though her eyes were closed, the lazy motion of her hand on the arm of the couch told him she hadn't fallen asleep. He touched it gently. "Steak, Lex?"

Not until they'd finished their meal, their plates stacked on the coffee table and an episode of Dragnet playing on the TV, did Joe and Alexa finally talk. He almost didn't risk another awkward moment, but his father's words—ones he'd heard all his life—pricked his conscience. Avoiding conflict wasn't the right way to treat a friend—even if it was the easy way. "Lex?"

"Hmm?"

"Can I ask you something?"

Her sigh nearly made him change directions and suggest a walk to The Confectionary for dessert, but she preempted him. "Why do I get the feeling that I'm going to get rebuked for something?"

He nudged her knee with his toe and shook his head. "Not rebuked, but I've noticed something—something that I think will be a problem between us. I don't want it to be."

"Okaaay..."

"I've noticed, for years really, that you keep yourself aloof from everyone around you."

Shaking her head, Alexa protested, "That's not true! I involve myself in all kinds of things."

"Only on your terms, though. You carefully let a few safe people into your inner sanctum. You occasionally insert yourself into the lives of people around you, but you don't usually allow them to be a part of your life."

Emotions flickered across her face as she considered his

words. He knew she considered it a necessity of life, but she took it to an unhealthy degree. Right on cue, she said, "But I don't hold myself aloof. I'm just careful—" He knew his expression betrayed him when she added, "Okay, what exactly do you mean, Friday?"

Once more, he tried to explain his concern. The way she lived, the way she held herself apart from people around her—despite her defensiveness, it was all true. "Lex, you only allow people in your life on your terms. People need people. God made us that way. It isn't 'safe' but it is rewarding."

"We're not all extroverts, Joe. Some of us need more time alone than others. That doesn't make us wrong."

"Oh, I have no doubt that you need that time too. I know when I'm intruding—no, Alexa, there are times you need me to go home. I know that and I'm fine with it. But honestly, you don't *need* as much time alone as you *want*."

The words hung in the air between them. After what seemed like much longer than it likely was, she asked, "Why bring this up now?"

"Because when things got uncomfortable and unfamiliar between us, you ran." He swallowed hard, miserable that he had to talk about this. "I don't want to be afraid that what I do and say will send away my best friend. I need to know that when you do invest in people, they aren't disposable."

The moment his words hit her, he knew she felt foolish. He hadn't wanted that. He started to reassure her, but she sighed and spoke. "I took an awkward moment and turned it into a full blown tantrum. I'm sorry." Alexa twisted her hands together before she added, "Suzy and I have been friends for thirteen years. Does that reassure you at all?"

"Have you ever gotten mad at her?"

"When she married Mike." Alexa sounded ashamed.

"You didn't like him?"

She shook her head, grimacing. "No. He just ruined our plans. We were going to graduate, get a house, and live happily ever after. Suzy would be my agent, and we would travel the world while I created murder and mayhem on every continent—and in most countries."

Joe heard something in Alexa's voice—something heartbreaking. Proof that another of her dreams had been squashed. "She could still be your agent—"

"Not with Mike and the kids. They deserve her time and attention." She reached for a piece of candy from a candy bowl he'd never seen before. As she untwisted the wrapper, she tried to explain. "I got over it long enough to throw the best bridal shower you've ever heard of—blew a huge bit of my first advance with that thing—ridiculously extravagant, but so much fun."

"You're often ridiculously extravagant, Alexa. It's what makes you so... *you*. What's so odd about that?"

She popped the piece of hard chocolate in her mouth, chewing on both the candy and his words. Again he started to interrupt, to assure her that all was well, and again she continued before he could. "It was the first time I'd ever done anything like that. I rented out the honeymoon suite at the nicest hotel in Little Rock, hired a caterer—the works. My idea of 'fancy' was a cake from the bakery and using organdy ribbon instead of crepe paper streamers to decorate."

Joe's low whistle surprised her. He grinned at the confusion in her eyes and on her face. "You were destined to have wealth, Lex. It suits you. God knew what He was doing when He combined your personality and talent."

"Really, Joe..."

"No, really. You're never ostentatious about it; you know, naturally, what is in good taste and what is just expensive; and you aren't afraid to live simply in the midst of it all. You've taken less is more and made an art of it while still enjoying the privilege of having money."

"You've never said anything so insightful. We've spent hours together—hours—but we've had few real discussions. I know more about Darrin's philosophy of life, religion, politics, and personal preferences after just a few dates and visits than I do after almost a year of friendship with you."

"Well—"

She interrupted him. "Does my money bother you, Joe?"

"When I think about it—sometimes. Usually no, but—"

He swallowed hard. "It can be… intimidating."

She hadn't expected an affirmative answer. Her eyes showed her astonishment. "Intimidating how?"

"It's no big deal, Lex. I get over it quickly enough. It's not all the time, and it's not you ever. It's just—just…" He paused. "It's a guy thing." He smiled and grabbed the deck of cards she kept in the drawer of the end table. "War?"

Chapter 16

August arrived hot and sticky. Of all the wonderful things about her new house, the one Alexa loved most was the excellent air conditioning unit that pumped cool, dry air into her home.

Her finished manuscript sat ready for her to edit the first draft, but her heart wasn't in it. She deleted the ridiculous title, *Plagiarist,* and typed in the one she preferred — *Twist.* She refused to give the sensationalist papers the satisfaction of using their ridiculous name.

The laptop shut with a snap that was likely not good for it. Alexa grabbed a book she'd just purchased, a "sure thing" from Todd at Bookends, and flipped it open to page fifty-two. Two paragraphs later, she tossed it aside. Restless. After a week of lounging around the house, thanking the Lord for air conditioning and doing little else but starting and not finishing books, she identified her malady. Lonely — she was also lonely. Joe had been busy with the high school kids for the past couple of weeks, Wes was on assignment, Suzy was in Hawaii with her family — a vacation that had taken six years to save for — and Darrin and Lorie were camping somewhere for the last two weeks before school started.

She should have gone. The mental picture of tents, mosquitos, and charred food changed that thought. Going would have been worse than the boredom of staying. She should have flown to — somewhere.

A glance at the clock on the wall depressed her. Nine o'clock was too early in the day to wish it were over. That thought snapped her out of her funk. She held a particular abhorrence for the way people tended to wish their lives away, one day at a time, living miserably as they waited for their life to start.

The phone rang. A spa in Rockland informed her that she had a manicure, pedicure, and a facial scheduled for eleven o'clock. "But I didn't make this appointment—" Even as she said it, she decided to keep it anyway.

A laugh preempted her confirmation. "A Mr. Darrin Thorne called and arranged it. He asked that I say, 'Happy Birthday, Alexa. I wish we were there.'"

"Wow." Her eyes widened. "I'll be there. Thanks!"

She stared at the phone for several seconds once the call disconnected. *How did I forget my birthday?* she wondered as she stood to climb the stairs to change for her trip to town.

Another thought hit her. If she called her mother now, she would have an excellent excuse to get off the phone. She punched the house phone number she'd written down as practice in kindergarten and waited for her mother to answer.

Pedestrians gawked as Alexa strolled down Rockland's "Boutique Row" wearing one of her new dresses from Laidie. A group of girls—teenagers—wearing hip hugging shorts and t-shirts with charming sayings like "date bait" and "sure thing" tittered, making indecent comments as Alexa walked past.

She ignored them at first, but when the loudest girl called after her, "Didn't anyone ever tell you that you're old enough to pick your own clothes?" Alexa turned to face them.

As with most kids trying to be tough, the girls didn't expect a confident response. Why she did it Alexa didn't fully know or understand, but the girls wearing clothes that advertised themselves as unpaid prostitutes, while mocking the concept of individuality, struck her as heartbreaking. "Have we gotten to the place in this country where intolerance now extends to an individual's taste in clothing?"

Had she said anything else, Alexa realized it would have probably earned her an earful of foul language—or worse. However, the word "intolerance" and the hint at individuality struck home with the mocker. "You actually like that get-up?"

"I do. In my opinion, it is one of the loveliest things I own."

Alexa saw a glimmer of recognition in one of the girls and tried not to react. The first girl, hooking one thumb into a belt loop of her incredibly short shorts, gave Alexa another once over and said, "Are all your clothes like that?"

"Not really. This is turn of the twentieth century, but I wear anything from any century."

"Except this one, I bet." Their laughter rang out as loud and brash as the glittering words on their shirts.

"I have a pair of shorts almost exactly like yours. I don't roll them up that short, and wear a shirt that covers my belly, but they're very similar—Hilfiger?"

"I don't believe you." The accusation came from the back of the group.

The girl who recognized Alexa finally spoke. "Come on, guys. Don't you know who this is? She's that author—you know, the one who writes the mysteries? The one who had that guy killing people in Fairbury? Alexa something."

Another of the girls grinned as recognition hit. "Hey, yeah! She always wears weird stuff. My mom has all her books—even got one signed last year."

The first girl nodded reluctantly. "Okay, okay. So maybe you do have my shorts. You really oughtta roll 'em up and get a couple of good shirts—sex appeal, y'know?"

"Sorry. Not interested." She almost didn't say it. What was the use? The girl wouldn't listen. The look in her eyes told Alexa that she had life figured out and no one—no one—would tell her otherwise. Joe's fight for teens pricked her heart. Okay, maybe this girl wouldn't, but her friends might...

"I knew you didn't—"

Alexa interrupted before she lost her nerve. "See, I've learned over the years that showing everything I have is a great way to get attention but a lousy way to keep it. If I want a guy to really see me—who I am—if I want to see him more than a few times, I have to keep him guessing, or he'll just move on to the next girl with lots to show and little left to the imagination. I prefer to wait for guys who respect me—not just my body."

"But you're not married—last I heard, you aren't even dating. How come you're not married? You're old enough."

Alexa didn't know which girl had asked. She smiled, amused at the question. Should she be bluntly honest or try to interject one more thing to make the girls think? After a couple of seconds she said, "Frankly, because I've always just said no. Well, that and because the one I want hasn't asked yet."

She gave them a quick smile, turned, and continued down the street toward the parking garage. Each step pained her. Quite uncharacteristically, Alexa longed to return to the girls and beg them not to let Hollywood, Madison Avenue, or the peer laws of high school dictate the choices they made for their lives.

In her car, Alexa sat staring at the steering wheel, wondering where those girls' mothers were. Where were the fathers? Did parents really allow their beautiful daughters to dress like that—advertising themselves as a "sure thing"—or did the girls change clothes after they left the house? As sickening as both options were, she prayed for the latter and that they would stop.

Her phone drove the subject from her mind. She smiled at the sight of Joe's name as it flashed across the screen. Wes had probably told him it was her birthday. "Hey, Joe!"

"Hi. Look, I wondered if you could do me a favor."

So much for a "Happy birthday, Alexa," she mused as she said, "Sure. Anything."

"I don't know what you were planning for dinner..."

This was more like it. "What do you have in mind?"

"I wondered if you'd make enough for me. I don't get off until six, and I haven't eaten all day. The tourists are restless or something. I've arrested two shoplifters, one drunk driver, and given out four speeding tickets—two to the same person!"

Disappointment hovered for a moment before she shrugged it off. "Well, I wasn't planning to cook tonight. I'm in Rockland. I just had a morning at the spa, went to lunch—did some shopping. I won't be home until right about six, so I made a reservation at Marcello's—"

"Great! Can I join you? I'll even pay for it. That was my back up plan if you didn't feel up to dinner."

She stared at the phone. Joe had never sounded so eager. Whatever they said about men and food must be true. "Sure. I'll see you there." The phone went dead almost before she finished speaking.

In Fairbury, Joe pocketed his phone and pointed at a jaywalker as a warning. Inwardly, he smiled. *Happy birthday, Lex.*

Joe seemed distracted all through dinner. He mumbled where appropriate, but most of his responses were less than engaging. That is, until she described the scene with the girls in Rockland. "They were just so sad. Why do fathers let their daughters do that to themselves?"

"Do you really have those shorts? I don't think I've ever seen those."

"Yep. I didn't bother to tell her that I got them to wear over my swimsuit at the lake."

"Aha! Now that sounds more like it." Joe signaled for the check. "Feel up to a game or a movie or something?"

Tempted to tell him no, Alexa stared at the check as it lay on the table between them. She had originally planned to cover the bill herself, but irritation welled in her. She wanted tiramisu and coffee after her meal—had deliberately chosen a light dinner to save room for it. One look in Joe's eager face squashed that notion. She reached for her purse, but Joe's hand stopped her.

"I'll get it. It's the least I could do after I invited myself to your dinner." Outside, he followed her to her car. "I'll walk back for the Jeep later."

Alexa nodded but had a feeling he'd be taking her little car home by the time he left for the night. She wove through the streets, growing more irritated with each block that passed. It was her birthday. She should at least have a decent cake. That thought disgusted her.

"I think before we start, I'll put a dump cake in the oven. They're so good hot."

"Sounds...good..."

"Trust me, it is."

As she pulled into the drive, she frowned. She stepped from the car, staring at the dark porch light. Her eyes roamed around the yard, anxiety growing with each dark shrub and corner. "I could have sworn that these lights came on automatically at seven o'clock. This feels too Sycamore Court for me."

A slight tremor in her hand rattled her keys. Joe noticed and took them. As he unlocked the door, he grabbed her right hand with his left and squeezed. "I sure hope you will forgive me," he whispered.

"For what?"

Joe pushed open the door. Lights blinded them, and voices screamed, "Surprise!"

"Happy birthday, Lex," he murmured.

Alexa kissed Joe's cheek. As she did, she took a moment to whisper. "Thank you—oh, and I'll get you for this. Just you wait."

Lorie raced to hug her, looking healthier than Alexa had ever seen her. The girl's porcelain skin seemed more delicate than ever, but was assuredly less pasty and jaundiced. "Come with me. The band is just setting up."

"Band?" She blinked as she realized that it truly was Lorie. "Lorie! I thought you and your father went camping!"

Lorie grinned. "We did. We just told you that we were going to be gone longer than we really were—or rather, we didn't tell you that we were camping here for the last few nights." Her eyes slid across the room. "Joe insisted we come, and I brought you his birthday present. It's in your room. Come on!"

As the girl dragged Alexa up the stairs, around the Zoots who were setting up their instruments in her empty nook, and up the spiral staircase into Alexa's room, Lorie chatted about all of the guests, assuring her that everyone expected another grand entrance later. "We wanted you to get the official 'surprise' shout, but Joe had this dress, and—"

Alexa pulled the dress from its garment bag. Iridescent silk taffeta in an unusual shade of teal rustled as she moved it to examine it closer. The heavy beading around the neck and on the belt—breathtaking. As she turned the dress around, Alexa's heart sank.

"Joe bought me this? Are you sure?"

"Well, I bought it. He just paid for it. He had me research swing dresses online, and I found this one. Your seamstress lady made it for us. She said the beadwork was her birthday present to you. She didn't charge Joe for it, and I'm really glad, because even without it that dress was ridiculously expensive."

Lorie seemed so pleased with herself that Alexa didn't have the heart to say anything. Still, her heart sank once more as she stared at the back of the dress. The deep "V" would reveal most of her back—to the bra-line at least. Of all the styles Lorie could have chosen, she had to pick backless. Alexa wanted to cry.

"Would you do me a favor?"

Eager to help, the moment she heard Alexa's request for Joe, she turned to leave. On the first step, she paused. "Oh, and Mrs. Peters didn't want Joe to know about the beadwork being her gift—just you. She said to wish you the happiest of birthdays and that she wished she could be here."

"I'll send her a note tomorrow with a picture of me in it." She swallowed hard. "Please get Joe."

While she waited, Alexa deliberated. Should she put on the dress and let him see it that way or—a knock on the door startled her out of her reverie. "Come in, Joe."

"Hey, how—you haven't put it on. You don't like it." The disappointment in Joe's voice cut her. He'd be so disappointed.

"Oh no, Joe. It's gorgeous! It's just that Lorie—well, look at that back."

"What's wrong with it?" Joe turned the dress around and shrugged. "I don't get it. Won't it fit?"

Unsure how else to handle it, Alexa carried it into the bathroom. "Wait here, will you?"

Two seconds in the bathroom and she dashed out and raced to the closet, the dress flying behind her like a superhero's cape. She dug through the drawers for proper undergarments and mentally thanked Laidie for her brilliant use of side zippers to aid in the ability to dress herself. Taking a deep breath, Alexa slid the closet door open again, and stood there barefooted.

Joe stared, waiting for something. She turned slowly. Again, he waited and then said, "I don't get it. What's wrong with it?"

As she watched his disappointment grow, Alexa spun again, this time even more slowly, pausing for a moment to show her back before facing him again. His expression didn't change. Slightly irritated, she prompted, "The back, Joe. Didn't you see the back?"

"Yes. That beadwork is gorgeous. It is worth every penny. You look great! The Zoots are out there, I've got Dylan ready to sing, and you have a houseful of people dying to wish you a personal happy birthday. Let's go."

Determined not to ruin Joe's fun, Alexa opted to table the discussion of his fickle opinions on backless dresses and enjoy her party. "You really got the Zoots? I can't believe you did all this!"

"I asked Lorie what she thought you'd like best for your birthday, and this is what she said."

"A surprise party?" Alexa couldn't imagine what she'd ever said to give Lorie *that* impression.

"No... she said—" Joe paused, sounding embarrassed. "She said you'd like to dance—swing. So I thought I'd get the Zoots in here, and then I remembered Dylan, and it kind of snowballed from there."

As she watched him, she saw Joe tug at his collar. He

was hiding something. The moment she thought it, Alexa realized what it must be. Lorie must have suggested that the gift she would most enjoy would be to dance with him, and confessing it would embarrass both of them. "Well, if we're going to be dancing, I'll definitely need to get on shoes and stockings." She smiled at Joe. "Be right back."

"I think Lorie said that there are stockings with seams in back in the garment bag or something. She said she got them because they were more authentic."

Once more in the closet, Alexa struggled and fought to pull on the stockings correctly. Her natural tendency toward perfection made satisfaction with the straightness of the seams almost impossible. Her calves mocked her as the seam danced a little to the left or right until Alexa thought she would go mad. After a few futile minutes of struggling, she gave up, put on her shoes, and stepped out again.

On the way out the door, she caught a glimpse of herself in the mirror and sighed. Fine dress, nice shoes, wrong hairstyle, and stale makeup—it would leave a weak impression on such a big occasion. "Just a minute, Joe. I need to do something with my face and hair."

"You look great! C'mon, I hear the band starting."

"They're just tuning up. Go down and mingle. I'll be there in a minute."

But Joe didn't go anywhere. He stood in the doorway to her bathroom and watched as she tucked a towel into the bodice of her dress, pressed it against the countertop, and scrubbed her face. He nodded, satisfied. "You were right. It looks better without the makeup."

"Silly man. I'm not leaving it off. I'm just refreshing it. This dress deserves more than a lick and a promise." She stifled a giggle at his embarrassed expression.

Chapter 17

As Alexa sat at her dressing table, reapplying her makeup in what appeared to be an attempt at a glamor girl style from the forties or fifties, Joe leaned against the bathroom doorjamb and watched her in the dressing table mirror. He had never closely observed the semi-ritual of cosmetic application, but tonight he found it fascinating. Just a few flicks of a bushy brush, a swipe of a Q-tip looking thing, and she already looked like a different person. He winced and held his breath as she swiped a mascara wand over her eyelashes, certain that she'd gouge out her eye. The bright red lipstick that Alexa rarely wore fit perfectly with the outfit.

Once satisfied with her face, Alexa brushed her hair, smoothing the long waves until they hung free below her shoulder blades. Joe hadn't ever consciously thought of it, but that night he did. He loved her hair. As she separated it into four sections, he sighed.

Alexa heard it and teased him. "I can't leave it down again, you nut. Do you know how hard it was to dance on New Year's with my hair flying in my face all the time?"

"I didn't say anything," he protested.

"You didn't have to. You sighed. Every time I go to put up my hair, you get this look of frustration on your face. I don't get it. Why should you care if it's up or down?"

He shrugged. "I just think you go to a lot of trouble for nothing."

"It's no trouble and it keeps me cooler, my hair less messy, and with some dresses it just looks right."

With that, she swung her legs around the bench and faced him. "So, how do I look?"

He knew the question wasn't a fishing expedition for

compliments. One of the things Joe appreciated most about Alexa was her carefree attitude in regards to her appearance. She dressed to please herself, but this was one of those times that proved that, like most women, she still liked to know the results were satisfactory.

"Incredible—as usual." He grabbed her hand. "Let's go! My toes are itching to dance, and there's a huge cheesecake down there waiting for you to cut into it."

Dylan stepped up to the microphone as Alexa descended the stairs. Strains of the opening to the "Anniversary Song" played, confusing her for a moment. However, by the time she reached the floor to greet her guests, Dylan began to sing.

> *Oh, what a thrill on the night you were born!*
> *They loved your sweet smile at the first light of morn.*
> *Your life in fresh bloom, stole the stars from the skies*
> *And twinkled all day reflected in your eyes.*

Joe slowly spun her into a waltz. As they reached James, he took up the dance, stumbling over the old-fashioned steps. Darrin rescued her toes a moment later. She drifted from one guest to the next, dancing with friends—young and old, male and female.

> *As your dear mother held you in her arms*
> *Your father thanked the Lord for all of your charms.*
> *While recovering she murmured quite low,*
> *Darling, I love you so.*

> *That night seemed to fade into blossoming dawn.*
> *The sun shone anew, and your life rushed along.*
> *Could we but relive that sweet moment sublime,*
> *We'd say that your charms ne'er changed with time.*

As the band played a little more quietly, Dylan spoke. "I want to apologize for my weak change of words. I didn't know any birthday songs other than the usual one, and I thought a waltz made more sense for a dance." Dylan bowed at the polite applause and stepped away from the microphone as Joe's mom wheeled a cake into the room on a teacart.

The room burst into "Happy Birthday" as they urged Alexa to blow out the single candle. She hesitated and plucked the candle from the top of what appeared to be a three-tiered cheesecake, and turned toward the rest of the room. With a light puff, she blew out the candle. "Thank you! This is just beautiful—wonderful. I am so thankful that you all came."

Joe stood near as she cut and served cake to each guest. He started to urge her to take a piece and let others serve themselves, but she showed genuine delight in welcoming and speaking to each guest. He couldn't have done it. She greeted her editor, publicist, Adam, Silva, and Rhette. Wes and Heather corralled Sarah and Zach ahead of them, pausing only long enough for hugs and a moment of celebration before they urged the children toward the kitchen to eat their cake.

Several of the guests kept her talking or dancing, leaving Joe with the responsibility of ensuring the others had a nice time. He found Martine and Elise, Alexa's editor and publicist, sitting in her little-used living room and chatting with Darrin and the Varneys. Martine smiled up at him. "Your Chief Varney was just telling us about all you did to help Alexa last winter. I want to thank you for your part in stopping that man."

"I just did my job, ma'am. We all worked equally to catch him—even Alexa did her part."

"I heard about the poker," Elise laughed. "That was genius."

"And could have been dangerous," Joe admitted. "I let my desire to catch him cloud my judgment. I should have been reprimanded."

Chief Varney wagged his finger. "Bad, Joe. Bad." He nudged his wife. "Does that count or should I slip a note in his file, too?"

Joe started to protest, but Martine said something that

soothed a part of his conscience that had chafed for months. "Look, Joe. I don't know much about police work, but as long as what she did was not illegal, I don't think you could have stopped her. By being involved, you probably kept her safer than anything else you could have done."

Soon Silva and Rhette found them, and began a publicity discussion with Elise that left Joe feeling like the party had morphed a schmoozing event.

Zach raced past the living room, nearly sliding into a couple dancing on the outskirts of the dance floor. Joe moved into cop mode and pulled the boy aside. "Hey, Zach. Do you want to go throw a Frisbee on the beach for a few minutes?"

"What if it goes in the water?"

The kid had a point. "Then what about across the front yard?"

"It's dark out there."

"That'll make it more challenging," Joe urged. "C'mon. Let's go play somewhere that won't knock people over."

Twenty minutes later, Heather burst out the front door, screaming frantically for Zach. "If you're hiding, you show your fa—" She glared at Joe. "Really? You didn't think I'd panic when I couldn't find him?"

"Sorry."

Zach interrupted. "Joe taught me how to throw it straight. Watch!"

"No way, you little monster," Heather laughed. "Get over here. We're leaving." She glanced around for her daughter before rushing inside, calling Sarah's name.

Joe gave Zach an exaggerated wince. "Sorry, buddy. I didn't mean—"

"Mom's probably got to pee or M.S."

"Or M.S.?"

"I think it's some stupid way of saying poop—like 'make stinky' or something. She's always telling Grandma about peeing and her MS."

Joe's lip twitched. PMS. "Well, maybe she's just tired from working all day, setting up for a party, and then searching the house because I didn't think to tell her we were going outside. My bad."

Sarah burst through the door and rushed to their side. Heather followed, sending both children to wait by the end of the drive. "—don't go in the street!" She rolled her eyes at Joe. "At her age, you'd think I wouldn't have to say anything. Hey," she added a little less abrasively, "this is supposed to be Alexa's birthday gift, right?"

"Yeah..."

"Get in there and dance with her. From what I heard Lorie say, that's what this was about—a chance for Alexa to dance." She smiled. "With you."

He nodded, glancing around him instinctively before he went inside. *All clear.* The thought amused him. He didn't have to protect her house like that anymore. That nightmare was locked away—likely indefinitely.

Alexa smiled at him from Darrin's arms as she waltzed to some number he didn't recognize. A glance at his watch told him the band would still be there for another hour. He didn't *have* to cut in, but the temptation nearly pushed him across the floor. The sight of his sister talking to Alexa's agent steered him to her side.

"C'mon, Jocie. Finish this one with me."

"Where've you been? She's danced with everyone at least twice—you once. This is about you guys. What girl wants her boyfriend—"

He pulled her closer and murmured, "Jocie, I'm not her boyfriend—never have been."

"But you said—she said—wait, what?"

"Everyone assumed and Alexa said that they wouldn't believe us if we denied it, so we're just letting you guys figure it out in your own time."

"Well, Dad's about ready to chew you out for abandoning your girlfriend, so you'd better 'fess up soon."

"I'll let you do that on the way home. They'll accept it more, coming from you."

Her eyes followed Alexa around the room before returning to his. "Joe, are you sure? She watches you. I've noticed it before."

"She watches *people*, Jocie, not just me. Right now, it's me, for some reason I may never know. Maybe we look like some odd character couple that would look suspicious in her next book. Who knows? It's just her."

"Mom is going to be so bummed. She's been telling everyone about how you're dating the incredible Alexa Hartfield. She's practically planning a rehearsal dinner already."

Joe groaned. He had never imagined his mother being that invested in any relationship of his. "Why? What's so special about Alexa?"

His sister's eyebrows rose. "Really, Joe? Really?"

"You know what I mean. I've been more exclusive than this a few times, and she hardly noticed."

"If you saw what we see, you wouldn't ask. You're different with her."

The song ended and Jocie stepped back. Her eyes slid across the room to Alexa before she jerked her head and turned as if to walk back to where James still stood. "Hey Jocie," Joe murmured.

"Yeah?" She stared up at him, smiling.

"Thanks—thanks and do me a favor."

"What?"

"Find someone else to talk to. That guy is giving me the creeps."

"He's full of information about Alexa, though." Her eyes roamed the room. "And it's not like you invited any cute guys for me…"

"Go flirt with Dylan then."

Interest flickered in her eyes. "Who's Dylan?"

"The singer."

"He's not married?" She took a step toward the stairs.

"Nope… just a couple years older than you, I think."

A grin split her face. "Can you imagine going out with a guy who could sing like that?" Another step away and she turned again. "Wait! Did you just encourage me to flirt with a guy?"

"Sure."

Her eyebrows rose in question.

Joe crossed his arms over his chest. "He lives six hours away. An hour or two of flirting is safe enough."

By ten o'clock, Martine and Elise departed for their hotel in Rockland. The Varneys left soon afterward. Joe's parents and Jeremy left with the band at midnight, but the rest of the guests stayed at Alexa's house. As the band dismantled, Alexa showed Silva and Rhette into one room and Lorie and Jocie into another. Joe showed Darrin and James the other two guest rooms, and Alexa pulled out extra pillows and blankets, leaving them on the couch for whoever might need them.

Doors opened, closed, and muffled voices drifted downstairs while Alexa wandered through her house, shutting off lights, picking up plates, and dumping the contents glasses into the sink. Soon the sounds quieted to only muffled giggles from Lorie and Jocie's room. Joe sat at the bar in her kitchen, waiting for her to return, and shook his head as she wandered through the door, arms laden with dishes and flatware.

"Joe, can you go grab the glasses I put on the entry table? I couldn't carry them all."

"I'll get them, but then you need to leave it alone. I've got Anita coming to clean all this up for you tomorrow."

"I'll call her in the morning and tell her not to come. She'll be here Monday anyway. I just need to put these things in the dishwasher and that'll be the bulk of the work right there."

Joe skirted around the bar and pulled the dirty dishes from her hands. He set them on the counter and loaded them, one by one, into the dishwasher. Once finished, he closed the door and glared at her. "Wash your hands."

"Oh, come on, Joe. It'll just take a minute."

He shook his head. "No. It's your birthday present, Alexa. Don't ruin it."

Beaten, she washed her hands, dried them, and turned to face him, leaning against the counter. "Okay, now what? I'm too wound up to go to sleep. Slapjack?"

Again, Joe shook his head. "We get too loud for that. We'd probably wake the whole house. How about a walk? It's probably pretty nice out there along the lake."

They slipped out her back door, onto the terrace, and down the steps to the sandy beach. Once she stepped onto the sand, Alexa pulled off her shoes. She pointed up at the sky. "Why don't you count stars for a moment. I want to get these stupid stockings off. They're driving me crazy!"

He gazed upward, chuckling at her as she muttered about her hosiery. "What's wrong with them?"

She dropped her shoes and stockings on the bottom of the terrace stairs and stepped back into the sand with a sigh. "Oh, this feels good." She glanced at him, her forehead wrinkling. "Right—stockings. It's those stupid seams. I can feel that they're not straight. Thankfully, this dress is long enough not to show it, but I could feel it on the backs of my legs—drove me crazy."

They walked several hundred yards up the shore, neither speaking. The moon shone brightly overhead, leaving just enough light reflected on the water to see. Alexa shivered. Joe paused. "You're cold. Maybe we should go back."

"No, I really needed this. It's been a busy day—lots of people and busyness. I like it out here." She shivered again. "I just should have brought a shawl."

Hoping it might be of some help, Joe removed his shirt and draped it over her shoulders. It felt strange and a little silly to walk along the shore in his dress shoes, pants, and undershirt, but it was the best he could do. "It's not warm, but it might keep off the chill."

She slipped her arms into the sleeves and rolled up the cuffs to her wrists. "I can't believe, as hot as it was that you didn't wear short sleeves!"

"I wasn't thinking or I probably would have. I just grabbed the first shirt in my closet and rushed to Marcello's before you decided to leave and go home without me." Joe stopped, pulled off his socks and shoes, and rolled up his pant legs. "There, that's better."

Again a few yards passed before either of them spoke. Alexa didn't turn to him or even change her rhythm as she said, "Joe?"

"Hmm?"

"Want to clear up a little confusion now?"

"Sure..." Something told him that he should know what she alluded to, but he didn't.

"Did you really think this dress was okay, or were you being nice because Lorie bought it and it's my birthday?"

"You don't like it." He felt like a fool. She probably had a dozen perfect dresses in the closet. He should have just suggested that she change into one rather than trying to shop for her. What a stupid idea that had been.

"Actually, it'll probably be one I wear often if I can get past one little problem."

Relief filled him. She did like it and wasn't offended. "What's the problem? Doesn't it fit?"

"It fits perfectly—not so tight that I can't move freely and not so loose that it looks sloppy." Her fingers traced the pattern of the beadwork around the neckline. "This— exquisite. Laidie outdid herself with this one, but the back—"

"I'd look, but I can't see it. What's wrong with it?"

She slipped one arm out of his shirt and turned away from him. "Now do you see it? I don't get why you didn't say something."

"I don't know what you're talking about." He helped her slip her arm back into the sleeve and pointed to a few nearby boulders. "Let's go sit down. I feel like we're dancing around something."

Once settled on the rocks, Alexa faced Joe, looked him square in the eyes, and demanded, "Why is it okay that there is no back on this dress, but the other one was a problem?"

"The other one what?"

"Dress."

He blinked. "What other dress?"

"The one Rhette made for me for the boutique opening. You practically said it was trampy."

The shock he felt was mirrored in her eyes. "I never—I didn't mean to imply that. That dress is so different—it's—" He sighed. "Lex, the back of that dress dipped so low that when you moved—well, it just made the mind go where a decent guy's mind doesn't want to go." He shook his head. "Okay, that's not true either. His mind does want to go there, but it shouldn't—oh, you know what I mean."

"But this dress—"

"Covers twice as much as the other one." He tugged at the shirtsleeve. "Let me see it again."

Alexa dropped the shirt from her shoulders, allowing it to hang around her waist as he glanced at her back again. "See?"

"I don't see. It's hard to explain, but aside from the fact that this has more fabric, there's something about it that is styled differently."

"Differently." She wrapped the shirt around her a little more tightly. "That's so helpful."

"I don't know how to explain it, other than you can't just say that if it shows more than the top of your shoulder blades, the dress is indecent. It doesn't work like that."

Alexa had never looked more confused. "I'm so lost. You're saying that the problem isn't showing the back but something else. What? You told me—"

"Back, sleeves, shorts, pants—even the woman." Joe wished he had never said a word about the other dress.

"Okay, try again, Friday. Give me the facts."

"Women never get it. It's not about whether sleeveless shirts tempt guys to lust. It's about whether one particular sleeveless shirt on one particular woman is indecent for that woman alone."

"If a shirt is indecent, it's indecent. What you're saying sounds like situational ethics. It's not that complicated. It's either revealing or it's not."

She didn't get it. He wondered if he should even try to show her, but he'd heard the same arguments over the years and they bugged him every time. "No, you're missing the point. The same shirt on someone else might be fine, or another sleeveless shirt—or backless dress," he joked, "might be fine."

He had to give her credit. She kept trying. She crossed her ankles, smoothed her hemline, and stared back at him. "So tell me why it's okay for me to wear the sleeveless shirt, but it isn't okay for Jocie or Heather. Why can I wear this one but not that one?"

"It's all in how it fits them—or you—how they wear it. Even their attitude can change how it appears. Women need discernment." She started to speak, but Joe added, "And men need self-control rather than expecting women to skip every kind of potential stumbling block that they might possibly run into. I don't think a burka is the answer to the modern modesty issue."

"Where were you in high school when all I wanted was someone to tell me to use my head instead of give me laws about what was or wasn't 'godly apparel?'"

"Let me guess," he joked. "Your mom made the rules?"

Laughing, Alexa shared a few of the rules she remembered from her teen years. "They changed," she admitted. "Whatever was spiritually correct one year might be out the next. Mom was always on the upswing of godliness."

As they walked back to her house, Joe slipped his hand into hers. "Did I say 'happy birthday' yet?"

"It's not my birthday anymore," she teased. "Did I say thanks for the dress?"

"I think so. I'm sorry for sending odd signals."

She shrugged. "I'm really sorry about that other one. I knew it was low, but I didn't think—I mean, people wear swimsuits that show more. I just assumed—"

"Not that all swimsuits are easy to ignore, but it's just different. That's all I can say. I don't know how to explain it, but I'm really glad you aren't ticked at me about it."

At Alexa's steps, Joe pointed to the side of her house. "I'll just go around and head out front."

"You don't have your car."

"I'll walk over to Marcello's and get it. See you tomorrow." He felt like he should kiss her or something—wanted to even—but he refused to consider it.

She removed his shirt, handing it to him. "Thanks for everything, Friday. Dinner, the party, the dancing, this dress—"

He cocked his head as he tried to remember other garments she'd worn. Even in the moonlight, he could see her skin darkening as she blushed. "What?"

"You don't wear jewelry. I just noticed—why is that? Someone so into details..."

"I have a few pieces—not many. Occasionally you have to have something, and I try to wear earrings in pictures, but—" She stopped abruptly.

"Go on. What?"

"I just can't stand spending a lot of money on rocks and metal."

Joe snickered. The idea of someone as fashion-conscious as Alexa—someone as decidedly feminine as she was—not liking jewelry sounded preposterous. "That's rich," he laughed. "That's really rich."

"It probably sounds ridiculous, but it's true. Sometimes I look at a dress, especially with a wide neckline like this, and I think, 'You've got to get over this.' Then I remember how much quality jewelry costs and how I'd probably hate the weight of it against my skin. Cold, heavy metal. Ick."

"You could just buy costume stuff. They make really nice simulated stuff these days."

"Seriously, Joe? Can you see me buying imitation sapphires or cubic zirconia and gold plated settings?"

He eyed her dress critically. "Well, I can't say I'm sorry you don't. I think that dress looks perfect without any necklace."

"I'd never let anything compete with this beadwork." She picked up the shoes she'd left on the step. "You probably haven't noticed, but most of my clothing has something around the neckline to accentuate it without jewelry. I didn't notice that I did it until Laidie pointed it out one time."

"She's a very nice woman, your Laidie. I think she undercharged me for your dress."

Alexa squeezed his hand. "I doubt it, but if she did, be assured that I overpay her more often than not. I want to keep her on my side for a very long time."

"She was going to come, you know." The disappointment and surprise that flooded her face made Joe regret mentioning it.

"Really? Here? Tonight? I'm sorry she didn't. What changed her mind?"

"She said her husband and son were going to be gone fishing this weekend, so she'd come down for the party, but she called yesterday morning and said she wasn't coming after all. She said she woke up with a scratchy throat and a summer cold."

"Knowing Laidie, she's holed up in her living room with a stack of movies and a pot of chicken soup."

His laughter filled the night air. "That's exactly what she said—almost, if not, verbatim."

"Still," she sighed, "it would have been so nice to see her again. We've only met twice, you know."

"She mentioned that."

"I'll have to send her flowers in the morning. She's been working on our things so much this year that I suspect her flower garden has suffered. Laidie loves her flowers." Alexa smiled at him before turning to go inside. "Goodnight, Joe."

"Night."

He stood at the base of the terraces steps and watched as she slipped inside the house. An emptiness crept over him as she disappeared from view. Joe pulled on his socks and shoes, rolled up the sleeves of his shirt, and took off for the town square. It was no time to grow introspective.

Chapter 19

Wes grumbled as his phone rang. "'llo?"

"Hey, Wes. Get Joe. I need him."

"'bout time you figured that out. Hold on." Wes, tempted to continue the teasing, was too sleepy to think of anything else. He opened the door to Joe's room and tossed the phone on the bed, hitting Joe's elbow in the process. "It's the sister of mine that you pretend not to adore."

Rubbing his funny bone, Joe grabbed the phone and covered it as he growled back at Wes. "At six in the morning, 'adore' is the wrong word, my man." He grabbed the bottle of water from his bedside table, took a swig, and attempted a chipper, "Mornin', Lex."

"I'm not going to apologize for waking you up, but I am going to apologize for what comes next… and I'm going to suggest that you find your phone."

"What?"

Alexa tried to sound cheerful as she said, "Well, you brought me a houseful of hungry guests and not enough food for me to feed them. I need eggs, mushrooms, juice, and more half-and-half."

"When?"

"About thirty minutes ago, but The Market just opened, so hurry up. I'll feed you."

"You sound out of breath—you okay?"

Wiping her brow with the back of her arm, Alexa continued kneading her dough and speaking into her speakerphone. "I'm just kneading dough for cinnamon rolls."

"On my way."

Joe found Alexa in the kitchen mixing icing for the cinnamon rolls. Minus pearls and heels, she looked like Donna Reed in her black and white gingham fifties house dress. What modern woman would wear a red kerchief to tie up her hair out of her face? He glanced at the belt around her waist. How many would choose a belt to match their kerchief or vice versa? It was a delightful kind of insanity.

"Cute dress." Whatever made him say that, he didn't know.

"It's one of my new ones from Laidie. Can you hand me the bowl up there?"

"Sure." Joe handed it to her, amused at the distracted way Alexa worked.

She cracked eggs into the bowl and passed it to him. "Whip these please."

While he beat the eggs, she sliced mushrooms, onions, and tomatoes; mixed orange juice concentrate into a pitcher; and began chopping fruit. He set the bowl aside and watched the process, strangely intrigued. She must have felt somewhat self-conscious under his scrutiny, because he found the morning paper thrust into his hands and a cup of well-doctored coffee set beside him.

Joe made a good show of reading the paper. He shuffled through the pages, pausing for a moment, moving his head up and down and from side to side, but he watched her work. For someone who rarely cooked for more than two or three, making a large breakfast for nearly a dozen people didn't seem to faze her. Joe couldn't help but wonder how she managed to adapt so easily.

Ready to begin cooking the eggs, she beat them once more, adding a bit of half-and-half to them. So that was her secret. His never got as fluffy or creamy as hers. Then again, he hardly tried. Once satisfied with the amount of beating she'd given to the eggs, she poured them into a hot skillet and sprinkled the toppings over it.

She lifted the pan from time to time in order to slow the heat, but in minutes, she placed a perfect omelet in front of Joe, handed him a fork, and passed him juice. "Oh, napkin.

Sorry." She jerked one from the basket and tossed it at him.

Not until Joe had taken his third bite did he realize that she had cleaned the kitchen. "How do you do it?"

"The eggs? Cook them slower. Most people try to cook eggs too quickly, but that just makes omelets that are both undercooked and burned."

He took another bite, watching her again for a moment. Had she dodged the subject? Did she think he was upset for cleaning after their discussion? "No, not the eggs. You do that because you're an incredible cook. The kitchen. This place was a mess last night and now…"

"I can't work in a mess. I just popped most things in the dishwasher before I went to bed last night, started a new load a few minutes ago, and voila. One clean kitchen. The rest of the house needs work, but Anita can handle it. I just can't cook without a clean kitchen."

A timer beeped, sending her for oven mittens and pulling out the largest pan of cinnamon rolls that could fit in her oven. She'd brought that pan to the station a time or two. When he saw her replace it with another pan, Joe's mouth almost watered. "Those are my favorite cinnamon rolls."

"You on duty this morning?"

"Nope. Go on at two—in the morning. Day off." He took the last bite of his omelet and wiped his mouth in anticipation of the rolls.

"Good. Can you take these over to the station? I made them for the guys and Judith. You can have one from the next batch when you get back, but leave these alone. I'll ask Judith."

Groaning, Joe took the oven mitts, and, using them like potholders, carried the rolls out the front door.

Once the door shut behind him, she smiled. "Serves him right for pretending to read that paper."

On his return, Joe found James and Alexa discussing her fall appearances and her upcoming trip to California. He knew James flirted with her—he had seen it at the party—but he hadn't been able to imagine why girls of any age would be interested. Sitting at her breakfast counter, his hair tousled and looking quite boyish in his sleep-induced stupor, Joe now saw what might appeal to women like Shannon and his little sister. James exuded a certain confidence in his charms, but Alexa showed no signs of notice or interest.

Joe decided to table the relieved sensation that welled up in him for consideration later and in privacy—or not at all.

James accepted his omelet, making half-hearted protestations about the effect it would have on his cholesterol. He ate the fruit she passed him, drained the juice and coffee, and nodded his thanks when she offered more. Joe's eyebrows rose and he frowned when James commented on how long it was taking the cinnamon rolls to bake.

Alexa had clearly reached the end of her patience as well. She leaned over the counter, crooking her finger at him and beckoned him closer. James, obviously not very astute at reading Alexa's body language, leaned forward—too eagerly. "I knew you'd—"

"Breathe."

"What?" James pulled back, looking as confused as he sounded.

"Lean forward again and exhale."

He jerked back, guilt written in invisible block letters all over his face. Alexa crossed her arms as disgust filled her features. "It's not yet eight o'clock, James. How dare you! I'm quite certain that Joe didn't add BYOB to his invitation."

"Just a bit, 'lexa. I had some left from my trip to Milan, so I toasted you—"

"Stuff it." Alexa poured another cup of coffee and passed it across the counter. "When you're done with that, we'll start on water." She tapped the counter in front of him until his eyes met hers. "And stay away from Rhette. I'm warning her about you."

"How'd—"

She stared for a moment before shaking her head. "I'm not blind, you idiot!"

"Well, if you'd just—"

Alexa cut him off by turning to Joe and offering a coffee refill. As she poured, Darrin entered the kitchen wearing long shorts, a loose polo shirt, and leather strapped sandals. Joe had never seen the man so casually dressed.

"Morning, Darrin." Alexa held up the coffee carafe. "Coffee?"

James slipped from the barstool and stormed from the kitchen. Alexa threw the men an apologetic glance and passed Darrin a fresh mug. "Sorry about that. He's impossible if he's been drinking. Any time he feels rejected by a female — which is much too often, by the way — he drinks more and gets maudlin, resulting in more drinking. Vicious cycle."

A shout upstairs sent Joe bolting from the room, toppling the barstool to the floor in his haste. "I'll get him, Lex."

Seconds later, he yelled for her to come. Alexa pointed to the oven. "Darrin, will you please take those out and drizzle the icing on them if it beeps?"

Without waiting for an answer, Alexa raced from the kitchen, took the stairs two at a time, and burst into Rhette's room. The woman wailed and sobbed uncontrollably. "What happened?"

Joe, with Rhette clinging to him like a life preserver, pointed to the phone that lay on the floor. "Will you see if Adam is still on the line? It's something about Silva being hurt."

"Not hurt! He said she's dead and there's blood and—" Rhette erupted into a fresh round of hysterics.

Shaken, Alexa picked up the phone. "Adam? You still there? How is Silva?" Nothing he said registered over the piercing screams and intermittent wails. "Just a minute, I can't hear."

Alexa slipped from Rhette's room, climbed the stairs to her bedroom, and shut the door. "Okay, I'm sorry. Rhette is a little upset." The understatement mocked her. "What happened? Silva was in bed—"

Adam, audibly shaken, tried to explain. "I started to

sleep on your library couch. I wasn't around when you were doling out rooms."

"Why—"

"Alexa, I'm sorry. I just wanted to relax a bit so I went down to that Aphrodite place. Anyway, when I got back, the rooms were all taken, so Silva said to sleep on the sofa—she even brought me a blanket and pillow." The man's voice choked. "She wanted me to sleep in the library because she thought it would be quieter, and the couch in there would be more comfortable than the living room. You might freak out to see me on the one that goes to your landing." Adam paused. "You know, Alexa, you have a lot of couches."

The irrelevant statements nearly drove Alexa insane. She ached to scream, "Out with it!" but managed to keep herself in check. "That would have been fine too. I don't know how I missed you. Sorry. But Adam, if you were asleep on my couch, how are you—not here? Where are you?"

"Rhette got a call from the buyer at Bergdorf's asking for a nine o'clock meeting at the boutique this morning. They said they wanted enough for a display of nine pieces and wanted to compare samples and stuff. Rhette got all nervous and freaked out, so Silva asked me to drive her to the airport. We flew back here and got in at four this morning. I went home, but Silva wanted to put together a presentation for the boutique."

"When is the last time you spoke to her?"

Adam's voice wavered. "When I dropped her off. She asked me to arrive at ten till nine this morning so that I could be 'fresh eyes.'" He sighed. "Right, like I could with four hours sleep."

A familiar feeling of dread slowly crept into her heart as he spoke. She had endured more violent deaths, despair, and unease in the past year than some experience in a lifetime. "Okay, so you showed up at ten till?"

"Yeah." Adam choked again. "When I got there, the door was open—unlocked. That was weird because Silva is such a stickler for keeping it locked unless we're open for business. I went in." A pause—long and ominous, working as effectively as mood music in a movie—set the tone for his next words. "Oh, Alexa. It was quiet—too quiet. Then I saw her—"

Hearing a grown man sob out of fear and grief—nothing could have been more horrible. She waited until he gained some bit of control before she choked out, "How did she die, Adam?" Rhette's outburst hadn't convinced her of Silva's demise, but the longer Adam talked, combined with his fits of weeping, confirmed it for her.

She didn't hear the door open or shut behind her, but she did feel a hand on her shoulder. The phone dropped and Alexa clapped her hands over her mouth to stifle a scream. Joe grabbed the phone, demanding that Adam tell him what happened. Silent sobs wracked Alexa's body as Joe listened and then disconnected the call.

How long Joe sat holding her, he didn't know. Several times, she seemed to gain composure, only to have a fresh wave of grief flood over her. Darrin knocked on the door, offering cinnamon rolls, but Joe shook his head and whispered, "Silva's dead."

Months earlier, Joe had held her awkwardly as she sobbed out her fear and frustration regarding the murders in Fairbury. He had hoped never to have to console her about anything like it again. His habit of detaching parts of himself from a situation to see it from another angle allowed him to wonder, amid his attempts to soothe and comfort her, why it didn't feel as awkward this time.

"Joe—why? I don't understand—"

"I don't know." It killed him to add the next words. "Adam wanted me to make sure you knew that it isn't suicide."

"But he said—" Her confusion prompted a new round of sniffles.

"You dropped the phone too soon. It's murder, Alexa. Someone smothered her—with one of those plastic bags you have to cover clothes in the shop. Then they slit her wrists to make it look like a suicide, but—" He sighed. "Lex, any cop worth anything would have known from the sight of her face, the struggle bruises, the position of her body, and the location of it—" Joe paused at the sight of her horrified face.

"Go on, Joe. I'll have to hear it sometime."

"Sorry. Occupational hazard, I guess. I tend to compartmentalize this stuff. Where she was found—just lying on the floor in the doorway to the back—made them suspicious, the color around her mouth and plastic inside showed that she was suffocated first."

He watched, confused and concerned, as Alexa shuffled across the room and into the bathroom without a word. When she returned carrying a box of tissues, he relaxed. Such a normal thing to do, but not detached. Maybe she would be all right.

She untied her kerchief, untwisted her hair, and began brushing it, lost in thought. "Joe?"

"Hmm?"

"Can you hire one of those crime scene cleaning services to come out to the shop? I don't want Rhette or Adam even to have to think about having it done. Just knowing they're coming will probably be a huge relief. If someone slit her wrists…"

"Yeah. It'll be bad. Bill to you or the business?" How had he known to ask the question? Strange.

"Me. I'll do it in lieu of flowers."

"No, you won't, but it's nice that you think you will." He took the brush from her hand. "You're going to pull out every last strand if you don't give it a rest. Your hair looks great."

She stared at him, stunned. "Do you really think I care about my stupid hair?"

"Lex, I'm not the enemy." He pulled her close again, but this time Joe wondered if it was more to comfort himself than for her benefit. "I'm just worried about you."

"It'll be okay. I'll go to Chicago and figure out what to do now."

He hesitated. How ready was she to accept reality? "Alexa, you know that this is another attack on the business, right? We need to ascertain if it's because of your presence, or if it has something to do with your employees, or what."

Her eyes rose to meet his, tears swimming in them as she choked, "If it has to do with employees, wouldn't you assume that they hit the target?"

Joe closed his eyes briefly. "We can only hope."

Alexa arrived in Chicago late Monday afternoon. She checked her phone as the taxi drove her to Rhette's of Chicago, frowning at the lack of messages. Joe obviously was still angry.

He had argued with her from the moment she said she was going to the boutique until she entered security at the airport, insisting she not go. He saw the move as dangerous and irresponsible, but Alexa insisted. Her business partner was dead—murdered. Rhette and Adam, shocked and unsettled, floundered without Silva's direction.

Joe insisted she had gone mad—insane. Her connection with the business would make her a person of interest—if not a suspect. Her arrival also made her too easily accessible to the Chicago Police Department—almost like a burglar fencing his wares on the station steps. However, nothing he said changed her mind. She had to go and had nothing to hide.

Despite her protests, he had called Darrin and his parents and asked them to keep an eye on her—to call often. Though she argued that he knew it wouldn't be effective, he had even called the Chicago Police Department and asked that they keep a secure watch over her and the shop, hoping for both protection from the murderer and deflection of her as a suspect. She still didn't know if they took him seriously or not. Joe didn't either, making his frustration thermostat hit the boiling point.

She checked her phone again as the taxi pulled up to the boutique. Still no call from Joe. Her fingers hovered over the keys. Would he be ticked? Probably, but it might also make him laugh enough to relax again. She paid the driver and stepped from the car. Before entering, her fingers flew over the keys. POUTING IS MOST UNATTRACTIVE IN A MAN.

That done, she unlocked the door, entered, hurried up the back stairs, and slipped into the small office at one end of the workroom. Adam and Rhette crowded in with her. They chatted and sniffled as Alexa laid out her plan of attack.

"First, I'm going to call Bergdorf's and see who was supposed to come. I know the police are likely doing that too, but I doubt they'll tell us much. They'll claim it compromises the investigation, or I'm a prime suspect so they won't tell me anything or some such nonsense."

"You! Prime suspect!" Adam shook his head. "How! You were in Fairbury the whole time."

"Technically, I might have been able to fly there and back in time, but then there'd be a record of that. But until that is proven, I'm going to be up there," she insisted.

She glanced sideways. "Rhette?" The young woman's head snapped up. At twenty-four, she was young and inexperienced, but once she got her head back together, Alexa knew she'd keep working with the same tireless energy she'd shown during the pre-opening weeks.

"Yeah?"

"I need you to make sure all orders are in process and then get to work on the spring sketches. We need those at the patternmakers by the first week in September—right?"

Rhette nodded. She pulled out her cellphone and punched in a few numbers. Alexa turned to Adam. "You need to go downstairs, check inventory, and then get that door open. The police cleared us for business, and we need to get the stigma off us immediately. I've ordered flowers and a headshot of Silva. We'll put them on that table near the front door with a guestbook for customers to sign. It can go to Silva's family."

The bean counter in Adam surfaced. "Can we recover from this?"

Alexa sighed. "Yes and no. From Silva's death—never.

From the negative press and blows to our reputation? Definitely."

After four calls to Bergdorf's, talking to three different departments and two supervisors, Alexa confirmed her suspicions. No representative from Bergdorf's made an appointment at eleven o'clock on Friday night to see the Rhette Collection the following morning. She would have been astounded if they had. How had Silva not seen through such an obvious ruse?

She sank into the office chair, closed her eyes, and prayed for strength. Her faith wobbled. For years, it had held her firmly, but it unraveled now, leaving holes all over the fabric of her life.

The phone in her pocket tempted her. She pulled it out and punched Joe's number. "Hey—"

"Call you back in five. Sorry."

Her fingers drummed on the desk. Was he busy or did he need a minute to diffuse refreshed anger? That idea produced a nervous round of giggles. "I need to write," she muttered.

Several minutes later, the phone rang, further jarring her nerves. Joe sounded strained. "Sorry about that, Lex. Had to ticket the Cox boy again—no helmet." At her silence, he added, "Kid's probably grounded until Christmas now. Not that it means anything—he'll be out there without it tomorrow most likely. What's up?"

Awkwardness flooded her. He was going to let her have it—she just knew it. She tried to preempt him. "Should I call the police? I mean, I can't imagine they don't know it yet, but—"

"They'll question you at some point, and you can show them whatever you've found then."

"Okay." There were so many questions she wanted to ask, but Alexa choked.

"Lex, listen. Go over the books. See if you can't find something in there that explains the original vandalism. Someone had to profit—probably the murderer. My guess is that Silva found out."

"What? What do I look for?" Defeat smothered her.

"Things like the boxes being shipped to you after they were already delivered to the store. Call UPS and see who arranged the pick-up. Look for things like that."

It made sense. Usually, she would have thought of something similar. Exhaustion, frustration, and grief choked her mind as well as her heart. "I wish you were here," she whispered. Without waiting for a response, Alexa disconnected the call.

In Fairbury, Joe stared at his cellphone screen. What did she mean by it? She sounded lonely—as if her usual comfort in being alone with herself had been stripped from her. "I wish I was there too, Lex," he whispered.

Chapter 20

Darrin wove his way through the tables of the restaurant and hugged Alexa as she stood waiting to be seated. "C'mon. Our table is over there. How are you doing?"

She almost hadn't accepted. With all that had happened around her, Alexa's natural response was to pull into her own little world and protect herself from further pain. Dinner with Darrin felt like the ultimate sacrifice. Joe was right. How selfish could she be—how shallow? Silva's family had lost their loved one forever, and she dared consider going out to dinner a sacrifice.

"I feel numb. The police questioned me today. It was mostly a formality. I have an excellent alibi, despite no one seeing me during the hours of one-thirty and seven when Joe left and arrived."

"But you didn't fly and no one could drive that fast."

"Exactly. Adam is the prime suspect right now. They confirmed that the cab did drop him off at the time he stated, but no one saw him go in or out of his apartment. They're reviewing security camera footage now."

Darrin leaned back in his chair, eyed her, and then leaned forward again. "I'm so sorry, Alexa. Are you sure this business is worth the trouble?"

Rubbing her temples, Alexa smiled at the server and reluctantly ordered a glass of wine. At the look of surprise in Darrin's eyes, she shrugged. "My stomach is in knots. I'm hoping it'll help soothe it or digest the food—something."

"And the business?"

"I've thought about it—really." When the server returned, Alexa accepted the glass gratefully and took a sip. "Silva just invested so much of her own money—twenty-five thousand dollars—in the venture. It's not a lot overall, but it was all she had. This isn't about me losing half a million dollars."

"Alexa..."

"Look, Darrin. They took that little bit of money and made an impressive presentation. They risked it, even before they had backing, trying to ensure a presentation that would tempt me or another investor. They planned to present their prospectus to five people, you know."

"Five?"

"Smaller increments—hoping that with requesting less, they'd get the backing."

"So why did you invest the whole amount?"

"I thought it would make it easier if there weren't half a dozen people that they had to answer to."

"Okay, but the money has been spent now. You gave it to them. Do you have to stay involved? Can't you be a silent partner?"

It was something she'd considered. It had never been her intention to be anything more than the financial backing for the endeavor. Silva had always brought her into it, asked her opinions, sought her input. "I can, but until it's successful, I'm going to help. I can't help Silva now, but I can do this in her memory. She deserves that." Alexa took a deep breath, trying to steady herself. "She must have been so scared..."

Darrin left her to her thoughts and ate the food the server brought, giving Alexa the opportunity to compose herself. It seemed strange to be relieved that he didn't try to comfort her. Alexa hadn't been one to seek that kind of reassurance until Joe. That thought terrified her. Becoming too dependent upon someone else for emotional stability would destroy the life she'd built and she wanted that life. She wanted it exactly as it was.

Her eyes slid toward Darrin. He hadn't pushed, even after she ignored his advice regarding the money. He had become a good friend—a treasured one. Alexa suspected that he knew her nonchalant attitude over the potential loss of so much money had been deceptive. Despite her apparent indifference, it grieved her. Her ability to invest that money had made murder possible. First people died because of what she wrote before she earned the money, and then someone died because her profits made Rhette's dream possible. While she might not miss the money, no one could "afford" the kind of financial blow it would be if the business failed.

"What will you do now?"

The words jerked her from her reverie. Alexa stared at him, grateful for the chance to swallow the lumps in her throat and blink back the threat of tears. After a few deep breaths, she managed a weak smile. "I'm going to stay until the Thursday before Labor Day weekend. After that, I'll fly home and work on my manuscript until my trip to California. I really hope this is settled before then. My parents—dealing with this with them would be a nightmare."

"Your parents? I wasn't aware you visited them on those trips."

Weariness fluctuated with annoyance in her heart. Alexa searched for the source of her reaction and sighed. It wasn't Darrin—not really. Once more, her parents had managed to drive an invisible wedge between herself and a friend without her realizing it. The simple mention of them made her back away in self-preservation.

"I go every other year—can't take more than that."

"Oh, Alexa. I can't imagine…"

Fumbling for an explanation, Alexa didn't answer for a moment. The last thing she wanted to do was be unjust in how she portrayed her family. "You know, I know my parents love me in their way. I know that. It keeps me from saying or doing things I'll regret later. The problem is, I can't win."

"I don't get it? If it's that bad, why not just call and visit in a neutral place?"

"They're family. They're my parents. They haven't written me off yet. It's just that if I visit, they're bothered by my presence. If I don't visit, then I'm the ungrateful prodigal refusing to return from the pigpen." Alexa shrugged. "Like I said, I can't win."

"It sounds to me like you're putting yourself in the line of fire. I don't really understand why you'd do that."

"Because it's right, Darrin. I need to know, for my own conscience's sake, that the rift is there because they choose to have it. I need that."

"I guess you never lose that desire to please your parents."

Alexa pursed her lips. "No, you sure don't."

They strolled lazily along the walking paths in Grant Park. As they walked, Darrin and Alexa talked of Lorie's exciting health improvements, Alexa's weak editing, and her transition to her new home. As if by unspoken agreement, they deliberately avoided all reference to the business.

"I'm not sure it's the place for me," Alexa admitted. "I loved having the space for the party. The closet—heavenly. Truly, I love it. But I miss the coziness of my home. I miss the drive-bys after a walk to town for a movie or an evening out."

"You felt at home there—from my perspective anyway. Lorie and I talked about it on the way home. She's never been in your cottage, but the pictures Joe has shown Jeremy gave her a feel for it. She said, 'Why does the first feel like a step into Alexa's heart and the new one a step into her life?'"

"That's a great way of putting it. That's exactly how I feel." She glanced up at him. "I'm already very private. It almost feels like I've put a fortress up around me, withdrawing even more." Laughing, she added, "Wouldn't Joe be torn if he heard me say that? He'd go crazy wondering if he should encourage me to take his house back or give me up for lost so he could stay."

"So use your house to reach out. Don't hide behind the walls. Pull others into the walls and open them."

"I'll think about it. You have a point."

Darrin slipped his hand in hers and led her to a nearby bench in full view of the lit sprays from Buckingham fountain. "Can we talk?"

"I thought we were..." She sounded coy. Alexa hated it, but exhaustion meant she didn't have the resources to correct her tone.

"A few months ago, when I was in Fairbury, we talked about the idea of exploring an 'us.' I thought at the time that I didn't want the kind of relationship it would have to mean."

"I understood, Darrin. Really. I've lived alone with no one else to answer to for so long that I just don't know how to respond to change like that. Truly, I wasn't hurt. Don't give it another thought."

"But I *have* given it a lot of thought—months now." He covered their hands with his other one. "I almost turned around that day and came back to ask if we could rewind and erase the conversation." Darrin sighed. "I wish I had. I just wanted to be sure."

As plain as the words sounded, Alexa didn't want to make any assumptions. After weeks of sleepless nights, she didn't trust herself to read his desire to revisit the idea of exploring a relationship accurately. "Can you be clearer? I really don't know what to think."

"I'm asking if I burned bridges that day. You're here for a few days still. I'd like to try again while I have the chance."

"I see." She didn't.

"Listen, Alexa. I realized that I was incredibly selfish that day. I based a decision that affects both of us on my reaction to a dream. I think—" She watched, amused, as he stared at their hands almost as if they were a crystal ball. Did he expect their depths to reveal the right words? Just as she started to reassure him that she understood, Darrin took a deep breath and said, "I think I wasn't as ready for a relationship then, and I used that dream to push you away."

The ambiguity had become a little annoying. "That still doesn't help me, Darrin. What specifically do you suggest? I take it you're attracted to me—I'm not playing games or fishing for compliments—but what are you suggesting we do about it?"

Darrin stood, leading her back down the paths they'd already walked, hand-in-hand. After a few steps, he cleared his throat. "I don't have the luxury of just allowing a friendship to grow into something else. You don't live here. You come just often enough to keep things interesting, but not often enough for that. If I lived in Fairbury or Rockland, it would be different. If you lived here—"

"Well, that's not going to happen at this point, so—" As the harshness of her tone registered, she stopped. "I'm sorry. What I mean is that I want to know what you want to see happen in the next four days."

"I'd like us to spend time together—purposefully—actual time doing things together. If things were different, we could take time slowly learning about each other. I don't have that luxury. I have four days to try to knit our hearts together enough to keep that connection while you're gone." He paused, gazing at her. "And if you're curious, yes. I worked on that line all day."

The whole thing sounded delightful and a little silly at the same time. Her experience with dating had been less than encouraging. She had watched a few relationships crash and burn. The last thing she wanted was to ruin a good friendship that way.

"And if it doesn't happen? If you wake up in six months and realize I'm not the woman for you, will I lose a friend? Have you ever been able to continue a friendship that crossed romantic lines?"

"I've never done it—the last time I did any kind of dating I was young and immature. I'm older though. I value people and relationships more. It would be hard, but I think I could do it—eventually."

"Okay, give me a few ground rules. Exactly what am I agreeing *to*?"

Darrin pounced on this eagerly. "I've been thinking about it, and call me a bad father, but I'd like to leave out Lorie and Jeremy. I'd like *not* to discuss the murder or vandalism. I'd just like to discuss *us* and do things that are about *us*."

"Lead the way, Galahad. I can agree to that."

Chapter 21

"Something is iffy with the books, Joe. I've gone over everything, tried to come up with every explanation I can, and it still doesn't work. When can I get you a copy of what I've found?"

The panic in her voice alarmed him; he glanced at the clock. He could take a break. "I'm at the station. Send it here and I'll call you back after I look at them."

Joe watched the printouts of Alexa's bookkeeping drop into the fax tray as he filed a few reports and recorded court dates on his schedule. Before he reached his desk, Joe saw the problem. He pulled out his phone as he spread the sheets across his desk. "Hey, got them. It's the insurance. You have two identical policies with two companies. Unnecessary, but no one would think anything of it unless they examined the books and were already suspicious."

"Two policies. That's what I was afraid of. I kept trying to come up with some—any—other explanation, but it kept coming back to that."

"Who do you think did it?" Joe tried to find something that would make more sense than the obvious answer.

"It has to be Silva. It is completely illogical; she's the signer on both of them, but she's also the one who is dead."

Joe examined the pages of policies and financial records before him. Silva had to be the culprit—and couldn't be. "Okay, Rhette or Adam are the only options. Since Silva signed, I'd say her, but maybe Adam told her that he canceled one?"

"That actually makes sense. I could see that happening. So Adam. And he found Silva, so maybe he's a really good actor." She sounded wounded as she asked, "Should I take this to the police?"

"You have to, Lex. Want me to call?"

"No, I'll go. I want to see the detective's reaction. I'll call back when I know." Dead air hung between them before she whispered, "Pray, Joe. I'm scared." The line went dead.

He stared at his phone, wondering. Hungry, he decided to take a walk to think. "Chief, I'm going to The Deli. Want anything?"

"Yes! Darla is on another health kick. I have sliced tofu loaf and sprouts on Bible bread."

Joe laughed. "I'll bring you real food."

"Did you figure out Alexa's problem?"

"No..." he stepped in the door. "We just increased the problem. I mean, we know one thing we didn't know before, but it just opens up more questions instead of answering other ones."

"Is she safe?"

The question vocalized the dread Joe hadn't been willing to acknowledge. "I don't know. I don't think she can be."

Chief Varney stepped into the main room, leaning his ample belly over the counter. "Why?"

"Because the most logical suspect of everything happening at the boutique is now dead."

Alexa's impatience mounted as the cab crawled the four miles through busy streets to State Street and the First District building. Her fingernails tapped a steady rhythm on her leather portfolio, and her mind tried to remember every word she'd spoken to Silva about the business, about her store in New York, and about the vandalism. Every word the woman said had sounded genuine. Alexa couldn't remember a single disingenuous moment.

Just outside the police station, she stepped from the cab, adjusted her hat, and ignored the gawks and rude comments as she entered the building. Her white afternoon dress hadn't been a well-thought out choice. Though better than the floor length dresses she often wore, the color, or lack thereof, would attract any dirt in her general proximity.

She found herself seated in an uncomfortable chair with Detective Tony Romano, who asked question after question. As she answered, she untied the leather portfolio and spread it open, pulling papers from it. "Here are the papers I mentioned. I don't know if they will help or not, but I thought you should see them. As much as I hope I am overreacting, this looks very wrong to me."

"I'm sure our guys will be able to figure it out. We've got a great team here."

She nodded, grateful for the hat that kept his eyes from boring into hers. The detective seemed to expect more, but what she didn't know. "I thought I should also tell you that I called a private auditing company as well. Obviously, if something is wrong with the books—related to the case or not—we need to know it. So the firm of Stanovich and Wagner will also have copies of these by tomorrow."

The detective's voice softened a little. "Ms. Hartfield, we're going to get this guy."

She nodded. "I am certain of it."

"You've done what you can do. We'll take care of it from here."

"In other words, back off and let you do your jobs?" Alexa reached for the papers, but Detective Romano held them firmly and shook his head.

"No. This is helpful, and I appreciate what you've done, but it isn't your responsibility to solve this case. I think your experience as a writer—"

Alexa stood, almost knocking over the flimsy chair in her haste. She glared at the man before her, every inch of her quivering with fury and pain. "This is not about me wishing to play Nancy Drew, Detective Romano. My friend and business partner is dead. She's not a case to me. She's not a puzzle or a curiosity. Silva Hoffman was a daughter, a sister, a friend, a talented designer, and my business partner."

"I didn't mean—"

"I need—not want, *need*—to ensure that my other

partners and employees are safe. I want to ensure that her family knows that she will receive justice. I—"

She stopped mid-rant, tears streaming down her face, and turned. With her portfolio folded and tucked under her arm, she grabbed her purse and whispered, "Thank you for your time," before she rushed out the door.

Detective Romano followed and watched from the steps as Alexa hailed a cab and rode off into an afternoon that promised rain soon. Satisfied that he had convinced her to drop meddling in the case, Romano strode back into the building to his desk. As his partner came into the room with burgers from the grease truck down the street, he said, "Hey, let's get a move on, Frank. Ms. Hartfield just dropped off quirky books."

Joe reread every piece of information Alexa had sent for the tenth time while Jeremy rattled on about something. The expectation in Jeremy's tone told Joe that he'd better be able to answer something. "What? I missed that?"

"Joe, she's going out with him every night! Lorie is so excited she's driving me crazy. I can't believe you're just sitting there like nothing is happening."

"Whatever is or isn't happening isn't any of my business. Maybe you should mind yours as well."

"You know, Joe, when people ask me what it's like to have a brother fifteen years older than me, I tell them it's cool. They don't believe me, but I mean it. When you're being your usual great self, it's cool because you're cool. When you're being an idiot, it's cool because I learn what not to do."

"Stuff it."

Jeremy ranted in a dozen directions before he finally disconnected and left Joe nursing a headache, still a bit uncertain why his brother had called. Did Jeremy really think he would take off to Chicago and duke it out with Darrin over Alexa? "Knew I shouldn't have let them think we were dating," he muttered under his breath.

Judith passed, leading a gaggle of kindergartners on a field trip through the station. "Who is Officer Joe dating, class?" she murmured just for his benefit.

"You stuff it too."

The din of excited children, each wanting his or her question answered first, drove him from the building. He started toward the town square and hesitated. The heat and humidity nearly smothered him. Joe retraced his steps and climbed into his Jeep. At the corner, his blinker flicked, ticking like a metronome while he decided where to go.

"Rosita's," he muttered.

Burrito, chips and salsa, and a large Sprite—a lunch any man would love. He started toward home but, at Elm Street, he continued straight through town and toward Alexa's house. The larger homes loomed as he drove down toward the lake and turned into Alexa's driveway.

His feet echoed in her entryway. Strange—he'd never noticed an echo in there before. Alexa's personality almost seemed like a muffler for the house. That thought amused him. He'd been spending too much time in introspection. Either that, or Alexa had rubbed off on him more than he realized.

The heat felt less oppressive on the shaded corner of her deck. The breeze blew cooler air off the water, making the temperature bearable if not comfortable. Joe loved her deck. At first, his excitement over her move had been limited to his own change of address to the part of town he'd loved for years. However, of late, he had grown to appreciate the advantages of a house on the lake—particularly the view and the size.

The doorbell rang. Joe extricated himself from the deck lounge and hurried to the door. "Hey, Mark. Got something for Alexa?"

"Yeah, is she home yet?"

Joe shook his head. "Not until tomorrow. Can I sign for it or does she have to?"

The UPS driver passed the tablet, stylus, and a large flat envelope to Joe. "Nah, you'll do. Thanks. I've tried three times already..."

"Long trip."

"Man, if she lived in Rockland, they'd have sent it back by now."

Joe closed the door, glancing around the entryway for an obvious place to put the envelope. Finding nothing that would ensure she saw it immediately, he tried her office. He set the envelope on her desk and strolled from the room, but another thought stopped him. He couldn't remember her ever using or even having mentioned using the room.

Envelope in hand, he decided to leave it on the couch on the landing sitting area. The moment his foot fell on the first step, his cellphone rang. As he watched Alexa's name flash on the screen, Joe felt stupid. He could have called. "Hey, what's up?"

"It's the records," she blurted without ceremony. "The one insurance company doesn't exist. They've got Silva's financial records." He heard a hiccough that sounded suspiciously like the aftermath of tears. "She was definitely skimming the accounts on everything she spent. They even found a few bogus repair bills."

"Wow. I just wouldn't have guessed it of her. How do they know the bills were fake?"

"According to Detective Romano, she took receipts, and any aspect of a job that wasn't itemized, she created a separate, duplicate receipt."

Joe thought for a moment. "Okay, so were the receipts with the same companies?"

"Yep—letterhead and all."

"But easy to prove fake. Why would she risk that?" It sounded too easy to make a mistake that would give the entire scheme away. "One call to the company and—"

"That's exactly what the police did. They called the contractor, asked for copies of all receipts for Rhette's of Chicago, and found it in seconds."

"So why risk—"

Alexa interrupted him. "Think about it, Joe. Who would look? You have the receipts for stuff you saw get done. You have identical receipts for things marked 'labor' or 'miscellaneous' and it's the same company that you know did the work. Why would you call?"

His low whistled echoed in her foyer. "Wow. Do they have an estimate of how much she was skimming?"

"At the rate she was going, she would easily have managed about fifty thousand a year without anyone ever noticing—assuming she didn't get greedy. With her salary, profit sharing, and the rest, she was on her way to becoming quite wealthy."

The idea that Silva, the designer of one of Alexa's most delicate and exquisite dresses, had been stealing from her—Joe tried to wrap his mind around the thought, but it seemed ridiculous. "What does the detective—whatshisname—Romano. What does he think?"

"Detective Romano insists that Silva never intended the business to be anything but a scam. She wanted it going long and well enough for me to release all the funds and then either skip out with them or milk them into her own private account while letting the rest of us think that we were hemorrhaging losses."

Pacing up and down her deck, Joe nodded as he listened. "Yeah, that'd explain a lot of things—like the vandalism. She got to skim there, but she couldn't go too far or you might quit."

"You know what this means, Joe…"

"That we don't know anything more than we did." Joe wanted to throw something. "Why did she cancel the models, though?"

"Well, we still don't have confirmation about that, but I expect to get it today. My only guess is that she thought it would limit the sales from the event but not kill them all together. That was the goal. Enough sales to keep me interested—oh, I don't know."

He heard the frustration and hurt in her voice. "I don't think we can understand what she was thinking—not yet. I bet we'll understand more later when the rest of the scheme is revealed. I seriously doubt that you've found it all yet."

"That's probably true. None of it makes sense. She loved designing, Joe. That wasn't an act. Why would she go from that to embezzling from a company—"

"But she didn't design for this company, right? Rhette was the designer."

Alexa didn't speak. He waited for a word, a hint of a word, an exhale even—nothing. "No, she didn't. Joe?"

"Yeah?"

"Do you think we have cause to request a look at the financials for Cutting Room Floor?"

"Her New York business?"

She sighed. "Yes. I mean, she might have been taking the money to infuse that business, but if there were investors there and she was skimming from them too…"

The unspoken question hung between them as they allowed silence to zip back and forth across the miles of airwaves. After several seconds, Joe asked the obvious. "So who killed her? Now that we have a good idea as to why, who?"

"We're all suspects. I'm primary." He hated the weariness in her voice.

"But they established that you couldn't have done it!" Joe yelled, pounding his fist on the railing. A splinter smarted, causing him to mutter a few euphemisms under his breath and wonder why he'd left the smooth surfaces of the entryway.

"They're now suggesting contract killing."

"Motive?"

Her chuckle was exactly what he needed to hear. "Money. Apparently they haven't read our contract very well. I think once they do, they'll focus on someone else. I just don't know who. None of us wanted her gone."

"Who could have figured out what she was doing?"

They discussed the vendors, the repairmen, the contractors, and the office staff. No one should have caught onto her. "Okay, so let's say she slipped up," Joe began, thinking aloud. "She's requesting a receipt from someone when she already got one, or whatever the scenario."

"Okaaay..."

"Well, what if that person tried blackmail?"

"Wouldn't that have meant the death of someone else instead of her?"

Joe began pacing again as his thoughts slowly organized themselves into more orderly ranks. "Not if she lured the person there to kill them and lost."

"No signs of a struggle."

"What do phone records say about that time? Was she talking to someone? Did she possibly say something that the alleged-blackmailer would have found unnerving? Something about how she was going to take care of the problem?"

Alexa muttered thoughts as she worked though the possibilities. "I just don't see it, but it has to be something like that. Or—"

"Or what?"

"Well, what if it isn't related to the business at all? What if she ticked off a designer in New York or had an old boyfriend who is of a jealous nature. A random serial killer that will show up next week..." Alexa wailed. "I don't know, Joe. I just know that I am tired of all of this."

"Well, you're coming home tomorrow. Just make sure you bring copies of everything." He started to say goodbye but remembered something. "Wait!"

"What?"

"I forgot. You got a FedEx package today. Where should I put it?"

"You're at the house?"

"I came over to have lunch on your deck. I didn't think you're mind..." Suddenly, Joe felt like he had abused her hospitality.

"Oh, I don't mind at all. I feel better knowing someone has been in and out." She sneezed. "Can you do me a favor?"

"Sure! Just tell me where to put this thing so I can go." Joe fanned himself with the envelope while he waited for instructions.

"Who is it from?"

"Did you just end a sentence in a preposition, Madame Writer?"

Alexa's voice relaxed as she chuckled. "Did you just use the word, 'preposition,' in a sentence?"

"Touché. It says it's from Gilbert Brown of Chicago."

"I don't know a Gilbert Brown. What's the address?"

"Um..." Joe read the address, trying to picture where the street might be. "It says 1911 Blue Cross Road. Do you know where that road is?"

"No." Her sigh seemed to slice the air between them. "That street won't exist."

He could hear her fingers flying over a keyboard. It took a moment to realize why he could hear them so well, but then it hit him. She'd put the phone down next to a computer. "What's going on?"

"And you dare lecture me about my dangling prepositions."

She sounded angry—furious even—as she said, "Yep. I was right. The street doesn't exist. I'd bet my life on it."

"I'd rather you didn't." Joe teased, hoping to relax her again. "Why don't you think it exists?"

"Father Brown. Someone has a sick sense of humor. G.K. Chesterton—*Gilbert* Keith Chesterton—wrote the Father *Brown* Mysteries. The first book was The *Blue Cross* and was published in *nineteen eleven*."

"How could you possibly know or remember that?"

"If it hadn't been Brown and Blue Cross, I probably wouldn't have. I had to check publication date and name. I wasn't sure if I remembered Gilbert correctly or not. College paper."

Joe gave a low whistle. "I'm impressed. I bet it would have taken the police longer to riddle that out."

"They didn't immerse themselves in mysteries. I read junk fiction to deep, philosophical stuff—even as a kid. Look, will you open it for me? Maybe Silva—"

Joe stripped the pull-tab from the envelope and reached inside. Her scream nearly stopped his heart. "Wait! Stop! Do you have gloves?"

Such a rookie mistake. Joe nearly swore with frustration. "Man, Alexa. I nearly blew it. I'll call you from the station."

Her answer came almost before he finished speaking. "Don't. I'll be home tomorrow. Just bring it over when you can. If whatever is in there is something I need to know before I leave, call me back. Otherwise, I just want to deal with it tomorrow. I'll make sure Blue Cross Road doesn't exist. I've got that address."

"Okay." Joe closed his eyes. "Lex?"

"Yeah?"

"It's going to be okay."

"Joe?"

He could guess her answer before she gave it, but he played along anyway. "Yeah?"

"It can't be okay. A woman is dead. There is no way, no matter what she did wrong, to make that 'okay.'"

Joe stared at the strangest note he'd ever seen. As he examined it with tweezers, dusting it for prints he now knew wouldn't surface, he tried to make sense of it. Was it something he should call her about? Would it help her to know now?

Martinez leaned over the counter, staring at the envelope and note. "You doing research for one of Miss Hartfield's books?"

Chapter 22

Alexa's car in the drive announced her return. Joe jogged up the steps and knocked loudly. Silence echoed inside. His hand hesitated over the doorknob before he let himself in the door.

Up the stairs—two steps at a time—and he found an empty sitting area. The kitchen also proved empty, but a muffled voice drifted in from the terrace. He grabbed a glass and opened the fridge. Lemonade. After pouring himself a glass, he hesitated before taking the pitcher with him. She might want a refill.

"—course it was! I love their volcano cake. Thank you for taking me." She smiled at Joe and raised her empty glass at him gratefully. She listened as Joe poured, a man's voice occasionally escaping through the receiver.

"Darrin?" Joe whispered, pointing to his ear and gesturing to the phone.

Alexa nodded and shrugged apologetically. Turning her attention back to her conversation, she agreed with something. "Yes, that was amazing. I doubt I'll ever forget it."

Joe leaned his forearms on the railing and jerked them back as he examined the boards for protruding splinters. Once more, he leaned over the railing and gazed out over the water. Jeremy had been right. Alexa's relationship with Darrin had changed. How would it affect his own friendship with her? Was Darrin the kind of man who could share Alexa with other men who happened to be friends?

Lost in thought, he didn't notice when Alexa hung up the phone and crossed the terrace to stand next to him. "I love this view," she murmured. "I'm so glad Wes bullied me into buying this house."

The neighborhood sounds occasionally encroached, but other than the lapping of the water on the shore, a car starting, a boat on the lake, or a lawn mower, the area around Alexa's was quieter and more private than her former home. Back at Sycamore Court, the sounds of life constantly interrupted with cars coming and going, children playing in the streets, and even a vacuum cleaner or radio blaring from an open garage. It seemed as if the houses near the lake and the space around them muffled the sounds of the people's lives.

"You're quiet tonight."

Still leaning against the railing, Joe turned his head to meet her gaze. "Just thinking. Your flight okay?"

"Smooth and as worry-free as it can be." Alexa rubbed her calf with the back of her foot. "Hey, can you stay for dinner? I got steaks. I'll make a salad and double baked potatoes if you do the grilling."

He listened, watching her for any sign of change. No signs surfaced. His eyes sought the water again. "How would Darrin feel about that?"

"Why should that matter?"

He turned and leaned his back against the railing. Joe's eyes rose to meet hers. "Jeremy said something about you guys the other day. You're barely home and he's already called…" Joe shrugged. "Something is up, and I don't want to make things awkward for you."

"Well, you just did," she replied.

"How's that?"

"I was just going to ask you a question on that subject—Darrin—but you've made it clear you're not comfortable with it. You feel awkward, and if my best friend feels awkward, I feel awkward." She flicked tears from the corner of her eyes. "What a mess."

As surprised by the tears as she seemed to be, Joe's conscience kicked him. "Lex, I—"

"Oh, I don't know what's wrong with me!" A slow inhale and exhale did little to calm her. Joe watched as she tried again. "Silly."

Embarrassed, she flung another tear aside and grabbed his glass. "Would you like a refill?" Her eyes traveled to the envelope he carried. "Is that the one that came yesterday? Oh, and I've got those papers in the house in my bag." She frowned. "Did you ever answer about dinner, Joe?"

Without waiting for him to answer, Alexa turned and walked away. Dumbfounded, Joe watched as she carried the pitcher and glasses into the house. The phone she left lying abandoned on the deck lounge. He grabbed it and followed her through the house, up the stairs, and to the chair across from the couch.

"What is it, Lex? You're agitated. I've never seen you like this."

"Is it a terrible thing if you don't miss a really wonderful man and aren't looking for ways to go back to see him?" She blurted the question, and a second later, her eyes widened. Alexa clapped her hand to her mouth, eyes wide. "Oh, Joe. I'm so sorry. I had no business—"

"No," he answered. "It isn't terrible." Joe took a deep breath and said what he hoped would be the right thing, despite how much he hated saying it. "I'd also assume that it doesn't mean you aren't attracted to or—what's the word—fond of him." He leaned forward, nudging her knee before adding, "You've lived alone for years. It's only natural that you'd prefer solitude at times—and possibly often."

Alexa gazed intently into his eyes before she asked her next question. "But what if I just don't want to put forth the effort? Is that bad?"

Joe leaned back against the chair, his eyes roaming her face. "Why is the most confident woman I know acting so insecure?"

Tears flowed now. "I'm afraid that I've grown callous."

"Why callous?" He wanted to talk about anything but a possible relationship with Darrin. Why—he'd deal with figuring that out at home.

"He was good to me, Joe. He took me to dinner, we went on walks; he brought me flowers and a new CD. Hollywood and Harlequin would have had me swooning inside of two dates."

"You didn't enjoy it."

Even before she answered, he knew what she would say. Pain filled her eyes as she spoke. "But I did. That's part of the problem. I did enjoy it. I felt appreciated for more than my writing. I felt admired." She closed her eyes. "He made me feel like the most beautiful woman in the world. I'm not shallow—at least, I hope not. But I'm not immune to admiration either." Fingers flicked more tears away. "I felt cherished, Joe. I've never felt that before."

"I don't think I understand the problem."

She stood and brushed imaginary lint from her dress, smiling weakly at him. "There probably isn't one. Well, there shouldn't be one anyway. I just don't think that I'm what Darrin deserves in a woman."

As Joe watched her descend the stairs and disappear into the kitchen, their conversation whirled through his mind. He could hear water spraying in the sink, the rattle of a dish—was that a sniffle? Though not exactly sorry that she might be having second thoughts about pursuing a relationship with Darrin Thorne, the "why" of her struggle left him feeling unsettled himself.

"Joe…" Alexa's voice filled the lower floor and drifted up the stairs. "Do you feel like running to The Market? It looks like I'm out of that spice mixture you like on your steaks."

An errand—this he could do. He jumped up and jogged down the stairs. At the door, he paused, his hand on the knob. "On my way. Need anything else?"

As he took his last bite of potato, Joe set down his fork and sank back into the chair, satisfied. He watched Alexa behind half-closed eyes. Her earlier unsettled nerves seemed to have vanished, but had they? He didn't know. As much as he hated to disturb the serenity of the evening, he stood.

"C'mon. Walk with me."

Alexa abandoned her plate and followed Joe down her terrace steps to the shore. Half a dozen yards passed—a dozen—before Joe spoke again. "You said something earlier that I can't get out of my mind."

"It's okay, Joe. I didn't mean to dump on you like that. I'm really very sorry."

He shook his head, feeling like a frenetic bobble head doll. "I thought we were friends, Lex."

"Of course we are. Whatever—"

"Isn't that the first commandment of friendship? 'Thou shalt be there to listen in good times and in bad?'"

Relief washed over him as her laughter rang out over the lake. Alexa had returned. The absent mindedness of dinner, the insecure emotional outbursts of the earlier afternoon—gone. Oh, yes. She had returned.

"You're right. What did I say that has you puzzled?"

After forty minutes of silent rehearsal through meal preparation and dinner, he didn't quite know where to start. He needed to put his words into thoughtful, natural, well-articulated sentences. As a just-the-facts-man, he didn't know how to discuss feelings as if they were tangible. She called him Friday for a reason.

"You said Darrin makes you feel beautiful, and the way you said it—"

"Oh, Joe..."

He cut her off before she sidetracked him. "No, wait. I don't understand that, and I want to. I've been with you when *you* knew you looked incredible. The Sadie Hawkins thing and the New Year's Ball—the Policeman's Ball. You *knew* you were beautiful, and I'm certain I said something. So," he continued, cutting her off again, "I don't understand why that should be so unusual. You get attention everywhere you go."

Jaw hanging in a most un-Alexa-like fashion, she stared at him. "You've got to be kidding me."

"No, I'm not. I'm still in shock that someone like you—so strong and independent—can suddenly seem insecure, but as far as attention..."

Her head wagged as he spoke. "Joe, Joe, Joe—no. I get attention. I know I do—won't pretend otherwise. I don't really like it, actually. I wear what I wear because I like it— not for the attention. But, Joe, my clothing—my eccentricity, if you will—*those* give me the attention you're talking about."

"But—"

"No, Joe. Darrin's was different. He didn't pay attention to me because I stood out from the jeans and painted-on t-shirt clad crowd. He found me attractive. *That* was something new."

"That's what I don't understand, Lex. I mean, c'mon! Why is that new? I've heard Wes tell you how gorgeous you are. *I've* told you how gorgeous you are. So why is this something new?"

Alexa slipped off her shoes and curled her toes in the sand as she tried to explain. "You can take a plain woman, put her in a formal gown, do hair and makeup, and she'll look beautiful."

"Not sure what the point is. Of course she will."

She continued as if Joe hadn't spoken. "Very few people don't respond to formal attire. Put a funny-looking man in a tuxedo and suddenly, he's distinctive and debonair."

"And your point is?" Joe's patience slowly thinned.

"With Darrin, it didn't matter if I wore white capris and a navy sweater, or my favorite tea gown circa 1910. With him, I felt beautiful—always."

Waves splashed against her feet as they drew closer to the edge of the lake. The water's gentle undulation in the moonlight left him feeling a little unsteady. If her response was any indication, Alexa felt it too.

"Alexa, you idiot," Joe insisted, with a failed attempt at gentleness, "that's because you *are* beautiful!" Despite his attempt to hide it, irritation in his voice stung her.

"Joe—"

"Forget it. I didn't think you were that stupid."

A glance her way revealed a small smile. "Joe, you always become insulting when you're annoyed or worried. Thank you."

His eyes sought hers, trying to read her thoughts. "I don't understand—"

"I know you don't. I didn't say that I thought I am hideous or boring." Her elbow nudged him. "I like my looks well enough. Of course," she winked, "I'd rather have red hair, but other than that, I'm satisfied. You're just being Friday about this."

"I don't understand—"

"You're beginning to sound like a scratched record. I said the word *feel*. You don't know what to do with that word, so you try to change it to think. Usually that works in modern society, but right now it doesn't."

Joe watched as Alexa's eyes swept the lake and looked out over it himself. The lights of the houses around hers danced across the water, setting a romantic scene for a very unromantic conversation. He gazed down at her as he tried to decipher her meaning. "So what you're really saying is that you liked that Darrin treated you like an attractive woman rather than a famous author or a pal. Is that it?"

Turning around and tugging him toward her house, Alexa murmured, "Mmm-hmm. Something like that."

"Well, for what it's worth, you're the most beautiful woman I've ever met, and I realized that when you weren't wearing any makeup, your hair was just hanging down, and your clothes were almost as normal as yours get."

She took his hand in hers and laughed. "You're good for me, Joe. Thanks."

On the terrace, they loaded their arms with dishes and carried them into the kitchen in silence. The FedEx envelope lying on the counter halted the serenity that had settled over them. What had been a relaxing evening—if a bit emotionally charged—changed in an instant.

"I forgot about that thing. Do I really need to look at it?"

Joe nodded and reached inside. "I want to see if you can make anything of it."

"Stop!" she screamed instinctively. "Don't you have to put on gloves or something?"

"We already checked for prints—nothing there. It's

weird."

Alexa pulled the sheet of paper from the envelope. Hand stamped with rubber stamp alphabet letters, the note held only four sentences. Her eyes widened with shock as she read.

SILVA BETRAYED YOUR TRUST. I STOPPED HER. IF YOU TRY TO DISCOVER MY IDENTIY, THE OTHERS WILL HAVE TO DIE TOO. ADAM IS NEXT UNLESS YOU STOP LOOKING FOR ME.

Alexa sank to the floor, her back to the cabinets. Seconds later, the paper slid to the tile beside her. "Oh, Joe…"

"Hey, hey, Lex. Come on. You've faced worse." Joe hunkered on his heels, his hand reaching for hers.

"Have you ever noticed that when you're worried about me, you call me Lex instead of Alexa?"

Joe realized she'd grasped at the first thing she could to remove herself from the present threat. "Wes does it too. You must inspire that in people."

"Wes calls me Lex? I've never noticed that. How odd."

Joe lowered himself to the tile, sliding across the floor until he sat beside her. "No, he has his own name for you. He calls you Annie when you're hurting or he's upset with you. Why Annie?"

"It's my name."

That thought hadn't occurred to him. "Your name is Anne?"

Alexa shook her head. "Annette Ellen Hartfield."

"Where'd you get Alexa?"

She relaxed, her shoulders drooping and her eyes closed. "James. When he responded to my query letter, I mentioned that I was looking for a pseudonym but hadn't made a final decision. When he agreed to represent me, he asked for a headshot and called once it arrived."

"And he suggested Alexa?"

"Alexa or Leigh," she corrected. "I thought it would be easier to adjust to Alexa; it felt like me."

"What about that note?" Joe picked it up again. "What was your first impression?"

"Juvenile. It sounds like a kid but a slightly articulate one."

Nodding, Joe read over the words once more. "That's what I told the chief while I dusted it for prints." He passed it to her. "We also faxed a copy to the Chicago PD."

"It has to be someone who is loyal to me—for whatever reason. I don't understand why, though." She stared at the paper in his hands. Pointing to one word, she added, "But why else the threat and that word, 'betrayal?'"

"You don't think that Lorie—"

"Joe!"

Had the situation not been so serious, Joe would have found her indignation amusing. "I had to ask. She's the perfect fit. She's obviously loyal to you—especially after how you met and the ball and everything. She has the teenage angst and hormones going for her…"

"She's much too intelligent for that." Alexa stabbed the paper with her fingers. "She's also a natural writer. She'd never come up with something so… so…"

"Juvenile. You're right."

"Well, that and the fact that she was under my roof at the time of the murder." Alexa's words felt like a bucket of cold water.

"So, who does that leave out? Who else was here?"

Alexa ticked people off her fingers as she named them. "Your family, Rhette, James, Lorie and Darrin, Wes, Heather and the kids…" Her voice trailed off as she tried to remember everyone who remained at her house or in Fairbury the night of her birthday party.

"What about Martine and Elise?"

"They left early, remember?"

Their eyes met and Joe's training kicked in. "Ok, can you see either woman—"

"Not Martine," Alexa interjected. "Not her. She was fascinated by the publicity angle when my 'characters' started dropping last fall, but it also rattled her." She shook her head. "No, Martine was terrified, but Elise…"

Joe waited. She seemed to weigh the possibilities and

probabilities. "Well?"

"Elise could have, I suppose. I can't imagine her doing it, really, but…"

"But what. Come on, Alexa. Talk to me."

"Well, it's just that she could have seen it as a chance to make it look like it was about friendship or loyalty to the clothing company, but really she just used it to give me more publicity. It's her job to keep me in the news and keep me, as she calls it, 'in the minds of my readers.'"

"You don't like her."

"No. I avoid dealing directly with her. I leave most of that to James."

"I thought publicists work for the author or the publishing house."

"Elise works with both Martine and James. I take their collective advice." Alexa struggled to stand and wriggled her toes. "James has a good pulse on what is best for me. Agent or not, he's my real publicist, and Elise is his research assistant. She just doesn't know that."

"Would she go this far?"

"Let's see…" Joe waited as she reviewed her recent conversations. "Well, she has been becoming increasingly irritated by James' vetoes. They stifle her plans."

"So revenge?"

Alexa's head shook as he spoke. "No, no. That doesn't make sense. I mean, come on. Would you start killing people so you had a crime to investigate? Professionally speaking, it's kind of the same thing. No."

Joe had to admit Alexa made sense. But, an alternative idea didn't surface. "True. She's not mentally unstable… it might make sense to someone like that."

"No. She's passionate about her job. She's a good publicist for traditional authors. You know Wade Harrison?"

"True crime guy?"

Alexa nodded. "She has done wonders for his career." She jerked her head up and met his eyes. "But, if my publicity turned negative, it would be necessary for me to follow a more conventional schedule of appearances."

"Hmm..."

"Oh, Joe!" She gripped the counter, lost in thought.

"What?"

"I thought she might be trying to get me *more* publicity, but what if she's trying to hurt it?"

"Hurt it, Why?"

"Because, like I said. I'd have to follow her preferred track for publicity in order to repair my reputation. She'd get her way. She would, in her mind, prove her superior plan for my career."

Joe pulled out his cellphone and scrolled through his address book until he found the number he sought. As she heard him talking with Detective Tony Romano, the full impact of the situation hit her. Joe had a Chicago detective's phone number in his contact list — because of her.

The house grew chilly as she waited for Joe to conclude his discussion with Romano. She closed several windows and adjusted the thermostat. Another shiver sent goose bumps over her arms.

Gesturing toward the stairs and rubbing her arms to show she'd gotten chilled, Alexa raced upstairs to change her clothes. Her fingers slid along the rack, searching for something light but with coverage. A jersey dress with three-quarter length sleeves caught her eye, and she pulled it from the hanger.

The moment the dress slid over her head, she felt better. *It's amazing what a thin layer of fabric can do for temperature control,* she mused as she grabbed the brush and smoothed her tousled hair. A glance in the mirror showed the effects wilted cosmetics. It only took a minute to grab her head wrap, scrub her face clean of makeup, and grab the brush again.

Alexa's feet skimmed the stairs down to her sitting nook. She grabbed a stack of mail from the end table and began flipping through it as she brushed out her hair once more. Catalogs, solicitations, bills — she stacked each item in a pile next to her, but her mind still dwelled on the reality that someone reasonably close to her could be responsible for Silva's death.

By the time Joe climbed the stairs, Alexa sat reclining with her feet up on the ottoman, her hair spilling over the back of the couch. She focused on relaxing and breathing with her eyes closed, trying to calm the rising panic in her heart. Without moving or opening her eyes, she started to ask him what Detective Romano had said, but Joe spoke first.

"Hey, Lex-a."

"I'm fine, Joe." She smiled up at him, amused at his chagrin over almost using his pet name for her—again.

Though his hand moved as if to touch her, he shoved both into his pockets and said, "They're going to bring in Martine and Elise for questioning. Can I take those papers with me? I want to make sure you didn't miss anything." He rubbed the back of his neck. "I'm beat, and tomorrow isn't getting any further away."

Alexa forced herself off the couch and skipped down the stairs. He needed to see her refreshed and unbothered so he could rest. She retrieved a thick manila envelope and hurried to the kitchen. "Wait there. Your mom sent you some muffins. She said you'd been talking about them."

Just the sight of his mother's muffins made Joe hungry again. He accepted them and opened the door. "Thanks for these."

"Thank her, I didn't bake them," she laughed as she turned to go upstairs again. "Night!"

His voice called to her from the door. "Alexa?"

"Hmm?" She half turned and caught his eye.

"Go take a good look at yourself. I've never seen you look better. You're a good woman, and I know that's the most important thing, but you are most definitely a beautiful one as well."

Something in his tone caught off guard. She smiled down at him and whispered, "Thank you. That, from you, means more than from almost anyone."

The click of the latch told her he had gone, but his words

echoed in her mind as she started toward the stack of editorial corrections Martine had sent. She only paused for a moment before continuing up to her room. However, once there, she hesitated. A hint of her earlier insecurity resurfaced, urging her to return downstairs and forget his words.

Alexa felt silly—ridiculous—but forced herself to sit at her dressing table. She gazed into the mirror, trying to see and understand why Joe always preferred her with her hair down, face washed, and a hint of medieval in the style of her clothing. *Well, he's no knight wannabe, so who knows what to think. Still, he's consistent.* Her mind returned to their earlier conversation. *And he means it. That has to count for something.*

Chapter 23

The morning sun filled Alexa's living room, giving it a warm glow. She didn't use the room often, but anytime she walked past at just that time of day, she gathered whatever she needed and brought it in there. With papers laid out on the coffee table, her laptop open beside her, and a glass of lemon water on the end table, she worked for hours on corrections to her manuscript.

Joe found her there, lost in her fictional world. "Hey…"

She jumped. "Oh! I didn't hear you come in. How was work?"

"Not too bad. Had a double shift—almost. Martinez had some family thing last night. I'm beat."

Without a word, she stood and beckoned him to follow her to the kitchen. Once there, she scanned her fridge. "Looks like you can have an omelet, eggs and sausage, um…" She glanced back inside. "Oh, and I have left over ham—could make hash. And there's cubed steak—could do country fried steak, eggs and gravy…"

"I didn't expect—"

"I didn't say you did. Now what do you want or I'm making boiled oats and okra."

"How about whatever's easiest," Joe suggested.

"Then boiled oats and okra it is."

"I said easiest! I gave you an answer."

Alexa shook her head. "That's easiest."

"Fine. Omelet sounds easier than the rest of it. Let's do that." He reached for a couple of plates and pulled out a cutting board. "What do I do?"

She pulled tomatoes, onions, ham, and bell peppers from the fridge and set them beside the cutting board. "I need a small handful of each one."

As they worked, Joe told her about that morning's conversation with Detective Romano.

"Elise has no alibi. Martine evidently entertained someone in her room that night, but Elise was alone all night." He mangled the poor tomato as he tried to cut it into reasonably small pieces. "She keeps proclaiming her innocence, but it looks bad. She seems to know an awful lot about how the shop runs and everything."

Joe continued to give the details she knew were important, but Alexa's mind whirled in other directions. It would have been so easy for Elise to create some sort of alibi. Why hadn't she? It was as if she hadn't even attempted to cover her tracks.

"No room service?" she asked as she cracked eggs into a bowl. "No phone calls? No cell records indicating she spoke to someone during that time?"

"Nothing." Joe shoved the pile of mutilated tomato pieces to one side of the cutting board and grabbed the bell pepper. "Romano recreated her timeline and said they know she got off the plane and took a taxi to the hotel. She said goodnight to Martine when she—Martine—got off on the second floor. Then she rode to the fourth floor and as far as anyone is concerned, vanished until the following morning at ten-thirty."

"How do you know she got off on the fourth floor? I assume that was her floor?"

Nodding, Joe chopped. "A man identified her. He's been staying in the Presidential Suite on the fifth floor for the past month. From the way Romano describes it, it sounds like the guy tried to pick her up, but she wasn't interested—guy's ticked too."

"That doesn't surprise me. Elise has a thing for James. She's incredibly loyal to him."

"There's that word again—loyal."

Alexa poured the eggs into a hot pan and turned to face Joe. Seeing him struggle with the chopping, she nudged him out of the way and tried to cut them up swiftly. "James left a message on my voicemail a while ago. Here…" She grabbed ingredients, tossed them over the omelet, dumped some cheese on top, and handed him the spatula. "You watch the omelet. I'll go call him back, find out what he wants, and try to get a feel for his opinion on everything. Give me twenty minutes and you eat."

Leaving Joe to fend for himself, Alexa hurried to the living room and pulled up a fresh document on her laptop while she waited for James' office assistant to put her through to him. He came on the line immediately. "Hey, Alexa. Sorry about calling you so early this morning. Elise has two television offers for you. She'll be calling later today, and I wanted to get to you first."

"Smart move. What do you have?"

"I think you need to decline Faye's but accept the Paisley Duncan one. She's getting great ratings right now, and her style fits your demographic and your image better."

"Paisley Duncan it is," Alexa agreed. "Hey, a trip to New York—shopping! So, when do I go? When's the interview?"

"That's the trouble," James admitted. "Two weeks."

"I'll call Laidie and get her to make me something new—something that says, 'still a good author and not responsible for recent and somewhat-connected-to-her murders in her town or at her shop.' What do you think?"

"Perfect." James switched the topic away from his least favorite part of Alexa, onto the details of the trip, and then to how she should steer any conversation related to recent events. Alexa tried twice to turn the conversation to her immediate concerns, but first James insisted that they go over a few possible changes to her current manuscript.

That settled, Alexa asked, "Do you think Elise could have set these things up specifically because of Silva's death? I really don't want to capitalize on that."

"Not capitalize, no. I think she's wise to keep you in the public eye as an author, while promoting the idea of the clothing line at the same time. She also plans to prep you on how to dodge questions related to Silva's death and the murders last winter." James sighed. "As much as I hate to say it, that's where her strengths lie. Listen to her."

Alexa pulled the warning note from its envelope. "I have something to read to you." She read it aloud, trying to keep any definitive inflection from her tone. "What do you think?"

"I think you need to use this Paisley appearance to announce that you are not looking anymore. Do it around town, in emails, on your website—everywhere. And if you do keep looking," James dropped his voice just a little, "don't tell me. I don't want to know. I just don't want to be next after Adam."

His half-hearted, nervous laughter, and the weak attempt to divert his discomfort from the topic with humor, reassured her. James had to be innocent. The fleeting notion that perhaps he and Elise had concocted the plan together evaporated, leaving her relieved and more confused than ever.

James' voice called her out of her thoughts. "Alexa!"

"Sorry. Started thinking and..."

"And I don't want to know. I'll let you go solve some crime or other while I get back to work. Talk to you later." Without another word, James disconnected.

"Well, okay then. Nice talking to you too," Alexa murmured as her thoughts returned to the problem at hand.

The situation bothered her. Every day she became more and more suspicious of trusted friends and associates. Her particular genre already made her ridiculously analytical about everything, and people's actions often became mental exercises in possibilities or probabilities. However, until recently, she hadn't taken her crazed cerebral gymnastics seriously. In recent months, her mind wandered trails that made her uncomfortable.

The phone jarred her out of her thoughts. "Hello?"

"Good morning, Alexa," Elise chirped. "I've got great news for you. I have you scheduled for two TV spots in the next three weeks." Before Alexa could speak, the woman continued. "Now don't say I never did anything for your career. I'll make the arrangements and email them later, but—

"

"Whoa, Elise! Hold on." As much as she hated to ask, Alexa forced the words from her lips. "What TV spots?"

Elise jumped into a sales pitch of impressive proportions. Alexa knew by previous experience that she needed to let the woman talk. She exclaimed at the right places, murmured where appropriate, and almost sat on her hands to keep from hanging up the phone. By the time Elise finished, a less determined woman would have begun packing her bags for two trips instead of one.

"It sounds like you've done your homework. The offers sound wonderful."

"I knew you'd—"

"I'll have to run it by James, of course, but I think I'll pass on Faye this time. The last visit became a tribute to my success as a woman rather than as a person or an author. I didn't appreciate what felt like a bait and switch. I don't want to risk repeating that. However, I think you can safely schedule the Paisley Duncan appearance."

Undaunted by Alexa's refusal, Elise worked furiously to change Alexa's mind, eventually citing the recent murder as proof that she needed as many public appearances as she could garner to show herself as an innocent victim. "I really think you need to reconsider. I mean, it's already common knowledge that you're trying to find Silva's killer. Readers will begin to see you as another sensationalist author trying to create fodder for your books or at best—maybe worst, actually—view you as another Jessica Fletcher."

"Well, I've decided to leave the detective work to the police. When citizens in my town were killed, that was one thing, but Silva's death is too personal for me to involve myself. I'm afraid I don't have a fair perspective."

"Oh, I am so relieved." Elise sounded more calculating than relieved, making Alexa wonder why. The woman continued without pausing. "I keep thinking the killer might decide you're a threat and come after you! Did you know they took me in for questioning? *Me!* Can you believe it?"

Elise rambled for several minutes before rushing off to

call James regarding the offers. Alexa mulled their conversation for several minutes before she remembered Joe in the kitchen. She started to hurry to tell him what she'd learned when she remembered her plans for a new dress for the interview.

She tucked her feet beneath her and dialed the woman's number. "Laidie? Hello! I need you desperately."

"Alexa? How are you? I read about that horrible—ugh—killing. Are you safe?" Genuine concern filled every word that Laidie spoke.

"I am, thank you. The whole thing has the police baffled. Nothing makes sense. Apparently Silva had been skimming the accounts—you know, double posting, bogus receipts—things like that. I keep thinking that she's our best suspect, but she's dead."

"Oh, that's terrible. What a betrayal after all you did for her." Alexa listened as Laidie whispered to her husband and told him she'd be upstairs. "But you are safe?" she asked as she returned to the conversation. Do they know who did it? No, you said they're baffled. Oh, it's just so disturbing. And Tim wonders why I hate going to Chicago or Milwaukee—it's just too dark now."

Laidie asked questions and Alexa explained what she knew of the case. As an afterthought, she mentioned her intention to leave detective work to the professionals and concentrate on the editing and corrections of her last manuscript. "Martine needs it in the next forty-eight hours, so I have my work cut out for me, but that's not why I called."

"Oh, do you need something else done for Rhette's collection? I imagine with all the drama, things are really unsettled down there."

"Well, right now, things are going great, but they'll probably need you in a few weeks for prototypes. Rhette has been trying to find locals, but we'll see." Alexa relaxed, closed her eyes, and forced herself to enjoy the "shopping process."

"Sooo… what can I do for you?" Laidie asked.

"Well, I have an appearance on the Paisley Duncan Show in a couple of weeks. Is it even remotely possible that you'd have time to get me something new by then? I need something that screams chic, feminine, and bold but innocent too. The last thing I need to do is overstate or understate my personality and position in this appearance."

Laidie's voice filled with the delighted and excited tone so familiar to Alexa. Any time she called with a request such as this, Laidie sounded as excited as a child at Christmas. "Oh, I have a few designs left from the last box you sent. I didn't try to do them because they seemed more appropriate for fall, but it's getting close enough that maybe—"

"Actually," Alexa interrupted hastily, "I kind of hoped you might want another chance to surprise me. The things you did this time were so perfect that I thought I would leave the design up to you. I think I want to stick with something from the twentieth century—flapper era to say the eighties at the latest. I'm not a big fan of the seventies, though."

"Okay, and what about style? Pants, dress, skirt..."

There it was—that passion that told her Laidie had already begun to work her magic. "Definitely a dress or a skirt, but other than that, go for it. Please order a hat to match from The Cache as you have fabric and a design. I don't know if they can pull it off in time, but I'd like to try."

Laidie assured Alexa that she would have the outfit in the mail in five days and that she'd bully the milliners over at The Cache to get things done in time. Just as she started to disconnect the call, Alexa stopped her. "Oh! Wait! Don't use my last measurements. Since moving into this house, I've lost a couple of inches on my waist and thighs. I can thank—or blame is more like it—the stairs here. Anyway, I'll go over to the cleaners and get them to re-measure me."

"Okay, email me tonight. I'll cut everything out in the meantime. I can drape it to fit your measurements on the form later."

As Laidie disconnected, Alexa stretched. Joe stepped into the room carrying the distinctive white paper bag of The Deli. "I kind of destroyed the omelet, so while you were on the phone, I ran down and got you a pastrami on rye..."

"Yum!"

They ate on the terrace and between bites, discussed the conversations. "Elise said she was afraid the killer would come after me if I tried to find him—or her, I guess. She's afraid that I'll come off as some kind of cross between Miss Marple and Nancy Drew or something. James, on the other hand, sounded utterly relieved when I told him about the note and that I planned to follow the instructions. He said that if I kept looking, he didn't want to know."

"Really."

She nodded. "Yep. He joked about being next after Adam."

"They're either on their toes or just stupid enough to make themselves look guilty in spite of it all."

"Laidie though..." Alexa couldn't hide her unsettled feeling.

"What about her? She wasn't even here. She couldn't come, remember?"

Alexa shook her head, chewing swiftly. After a gulp of water, she rushed to explain. "I really can't believe she'd be able to do anything like that. She's such a quiet, sweet woman, but..."

Joe took Alexa's plate and glass from her and carried it to the kitchen sink. While he refilled their glasses of water, she sat thinking until her thoughts drifted into an unsettling quandary. As he set her glass in front of her, she gazed up at him. "Joe, I don't know what she said that bothers me so much, but something was off. I knew it the minute she said something, but we got sidetracked, and now I don't know what it was."

Joe shook his head as he passed the bowl of lemon and lime wedges. Taking one for his own glass, he said, "You're seeing suspects behind every tree. Everything will sound suspicious to you right now. It's the nature of the hunt. Laidie was in Wisconsin. She wouldn't and couldn't have known what was going on with Silva, so she had no reason to kill anyone."

Relief washed over her. "You're right. I don't want to lose my best seamstress—particularly because she started killing off my business partners."

"That would be a bit awkward to explain at parties." Joe's voice raised in a slight falsetto. "'Oh, this old thing? It was made by my seamstress. Oh, no, sorry. I can't give you her number, but she's at cell block…"

"Joe!" Alexa's laughter rang out across the terrace.

His phone buzzed and Joe sighed. "I forgot. I have to give a lecture on the evils of gangs to kids who cannot comprehend the reality of them." Absently, he kissed Alexa's forehead, wished her a nice afternoon, and jogged down the terrace steps to the side yard. Seconds later, the gate latch clicked shut with a gentle clink.

Alexa sat in her chair, stunned. More than the fact that he had kissed her, his obvious unconsciousness of the action surprised and confused her. She shook her head as though to clear her mind like an Etch-a-Sketch screen. When that failed, she stood and strolled into her kitchen. Her manuscript called from the living room, leaving her no time to mull over the incomprehensible actions of her friends.

Chapter 24

The gate swung open to her touch, the understated "Hartfield Cottage" sign swaying gently. Alexa glanced around the yard, missing days of raking leaves after a morning of murder and mayhem with her laptop. The door stood open, the screen unlatched. She pulled it, leaning in to call out for Wes, when she saw him sitting on the couch.

Lost in thought, Wes rolled a black pearl ring between his thumb and index finger. Surprised, Alexa stepped inside and watched as he gazed at the ring. "Wes?"

Her voice seemed to snap him out of his reverie. "Hey, Annie!"

"Is the decision that hard?"

Confusion clouded Wes' eyes before he caught her gaze and chuckled sheepishly to himself. "Not really. The decision was easy enough. Getting the nerve, however…"

She sat next to him and took the ring from his hand. Leaning her head against his arm, she examined it carefully. "It's gorgeous, Wes. It looks like Heather too."

"She said something once about loving Judy Garland's black engagement ring. I did a Google search on it, but I couldn't find a picture that was definitively hers, and those that did say it, all looked different. I think it was this setting with onyx, but then I saw this and…" He shrugged. "This just said 'Heather' to me."

"It does. Pearls are soft though, aren't they? She couldn't wear it around the house."

"No, but I know she only wore her band with her ex, so I thought maybe…"

Alexa handed the ring back to Wes and closed her fingers over his. "She'll love it. Of course, I think mostly because of the man who comes with it."

"It's not too early?"

"You've known her for what, nine months? How is that too early? You love her and the kids. They love you. What is too fast about that?" She lowered her voice a little and gazed up into his eyes. "But, Wes, is she saved? Does she know Jesus? I've never seen—well, anything. That's my only concern."

"Thanks to you, Annie. Yes."

The answer surprised her. "To me!"

"Heather says you preached at her until she couldn't help but be curious. I just answered the questions you raised."

"But—" Alexa shook her head. "No, Wes, I never said a word—"

"She said your life and how you treated them—especially after the stuff last winter—did it." Wes wrapped an arm around her and squeezed. "She couldn't ignore Jesus when you reflected His character in everything you did."

As she marveled at the unexpected compliment, Alexa kicked off her shoes and tucked her feet under her. "I never realized. I just didn't—wow."

"If only Mom—"

Anxious to change the subject, Alexa latched onto that idea. "Mom! Did you call and tell them about Heather? They'll have to forgive you now. Heather comes with instant grandchildren."

"She hasn't said yes yet, Annie. Don't you think I should wait until we have that confirmation?"

Alexa unfolded her legs from beneath her and jumped up to get a glass of water. She fought to ignore the dirty dishes, piled laundry, food encrusted stove, and the overflowing trash. It wasn't her home any longer, and she had no business making her brother feel guilty for not keeping it as nice as she liked it.

"Something to drink, Wes?"

"Yeah, can you bring me a bottle of root beer?"

As she entered the room again, she saw Wes tuck the

ring back into its jeweler's box and stuff the whole thing in his pocket. She smiled and handed him the bottle. "You bring the kids over to spend the night tomorrow night. Take her out, walk her home, and sweep her off her feet. She needs a bit of romancing."

"You think I'm unromantic? Did you know that we—"

"I do not want to hear this!" She protested, laughing. "Just make sure she feels like the only woman you could ever spend the rest of your life with."

"She is." He shook his head. "Have a little more faith in me than that. I know what says, 'I love you' to her."

Alexa kicked off her shoes and sank back into the same familiar corner where she'd written the bulk of so many of her books. Hands wrapped around her glass, as if a coffee mug on a cold morning, she drew her knees up to her chest and closed her eyes. Wes waited exactly half a minute before he spoke.

"Why are you here, Annie? You couldn't have known about the ring or my next assignment, so what's up?"

She kicked him gently with her stocking covered feet and murmured, "Don't let me forget to go to the cleaners and get my measurements retaken. Laidie is making me a new outfit for my next appearance on the Paisley Duncan Show."

"Paisley Duncan! That's good news, right? From what I've heard, she only invites the most unique guests and sticks to tasteful topics. I read just a couple of weeks ago about how she had successfully managed to distance herself from the 'I'm really an exotic dancer and not a mom of three toddlers' fare that got so popular for a while there."

"I think that's why James recommended that I accept her instead of Faye. Faye is good about staying away from that kind of junk, but the last time I was on her show, she invited me to discuss the success of my new book, and it became all about some feminist agenda. That's not exactly the goal of my writing."

Wes shook his head. "You know, that still doesn't tell me why you're here."

Despite her best efforts to appear unruffled, her fingers

fidgeted, giving away her nervousness. "Remember when I took off for Suzy's place?"

"Yeah... I've wondered about that for a while— especially as quiet as both of you were about it. It had to be big."

"That's just it, Wes. It wasn't. I blew up over nothing— overreacted. Well, actually he did. We both did. Whatever."

Wes passed her a throw pillow. "Take your angst out on that thing. You're going to ruin that dress." Her smile spurred him to continue. "Now, Annie, what happened? You guys make no sense to me. You're the biggest, mixed-up, non-couple that I've ever met."

"He kissed me."

Laughter filled the cottage. She watched as he tried to control himself and struggled not to jump up and leave. Talking about it—maybe not such a good idea after all. When she bit her lip, he stifled his next snickers and apologized. "Sorry. I know it doesn't feel funny, but it really is. I mean, think about it. This isn't exactly the first time you've been kissed, but you act like it's monumental."

She flung a stray tear away from the corner of her eye before she murmured, "Well, for our *friendship* it just might have been. I don't know."

Her natural inclination to protect her privacy warred with her need for comfort and advice. Twice, Alexa began to explain and stopped before she managed to tell her brother about their mutual overreaction to the kiss, her flight to Arkansas and the comfort of Suzy's much leveler head, his apology, and how things had become normal again. "Until today," she murmured miserably.

"What happened today—what changed?"

"He did it again." She waited for another eruption of laughter, but Wes seemed at least to attempt to control himself.

"I'm really having a hard time not saying, 'It's about time.' So what's the problem?"

"He didn't realize he did it." The blank expression on Wes' face told her that she either hadn't made herself understood, or she had overreacted again. "See, the first time you had been hounding both of us about how we needed to be a couple, and it was easy just to assume that he tried something and it went all wrong, but today..."

"Why all wrong?"

Alexa felt heat flood to her face. She examined her nails closely before meeting Wes' probing eyes. "I didn't explain it very well." She took a deep breath and in a rush, blurted out her next thoughts. "I mean, it feels like I'm betraying a confidence, but who else can I talk to?" Without waiting for a response, she continued while she still had the will to do it. "He kissed me that day in my kitchen, and it shocked me. I—"

"You pushed him away, didn't you? Pushed him away and left. And he apologized for it, trying to make things go back to normal? Dumb thing to do, by the way," Wes added for good measure.

"Dumb is right, but that's not quite how it happened. See..." She groaned, closing her eyes. "Wes, I didn't respond—not at first. I mean, I was stunned—shocked. I knew he wasn't looking for any kind of relationship, and he knew I wasn't—looking, that is. I'm just less adverse to the idea." At Wes' smirk, she hastened to correct herself. "I mean, to the idea of a relationship—not just one with him."

"Mmm hmm."

"Stop it. If I don't get this out now, I never will. So... right. We have such a good friendship as it is, that it took me a minute to process it. You know how I am."

"So you turned on your analytical writing process and looked for means, motive, and opportunity?"

"Something like that," she replied sheepishly. "Well, he'd taken the opportunity. I think I was focused on the motive. Means were pretty obvious."

"I'll say."

A smile tugged at the corners of her lips. Maybe she had overreacted. "Anyway, by the time I responded, he flipped out. I mean, totally—like—he flipped out. I mean he jumped up and pushed me away like—like—I don't know what. Like something."

"That was enough likes for a California Valley Girl from the eighties." Wes winked before he asked, "You said he pulled you onto his lap. He then shoved you off. That's when you ran out on him?"

"Yeah. I still don't know why he did that. I mean, all he had to do was pull away, and I would have stood up by myself. I—"

"I get it." Wes nodded thoughtfully. "It's a guy thing. And then he did it again today?"

She shook her head emphatically. "No, no. Today he just kissed my forehead—like we've been married for fifty years or something—and went off to work. I don't even know if he ever realized he did it. I mean, it was that absent minded."

"And you're telling me this why? I know you. You wouldn't share any of this unless you had motive. So spill it, little sister."

"I need to know what's going on with him. Why is he acting like this? You're a guy. Tell me!"

Incredulous, he stared slack-jawed at her. He shook his head as if to clear it and said, "Well, you tell me, Alexa. Why is a man—one who has never hidden his admiration for you, I might add—why is he being affectionate?"

"Look, Wes. I know you've got your matchmaker hat on. I don't know, maybe our last name has brought out the latent Woodhouse in you—"

"What? I think the word you mean is woodshed."

"No, Wes. Woodhouse—Emma. Jane Austen. Who lived at Hartfield—" She groaned. "It kills the joke when you have to explain it, brother mine."

"Okay, since you're explaining, so what's with Emma and Austen? I didn't read anything but the Cliff Note version of Pride and Prejudice—that I can think of."

"Well, she liked to play matchmaker. Kept trying to fix everyone in the area up with someone else—all the wrong people, I might add. I've seen you doing the same thing with Joe and me, but—"

"I."

Alexa's forehead wrinkled. "I what?"

"Joe and I. The author of the family should get her grammar straight."

She shook her head. "You never did grasp that simple rule, Wes. It's me. I wouldn't say, 'When it comes to I.' I would say, 'When it comes to me.' So, it's Joe and me."

Mid-lesson, Wes waved his hands for her to continue. Alexa sighed and gave him a feeble smile. "Joe isn't looking for a relationship. Remember? He made it very clear that marriage isn't an option, and I'm not playing with casual romance. It's a recipe for disaster—at least for me."

"Casual romance can turn into something deeper. There are a lot of marriages out there the resulted from a 'casual romance.'"

"Yeah, and a lot of divorces too. He's not interested in marriage, and I'm not interested in dead-end romantic relationships. We're friends," she insisted. "We're best friends, if we're honest with each other, but we're just friends."

"And you love him."

She stood and fumbled for her shoes. "That's not the issue, Wes. The last time Joe showed affection like this, I overreacted, but it was to *his* overreaction. I kind of expected this, but he didn't. What happens to our friendship when he realizes that he's crossing that line?"

Wes walked her out the door, down the steps, and to the street, his arm draped over her shoulders. "Annie, what happens is that he figures out that marriage *is* an option. This is all because of Darrin, you know. He's jealous."

"I don't think—"

"But I know. Look, I don't know much, but I do know how men think. Women always think they do, but they don't."

"How do men think, Wes? How?" She waited for some kind of encouragement that her fears were truly unfounded.

"Well, a big part of it is that we don't. Seriously. That's a big part," he added as she brushed him off.

"So..." Alexa stared at her shoes. "Will you be there to

help me salvage my friendship when this boils over and scalds one or both of us?"

Wes wrapped his arms around her, hugging her fiercely. "I'm always here for you." He tilted her head to meet his eyes. "Do you trust me, Annie?"

"Of course!"

"Then do it. Trust me. I'll talk to him."

Her voice shook as she whispered, "But—"

"Trust me."

A few yards away from the house, she turned and glanced back. Wes stood at the gate, watching. He didn't raise an arm, wave, or call out, but she knew his thoughts. *Okay... I'll try to trust him anyway.*

Joe stepped from the bathroom, fresh from a shower. Clad in nothing but swim trunks, he towel dried his hair as he shuffled through the living and dining rooms to the kitchen. Wes stood at the counter, guzzling water after a run.

Joe reached for a clean glass and frowned. There were none. Frustrated, he emptied the sink of dirty dishes and ran hot water. "This house needs a dishwasher."

"Where would you put it? Seriously, where?" Wes rolled his eyes. "Didja save me any hot water?"

"Yep. Just took a quick one." As Wes turned to leave, Joe called out, "Hey, Alexa says you're dropping off the kids at her house tonight. Going somewhere special?"

"She told you about the ring?"

Joe shut off the water and turned, gaping at Wes. "Ring? You're kidding!" Wes' expression said otherwise. "Wow! Congratulations, man!"

Wes' grin grew. "Looks like you'll be getting this place all to yourself. Maybe you can talk her into selling it—if that's what you really want."

Something in Wes' tone caught Joe's attention. "What? I know that tone. That's the 'you're being a fool, Joe' tone my dad uses when I'm dead wrong about something."

"Well, at least you admit you can be. Maybe there's hope." Wes leaned his arm against the wall. After a few seconds of observation, he shook his head. "Okay, maybe not."

Joe stared at the sink of sudsy water and gave up. He opened the fridge, pulled out the mostly-empty carton of orange juice, and carried it to the living room. "If you want to lecture me, you'll have to do it in here."

Wes started to lower himself into a chair, but Joe shook his head. "She'll kill you if she finds out."

"Right." Wes moved and dropped to the floor, flat on his back, one arm over his eyes. "Wanna guess what I want to talk about?"

"That's easy. You're sister. You have a two-track mind. Sister and wife-to-be."

"Can you blame me?" Wes rolled onto his side and propped his head on his hand.

Joe took a long drink of orange juice—nearly emptying the dregs of the carton—and tried to prepare himself for the semi-routine grilling about his "intentions regarding Alexa." Wes' approaches had become quite predictable. One look at Wes' expression and Joe placed his imaginary bet on the "don't let her get away" version this time. Her recent dates with Darrin would inspire it, surely.

He lost. Wes waited until Joe gave full attention to the discussion and said, "Alexa came to talk to me yesterday."

Joe leaned forward. "You make it sound unusual that you would talk to your sister."

"She came to talk to me about you."

"What!" Incredulous, Joe shook his head. "That doesn't make sense. She values her privacy even more than I do."

"Apparently, when you left her house yesterday, you kissed her goodbye."

"I did no—" The protest died in his throat. Suddenly the image of his phone buzzing, him standing to leave, bending to kiss her forehead—all exploded in his memory. "I didn't realize—"

Wes nodded. "She knows."

"Knows what?"

Wes sat up. "Knows you didn't realize it."

"Well if she knows that, then why come to you?"

"Because the last time you kissed her, it almost destroyed your friendship." He held up both hands and stopped Joe's intended interjection as he continued. "Hey, look. I get why you did it—"

"Did what?" Joe frowned. "I'm confused."

"Why you pushed her away last time. Alexa would figure it out if she thought about it long enough, but the fact is: your reaction spelled rejection for someone you claim is your best friend." Wes hesitated and added, "C'mon, Joe. Think about it." With that, Wes disappeared down the hallway—presumably to find fresh clothes for a shower. Or so Joe hoped.

Joe sat sipping the last dregs of the carton and considered Wes' words. She hadn't talked to him. She went to Wes instead. Their friendship—apparently irreparably damaged because he hadn't resisted the temptation to kiss her. And now he'd done it again.

She didn't run this time. Then again, I didn't make her feel totally rejected this time either. Still, improvement—such as it is. But what do I do?

He listened to Wes singing in the shower—some rock song Joe had never heard. The lyrics, if he understood Wes' stage-styled, under-enunciated wails correctly, sounded strangely applicable. "*...don't know where we're goin'. Don't know how we'll ever get there. Don't know why I'm doubtin', but I'm layin' my heart bare—for you...*"

Just as Joe started to jump up and pound on the bathroom door, shouting, "Subtle! Lay it on a little thicker and maybe I'll get it," he realized that Wes probably sang about himself.

He'd protested—used Alexa's career and wealth as an excuse—but that's all it really was, an excuse. Wes and seen through his overly-protested objections. His subtlety with Alexa had worked though. He left just enough doubt to keep her from expecting him to "go there."

236

And then you did. You deserve any blasting you get.

Wes stepped from the bathroom minutes later, still buttoning his shirt. "Well?"

"Well what?"

"Dodging the subject won't help any, Joe." Wes dug through a basket of clean laundry and pulled out a pair of socks. "What are you going to do about you and Alexa?"

Joe shrugged. "I don't know." Setting the empty juice carton on the coffee table, he leaned back and covered his eyes. "I thought about giving up my job, you know."

"She'd reject you in a heartbeat if you did."

"I know."

Several silent minutes passed as Wes moved in and out of the room, getting ready. The air conditioner "pinged" as the thermostat turned on again. Wes nudged Joe's knee with his toe as he sat on the opposite corner of the couch. "You don't have to have the First Church classic marriage, you know. The Bible has no law that says you have to be home by six, she has to have dinner on the table, and you can only spend nights apart for emergencies."

"I'm a selfish man, Wes."

"And she's an independent woman who is accustomed to doing her own thing. You have your mission to the kids in this town, and she has her book signings and shopping trips." He shook his head. "Joe, she's the perfect woman for you. She won't care if you're there for dinner or not, but…"

Joe's mind had already wandered to the word pictures Wes had created for him. "What?"

"Wouldn't it be nice to know you didn't have to go home? No ruined reputations if you stay, no other man carrying her off to who knows where. Wouldn't that be nice?"

"Do you really think—"

Wes stood and grabbed his tie from the back of the chair. As he pulled the zippered side into place, he grinned. "Love these things. Best invention ever." Once adjusted, he returned to the topic. "I don't know, Joe. I know she loves you. I know she values your friendship more than anything else right now, but she's used to being alone. As much as Alexa likes that, I think she's getting tired of having quite so much of it. You did that." Wes stood, hands stuffed in his pockets and stared at Joe. "You taught her to enjoy having someone around again. She might be at that place, or she's getting there quickly, where she'll sacrifice one thing for another."

"Yeah?"

Wes nodded. "Yeah. I just don't think you want that sacrifice to be you."

With that, Wes grabbed his keys and the small ring box off the end table and slipped them into his pocket. "Night, Joe."

"...don't want that sacrifice to be you." Wes' words taunted him. Hadn't he just gone through those thoughts while listening to Alexa's conversation with Darrin on her terrace? It was true. It could happen. And he'd have no one to blame but himself.

Chapter 25

Joe climbed the stairs, horrific sounds growing louder with each step. As he entered her room, he winced. "Whoa! It sounds like a cat in heat up here! Cut it out!"

"You're just jealous because you don't have my stunning pipes!" She winked and tossed another dress on one of several piles that littered the room.

"Packing?"

"Yep. I think I have it narrowed down to this side of the room." She swept her arm over several piles. "Care to put away those over there for me?"

Joe carried a dozen—maybe two—dresses into her closet and hung them on one end of the rack. She could organize them when she had the time. He stepped back into the room and started to ask about her books, but the doorbell rang. He reached for another half dozen dresses, when her cellphone rang.

"Can you get that, Joe?" Alexa called on her way to the door.

He answered tentatively. "Hello?"

A woman's voice came through the line, sounding confused. "I'm sorry; I think I have the wrong number."

"Who are you calling for? This isn't my phone," Joe admitted, unwilling to identify whose number the caller had reached until he knew who it was.

"This is Adelaide Peters. I'm looking for Alexa Hartfield…"

"Mrs. Peters. This is Joe—Joe Freidan. You made the dress for Alexa for me?"

"Oh, yes. Officer Joe. I wondered—"

"Alexa is answering the door right now, but she'll be

right back. While I have you, I wanted to thank you for all the work you did on her dress. I wish you could have seen it on her." He cleared his throat. "I think you undercharged me, but—"

"It was my pleasure."

"I can't imagine how you got it done so quickly—especially with all the extra sewing for Rhette and Silva."

"Oh, isn't that just horrible about that Silva! Her death was such a shock, but with the way she was cheating Alexa…"

Surprised that Alexa had shared the information with her seamstress, Joe fumbled. "Oh—I'm surprised Alexa mentioned that. She's given up trying to investigate Silva's murder."

"Oh, Alexa didn't mention it. Silva did—in a manner of speaking."

"Silva told you she was skimming off the books?" Joe began to question Laidie's mental stability.

"No, no. She and I were talking on the phone once—about the prototypes I think—when she had to switch over to take another call. It didn't switch right or something, because I heard her talking to someone else… Aaron or Darrin or something like that."

"Adam?"

"That could be it," the woman agreed after a few seconds of thought. "Anyway, they were talking about fixing discrepancies in the books and how it was more profitable that way. I was going to talk about it with Silva the next time she called me, but then she was gone…" A sniffle broke through the phone line before Laidie added, "You know, I really hoped there would just be a good explanation for everything."

Joe's mind whirled, trying to process the information without abandoning the conversation. "Well, you didn't call here to talk to me about unpleasant memories. Let me find Alexa."

He tried to step quickly down the silly little spiral staircase that led to Alexa's room, but the tight curves made it awkward. Joe reached the entryway just as Alexa sliced open a box. "Found her. She's opening a package..."

Alexa showed him the return address before continuing to unwrap the box. Joe grinned. "Actually, she's opening a box from you. She's so excited about it she didn't even take the phone."

"Oh, that's why I called. I wanted to make sure it got there in time. It was supposed to arrive yesterday, but then the tracking went all crazy and said it was in New Jersey!"

"Shall I have her call you back?" Joe snickered at the sight of Alexa preening in front of the mirror, swaying with it as if she'd found the perfect prom dress. "She's a bit obsessed with her new clothes."

"Oh, that's okay. Now that I know it's there, I'm fine. I'll talk to her another time." She coughed slightly. "Silly thing. I haven't been able to shake this cough since missing Alexa's party!"

"I hope you feel better soon."

"Oh, I feel fine," Laidie assured him. "I just have this strange residual cough. Anyway, I'll talk to her later. Please tell her that I'd like to know when the show airs so I can watch it."

Alexa disappeared into the bathroom as Joe disconnected the call. He wandered into the kitchen, poured himself a glass of water, and dropped onto a barstool. As he relived the conversation, he rubbed his temples — certain he'd missed something.

Alexa appeared wearing the outfit just a minute or two later. "Look! Isn't it marvelous?" She spun in circles, swinging her skirt in fans at her side. "It's just perfect."

"I like that color."

"Peacock blue. So rich!"

"It suits your strutting in that thing!"

Alexa rolled her eyes. "Ha. Ha. So funny." The distraction disappeared as she spun a hat on her finger. "Look at this hat! The netting... I just can't believe this hat. Miranda over at The Cache outdid herself."

"It is a nice hat..." He didn't quite know how to

compliment a hat, but it was a nice looking thing.

"It's exactly what I would have ordered if I had been looking for something to go with this dress. I just can't believe it."

As usual, new clothing sent Alexa into almost childish fits of delight. She rustled her skirt and spun in circles, watching the hem flare out higher and higher, until Joe glanced away in case it should rise a little too high. She collapsed against the counter seconds later, laughing and gasping. "There's something almost giddy about a new dress."

"Maybe that's where the old idea of telling a woman to buy a new dress as a depression solution came from."

Alexa nodded. "Well, maybe not for true clinical depression, but it sure works for me when I'm having a rough day. Laidie sure came through for me."

"She seems to know exactly what suits you best."

Her fingers slid over the smooth, silky fabric, inspecting seams and trim work. "I just don't know how she isn't worn out after all the work she did for us. Silva ran her ragged with all the troubles we had."

"Speaking of Laidie and Silva, did you know that she overheard Silva talking to Adam about the books?"

"No!"

"Yep. He knew about it, Alexa. I think he's in on it."

She beckoned him to follow. "Come talk to me while I change.

Joe followed her upstairs to her room, relating the conversation with Laidie. Alexa stepped into the closet room and closed the door, listening and commenting occasionally as Joe theorized about various possibilities. She emerged minutes later, wearing a delicately embroidered white dress.

Before he could hope to compliment her on it, Alexa suggested a theory of her own. "What if Adam killed Silva? He knew of the book tampering, got tired of his percentage, and decided to take over as chief thief."

"But the note—"

"Don't you see; it's perfect! What better way for him to

deflect suspicion than to make himself a supposed target? I won't be surprised if we get a call soon about an attempt on his life."

"He did go back to Chicago with her, and he was the one who supposedly found her..."

They talked as Alexa finished packing. Joe watched with half-interest as she hung dresses in a garment bag, packed hats, blouses, and undergarments in a large suitcase, and pulled full cosmetic and toiletry bags from a shelf in the closet. These she placed in an overnight bag and zipped shut. He'd never seen anyone pack so quickly.

Before she zipped up the garment bag, Alexa hung her new dress inside and stared at it for several seconds. Unaware of Joe's observation, she gathered several pairs of shoes and set them, one pair at a time, beneath the bag before choosing a pair of pointy-toed heels that looked miserably painful.

"I can't believe you would torture your feet with those shoes."

"They're not made for long walks or anything, but they're fairly comfortable for an afternoon of fun in the city."

"But—"

"I'll only walk from the limo to the studio, on and off stage, back to the limo, take a cab somewhere to eat, check out a few of my favorite shops, and then go back to the hotel. If I planned any serious shopping or house hunting, I'd probably wear these." She shook a pair of square-toed pumps."

"Those don't look any better to me, so I'll have to trust you on that. You complain less about your feet than anyone I know."

"It's all in the shoe. Buy fewer pairs and spend the money on only well-made shoes, and your feet will thank you." Alexa carried her rejected shoes back to the closet.

"But you must have thirty pairs of shoes!"

"And that is exactly the national average."

He shook his head. "I don't believe it. I know my mother doesn't have half that many. Even Jocie doesn't have that many!"

"Well, minimalist women out there with only three or four pair, help those with forty or fifty pair look less obsessive."

Joe gave up all attempts to hide his amazement. "Fifty pairs of shoes? Why?" At the amused expression on her face, he backpedaled. "I mean, you have a reason to have a lot of shoes. You have a public image to uphold, a really diverse wardrobe — it makes sense — but..."

"It's just a matter of preference. Suzy only has about four pair that I can think of. One athletic, one pair of brown sandals, one pair semi-dressy white shoes, and one pair of black pumps. She's also the scandal of her very proper southern church. She's been known to wear white shoes in November and black ones in July."

"Huh?"

"Very eloquent, Joe. I couldn't have said it better myself." Alexa handed him the large suitcase. "Care to help me carry down these bags?"

Joe grabbed the suitcase, garment bag, and overnight bag. He followed her to the car and placed them exactly where she asked, smiling to himself at how she even kept her car ordered precisely how she wanted it. "You know, I only see you let things get messy when you're working."

"Is that bad?"

He shook his head. "Nope, but it tells me when you've finished working out a problem. You go from leaving little bits of clutter around you to cleanup in seconds."

"Do I?" She closed the hatchback and turned, slipping her arm in his. "Interesting."

The movement — so natural and *her* — affected him in a way it never had in the past. He shrugged off the thought as the result of too much interference on Wes' part, and walked with her back to the couch, listening as she talked out her plans. "Okay, I made a quiche last night — half is still in the fridge. I guess I expected them to eat more than they did."

"Want me to take it home for Wes or over to Heather?"

"Either way — oh, and there's also fruit in the basket and a roast that I meant to make for dinner, but I didn't have time.

Take those home for you and Wes. Just pop the roast in the crockpot all day and it'll be ready." As she reached the kitchen, Alexa opened the fridge and pulled out the items in question. "Oh, and I forgot about this salad. If you don't want it, I'll go dig a hole for it in the flowerbed."

"Hole?"

"The lazy woman's way to compost. Bury your kitchen scraps where you plan to grow something sometime." She grabbed a small carton of cream. "Do you want this?"

Joe added it to the pile. "Got a box?"

Much to his chagrin, Alexa pulled out a market basket, complete with floral liner, and set everything in it. "Thanks. I hate coming home to green, fuzzy food in my fridge."

Joe swallowed a lump that rose in his throat. "I wish you weren't going."

"I'll be back on Wednesday. I'm not staying any longer than necessary." She pulled out a notepad with contact information on it. "I'll be at the Warwick again—here's everything—"

He ignored the ominous feeling that came over him as she mentioned the hotel and concentrated on the things within his control. "I'll call the Chicago PD and tell them what Laidie said. They'll probably call her and verify the information, so don't be surprised if she calls."

"She won't. She'll expect it. Laidie is, if anything, very levelheaded. That's probably why she could easily just disconnect a call like that and decide to talk to the woman later. Most people would have confronted it, called me, or done something about it. Laidie thinks and acts after careful thought. I bet she didn't want to accuse without cause."

That made sense—explained why she hadn't told Alexa yet. "Well, don't worry about it. You take it easy, relax, shop until you drop, and who knows, maybe Adam will be behind bars before you get back."

Alexa pulled out one of her kitchen chairs and sat. She rested her head in her hand and drew designs in the tablecloth with her fingernail. "I just can't imagine Adam... He was so shaken. It sounded genuine to me."

"Well, I hope he's innocent, but if he's not, I want him caught before he decides to make you a target."

Lost in thoughts he could only imagine, she nodded and then smiled up at Joe. "Hey, you know what? I just realized something."

"What?"

"My brother is engaged! We need to have a party."

Joe chuckled and resisted the urge to cover her hand in his. "Let's plan that for when you get back, okay? It would be difficult to plan, execute, and recover from a party in twelve hours."

"Spoilsport."

Joe crossed his arms over his chest and leaned back in his chair. "Got that right."

Chapter 26

The theme song of the Paisley Duncan Show swelled, and the backstage manager motioned for her to get ready. The rich, deep tones of the show host's voice, announced clearly, "Our next guest is none other than bestselling — and eccentric — author, Alexa Hartfield!"

The manager nodded and Alexa stepped onto the stage and strolled across to the chairs that made up the set, taking the one offered by Paisley. The woman immediately pounced on Alexa's ensemble. "That is one stunning dress, Ms. Hartfield."

"Alexa is fine, and thank you. My seamstress made it in record time for me to wear today." Alexa smoothed one side of the skirt. "I love it."

"Thank her for me, will you? I had a bet with my general manager. He said you'd wear paisleys. I said no. I won. He owes me tickets to the Mets game." The audience laughed and Paisley continued. "But tell me how you developed your particular style."

The question seemed trite. Every interview she gave mentioned it. Did they really think viewers wanted to hear the same story all over again? She tried a new approach. "That's odd. Most people say that I have no style." She chuckled. "Then they get embarrassed and say they mean I don't stick to any particular style."

Laughter, sounding more like a soundtrack rather than the genuine amusement of the audience, erupted around her. Paisley nodded and pressed her again. "You really must explain it, though. I've seen pictures of you in nearly every style imaginable."

"It's not a very exciting story — and one people have

heard often." Once she said it, Alexa felt rude. She continued, trying to make it simple and interesting. "I simply fell in love with a vintage dress once, and several women said they couldn't wait for that style to return so they could wear it again." She couldn't help a smile as she added, "I was a bit miffed."

"Miffed? I haven't heard anyone say that since the eighties!"

"See, even my slang is eclectic and somewhat dated." Determined to finish the topic, Alexa continued. "Yes, I got miffed. I hated the idea that people expected me to wait around for someone else to tell me what style I could or could not wear. So, I decided that day that I'd just wear whatever I liked."

Paisley urged her to stand and tell the audience about the dress she wore. Alexa stood and spun slowly. "Laidie—my seamstress—made this dress from silk dupioni. I think my favorite part—aside from the general style—is the polka dot netting around the hem."

"There are so many details. It is amazing. You'd think with so many elements, it would look overdone, but it doesn't. Tell us about how she decides what to put on them."

"Well, I think she tries to stick to authenticity. For example," Alexa pointed to the bottom of the netting. "The satin bound edge of the netting gives it that polished finish, and the netting itself holds the skirts out properly." She tugged at the cropped jacket. "This jacket keeps the dress from seeming too much like a fifties cocktail dress. I think Laidie may have combined two looks to update it for today. I think it's a period correct style, but I do wonder if all her work on the Rhette collection influenced it."

Across the room, Alexa saw Elise rise, shaking her head, and then sink back into her chair. After Elise's work to distance Alexa from the clothing line, she'd now tied a knot between them. Alexa waited for Paisley to pounce on that. It didn't take long.

"The Rhette Collection has had quite a bit of press lately. First the model strike and then the murder—after last fall and the trouble in your town, how did you react to the news?"

Alexa squared her shoulders and met Paisley's eyes. "I felt as terrible as anyone would when they learn that a friend has died. That she was murdered makes it even more horrifying."

"I've heard, and please understand, I'm not trying to sensationalize your grief," Paisley assured her. "I am very sorry for your loss. However, I have heard that they discovered the victim had been stealing from the business. Is this true?"

Joe would consider throttling her, but Alexa felt the opportunity was too great for her to lose. "I'm afraid that is true. I discovered only the other day, that not only was Silva skimming the accounts, but someone claims to have heard her sharing that information with my office manager. I haven't had a chance to talk to him as of yet, but I intend to."

"How has this murder, and the ones in your town last fall, affected your writing. *Have* they affected it in any way?"

"Not as you'd think, no, but yes they've made a big impact on it." Alexa continued, weighing each word as she spoke. The conversation hadn't been following the prepared script she'd been given. "I've always had a strong sense of justice. This is, of course, the purpose of my books. I pose an injustice—in my genre, it is the violent destruction of human life—and try to apply justice to the situation. Now that I've seen this kind of senseless death firsthand, I have an even stronger desire to see it righted."

"Would you say that your experiences have improved your writing?" Paisley's eyes almost seemed to apologize for the question, and at that point, Alexa suspected one of the managers was feeding her new approaches to the interview.

"I don't know." She folded her hands and tried to relax. "I would never write again if it meant that it would spare a life. However, since that is unlikely, I'll continue. Will it be improved? I don't know. But it is cathartic. Some of us need fictional characters to hate and despise in order to handle our angst in a healthy manner." She cleared her throat. "At least it isn't wrong to hate a fictional character."

"You think it's wrong to hate the man who killed your partner?"

"I do," Alexa insisted. "I believe that when Jesus said that to hate is to murder, He didn't exaggerate. In fact, I think He unveiled an understatement."

From there, the interview veered back onto the scripted topics of Alexa's faith, her family, and her soon-to-be-released novel, *Warped Justice*. By the time she stood, shook Paisley's hand, and exited the stage, Alexa breathed freely again. Image salvaged—check. Elise appeased—check. For now.

From her hotel room bed, she dialed Joe's number. He answered quickly. "How did it go?"

"Pretty well, actually. I do wonder why they always ask why I wear what I do. Don't most people know that story by now?"

"I'm sure if Thomas Edison gave interviews today, they'd all ask about how his teacher said he wasn't very bright and how that affected his life's course."

"I suppose."

Joe's tone relaxed into the comfortable camaraderie they shared. "So, when does it air?"

"Monday."

"That soon?"

She took a steadying breath and braced herself for his anger. "Got a call as soon as I reached the hotel. They had to scratch their previously scheduled show from the program, so they decided to move mine into that slot. Elise is furious. She wanted more distance between the murder and the airing."

"Well, I have Monday off, so I'll come over and watch it with you."

Alexa sighed. "Then I'll tell you now. You won't like it."

"Lex…"

"Well! She set me up and handed me a perfect opportunity. I had to take it." Room service knocked. "Gotta go. I'll talk to you when I get home." Just as Alexa punched the end button, she heard Joe roar out a warning. *Oh boy... Oh. Boy.*

The upbeat theme music dubbed over the end credits as the camera pulled back, panned the audience, and zoomed back in on Paisley and Alexa. Joe watched her from the corner of his eye before asking, "What were you guys talking about there?"

"At the end? She actually apologized for bringing up the murders the way she did. We ad-libbed most of it. We had a list of scripted questions to work from, but once I went off on the Adam tangent, it snowballed for a bit."

Joe watched as Alexa rubbed the back of her head into the couch cushions. Apparently unsatisfied with the result, she reached up and kneaded the base of her head. Tension on her face and in her posture told him how nervous she had been. Did she still think he'd be upset?

"I think you were amazing. If any of this hurt your reputation as an author, you did a great salvage job. And—"

Her head snapped up. "What?"

"I think we should warn Adam."

"Warn him, why? And how! I can't just call him and say, 'Oh, by the way, I might have hinted that you killed Silva, so either be sure to pretend that someone tried to kill you or be careful—whichever fits.'" She stared at Joe. "Really?"

"On the off-chance that this wasn't Adam, we have to warn him. If he didn't do it, he'll feel betrayed." Joe shrugged sheepishly. "There's that word again."

Alexa grabbed her phone and dialed the Chicago store, putting it on speakerphone. "Rhette? Is Adam around?"

She rubbed the back of her head as she waited for him and then began explaining the situation as Adam came on the line. "Someone mentioned that they'd overheard a conversation between Silva and another person—possibly you—and that person thought that you might have known about the book doctoring. So, I decided to use that information to drag the killer out of hiding. I mentioned it on the Paisley Duncan Show." She glanced at Joe for encouragement before continuing. "I didn't give your name, and I'm not accusing you of anything. I just wanted to call and warn you to be careful. Never be alone. Don't trust anyone but maybe Rhette. She's the only one with an alibi."

Adam, audibly unnerved by Alexa's words, promised to watch the interview as soon as he found it online. "I'll watch my back, Alexa, and thanks for calling. I mean, I'm glad I know I need to be careful, but I'm even more glad that you know I didn't do it. I'd never steal from you, and I couldn't kill anyone. I still get sick remembering."

Once Alexa disconnected the call, they sat, each lost in thought until she whispered, "I feel like a liar and a false accuser all rolled in one."

"You don't think he did it. You think it's possible, but that doesn't mean you consider him guilty. And," Joe continued, nudging her knee with his foot, "you didn't accuse him of anything. You warned him, remember?"

They sat—possibly for hours—staring at the blank TV, unspeaking. Thirst drove Alexa from the sitting nook, with promises of juice. Seconds after she descended the stairs, Joe followed. "Seemed like if we're going to stare at something, the lake would be a better view than a TV screen."

"Good idea."

Again, they sat in silence, side by side, staring out over the water in the last hours of daylight. After some time, Joe's stomach rumbled. Without a word, Alexa reached into her pocket, pulled out her phone, and passed it to him. "Call The Deli. I'd like pastrami on rye and the pasta salad. Then call Hunter and ask him to pick them up. I have a great cheesecake in the freezer. I'll go set it on the counter to defrost."

Once he finished with the arrangements, Joe followed her inside and passed her the phone. "Dinner procured." He stared at the cheesecake. "Yours?"

"Mmm hmm. I made two last time so I'd have one when I wanted it." As she spoke, Alexa cut two slices and slid them onto plates, covering them with cereal bowls. She returned the leftover cheesecake to the freezer and pulled out a pitcher of tea. "Plain, pineapple, or maybe mango?"

"Mango."

"Sounds great. Will you carry out plates and napkins?"

She kept busy—too busy. Joe couldn't tell if the uncertainty with Adam caused it or if she had work to do and had forgotten about it. Just as he started to ask, the doorbell rang. "That was fast." Joe glanced at the clock on the oven. "Twenty minutes from order to delivery. That's better than pizza."

"The food is too."

Laughing, Joe shook his head as he went to answer the door. "That's your opinion."

They ate, still speaking little, each lost in a private world neither seemed ready to share. The sun set, sending a riot of color over the shimmering surface of the lake. Twilight fell, and with it, the first star of the evening."

"Did you see that?" he whispered.

"Mmm hmm..." Seconds later, Joe unconsciously began humming, "Catch a Falling Star." Alexa chuckled and murmured, "Stop that or I'll sing along."

"Stop what?"

"Humming!" She gently shoved him before adding, "That song is going to be stuck in my head now." As he hummed louder, she laughed and shoved him harder.

Joe caught her hand and held it as he'd done many times, but the air between them changed. Something was different. He started to speak—to ask if it bothered her—but stopped himself. There was time. Why rush?

They might have sat there for hours again—possibly taken a walk along the shore—but Alexa's phone rang, jarring them from the serenity that had finally settled over them. "Hello?"

The color faded from Alexa's face—something Joe only

could have known from the ghostly pallor left behind. Her question to the caller told everything. "Is he going to be okay?"

He pulled out his phone and typed a text message, passing it to her without sending. She read it, nodded, and asked, "Detective Romano, could the wounds have been self-inflicted?"

The phone buzzed with words that Joe couldn't hear. "I see." She saw what? Joe wanted his phone back—to ask her to put it on speakerphone, but her next words stopped him. With an edge that Joe knew well, Alexa's tone changed as she said, "I *did* tell everyone that I had decided to leave the detective work to the professionals, Mr. Romano. This is why I expected the wounds to be self-inflicted. If Adam could not have—"

Tension slowly seized her body. Her ankles clicked together primly. Her shoulders squared and her posture grew rigid. When Alexa's eyebrows furrowed and her lips pursed, Joe leaned back and waited for the show. It promised to be entertaining.

Unaware of Joe's amusement, Alexa took a deep breath, and with great control said, "Detective, I am accustomed to dealing with professionals in law enforcement. I am not in the habit of presenting myself as a scapegoat for incompetent investigations and sloppy police work."

Now able to hear the detective's words, Joe lunged for the phone, but Alexa turned aside, taking the phone out of reach. As the officer continued his harangue, she punched a button on the phone and waited for the verbal assault to cease. "Are you quite finished? Good. I have recorded this call, and if you ever speak to me like that again, I'll file a complaint with your police commissioner. Good evening."

Joe cheered the moment she stuffed the phone back in her pocket. "Magnificent."

She shook her head. "He won't call again. If I want to know anything, I'll have to find someone else to keep me informed."

"I suppose you shouldn't have—"

Alexa interrupted him. "No, it's all right, Joe. I think we know what we need to know." She grimaced as she added, "I just don't think we know what it is we know."

He recycled her words several times in his mind, but it did little to enlighten him. "What?"

"I think we have all the information we need to figure this out. I just don't think we know what information is pertinent and what is extraneous—for now. We'll figure it out."

Joe forced himself to relax and ask the question he didn't want to ask. "So what happened to Adam?"

"Someone tried to strangle him while he was at the computer. Apparently, he took my warning very seriously. Detective Romano said he had worked out just about every scenario possible and how he could react."

"Sounds like him from what you've described," Joe murmured. He frowned. "But if he took it seriously, how did anyone get in?"

She closed her eyes and whispered, "He forgot to lock the back door when he took out some trash." Head waggling, Alexa continued. "So, when he sat down at the computer, he actually wrote out an email to several people—Detective Romano says my name was on the CC list—and kept it open in case someone came in with a gun or something."

"Smart…maybe…"

Alexa nodded. "Yep. He planned to click on the email first and then pretend to die quickly so that he'd have a chance."

Shaking his head, Joe asked incredulously, "And that worked?"

"Apparently. Someone came in and threw a rope around his neck. Romano says he took as deep of a breath as he could, leaned forward, clicked the email's send button with his mouse, made hacking noises, and fell off the stool. Laid there limp, even though I guess he cracked his head on the floor."

"No slit wrists this time?"

"Maybe she saw the email go out and wanted to get

away." She met his eyes. "Or maybe the blood was too much last time. Who knows?"

"You said she." Joe leaned forward. "Did Adam see someone?"

"No..." Her forehead furrowed as she thought. "I didn't realize I said that." She stood and beckoned him to follow. "I'm going to Chicago—make sure Adam is fine. Come talk to me while I pack."

Joe followed her upstairs. The sight—one that had become familiar—of her pulling out suitcases and a garment bag drove home that she would leave again. Just like that. Utterly spur of the moment. Those trips wherever she wanted to go personified her. "I'll go fill your car with gas while you do that."

She glanced up from a pile of dresses. "Thank you. That would be wonderful."

By the time he returned, the entryway held her luggage and Alexa worked in the kitchen, wiping down the counter. She smiled at him. "Cheesecake?"

As he accepted the plate, Joe asked, "Are you going to see Lorie while you're there?" When she didn't reply, he added, "Jeremy seems to think she's getting nervous about school—senior year and all that stuff."

"Probably," Alexa choked before reaching for a glass and filling it with water. "I'll probably take her over to Rhette's and have her pick out something for the first school dance."

Joe wanted to ask about Darrin—would she see him? Did they have a standing date? As he watched her finish her cheesecake, Joe realized that Alexa knew he was curious. Anxious to fill the now awkward silence, Joe gestured to the dessert with his fork and murmured, "Good cheesecake."

"Mmm... just the way—"

The phone interrupted her. By her surprised expression, Joe suspected Detective Romano had decided that his unprofessional behavior could cause him some trouble. Her next words confirmed it.

"I see. Thank you, detective. Yes, I certainly accept your

apology. I know I was out of line myself." Her lips twitched as she listened. "Well, that's kind of you to say, anyway. What—oh. Darrell. Interesting. Well, I'm flying out tonight. I want to see Adam for myself, and I need to do some shopping. I'll talk to him then. Will he be charged without a complaint against him? But I can file one when I get there, if I choose to, correct?"

Again the wait as she listened. Joe knew exactly what the man said. Seconds later, she disconnected the phone. "You heard that, right?" Alexa pulled up a barstool and sat down, staring at the phone. "Darrell. Laidie didn't hear Adam talking to Silva; she heard Darrell."

"Well, she said Darrin or Aaron... so that makes sense. My mind was already on Adam, so I stuck with the similarity of Adam to Aaron."

Alexa closed her eyes. "He turned himself in tonight when he heard about Adam. He was afraid that we'd find out and that it would look like he tried to kill Adam."

"And what are the odds of Darrell turning himself in to avert suspicion and get a lesser charge or let off the hook by an overly-kind author?"

She stood and carried the plates to the sink, rinsed them, and loaded them into the dishwasher. "That's Tony's idea. He wants me to press charges."

"Will you?"

"Unless Darrell can convince me that he's completely innocent of Silva's death, I'm definitely pressing charges. If he can, then we'll see."

Alexa yawned, and Joe took his cute to leave. "I'd better go. You have an early flight, I suppose?"

"I'll probably take the eight o'clock shuttle."

Joe hugged her at the door. As he opened it, he turned to her. "Lex, be careful. Whoever is doing this seems loyal to you, and I hope that means he wouldn't harm you, but..."

"But what?"

Swallowing the lump that grew in his throat at the thought of something happening to her, Joe continued. "But, if you did something that felt like a betrayal of that loyalty and trust, I'm afraid you could become a target yourself. Stay with others. Don't go out alone. Go with Darrin, Lorie, Rhette—someone." He saw the protest on her lips, but he rushed onward before she cut him off. "If you ever feel uncomfortable, either come home or go to my parents' house. Go to Darrin and Lorie's." A new thought hit him hard. "Oh, and rent a car."

"Drive in Chicago? Are you nuts?"

"Please. The idea of you getting into a cab—I'd feel better if I knew no strangers were driving you around. It's harder to take off with someone if you're not stepping into that car voluntarily."

Alexa hugged him again, holding on just a little longer than usual as she murmured, "I'll rent a car." Stepping back, she shook her head. "You know, you're taking all the fun out of this."

"Good. Maybe that means you'll come home sooner this way." He paused, the sudden urge to kiss her hitting him anew. "Call me when you get there. 'Night, Lex."

The door latch clicked softly as the door shut behind him. She stood at the tall window flanking the right side of the door and watched until his Jeep pulled out of the drive and drove out of sight. What a strange afternoon they'd had—nice, but strange.

Chapter 27

"'...you'll have a pocketful of starlight.' La, la, la, la, la, la..." Alexa sang quietly as she unpacked her suitcase. Joe's song had drifted through her dreams, followed her into the first-class lounge at the airport, and now filled her mind as she tried to settle in before going to see Adam. "Joe, I'll get you for this." Her mind drifted to the silly songs her dad often sang to annoy her and she added, "I guess it's better than one of those sunshine songs—barely."

The realization that she'd spoken aloud hit her hard. The last time she'd done that had been the first—last fall—at the onset of her foray into true crime. It unnerved her. "If I do it again—" she groaned and then finished the thought silently to herself. *I'll take one of those Valium tablets tonight before bed if the Rx is still good.*

Despite dragging out the inevitable, Alexa eventually forced herself to grab her purse and stroll downstairs to the valet booth. With Joe's words in her mind, she examined the backseat and trunk of the car before climbing in and driving to Northwestern Memorial Hospital. She didn't find Adam there. When he didn't answer his phone, she tried calling the shop, but the line was busy. Frustrated, she drove to the boutique to retrieve his address.

A few customers milled about the shop and employees tried to assist, but even without any retail experience, Alexa could see that many were there out of morbid curiosity. Crime scene tape forbade her to go upstairs, but Rhette pointed downstairs. "They let us take a couple of things down there. Adam is trying to—"

"Adam is here?" Without waiting for an answer, Alexa hurried down the steps and found him setting up a temporary office. She hugged him, relief washing over her as she saw for herself that he really was all right. "Are you okay? Shouldn't you be resting? What are you doing here? I went to the hospital and you weren't there."

Adam laughed at her barrage of questions and patted her awkwardly. "They let me go this morning."

"So you decided to kill yourself with work..." She winced at the joke. "Sorry. That didn't come out right."

"Trust me. I wanted to stay home, but I couldn't; since everyone I know is working, I came here. At least people are here until around nine o'clock."

"What if I take you to a hotel—" She groaned. "And that didn't sound any better than my last gaffe. You know what I mean. You can rest and watch TV and I'll be down the hall in my room—"

"I'd just as soon work." Adam took a sip of water and winced. "I really feel fine. My throat hurts, of course, and I sound awful..."

"That you do. Does talking hurt?"

"Some."

Disappointed, Alexa forced herself not to ask the questions she ached to. "Do you need something soothing for your throat? Smoothie? Ice cream?"

Adam shook his head the merest bit. "You want to ask questions. Go ahead."

"I just wondered if anything about this struck you—aside from the floor and your head."

He ran his fingers through shaggy blonde hair. "Yeah... mild concussion they said. Not supposed to go on any roller coasters this weekend."

"Very funny. So," Alexa decided to take advantage of Adam's willingness to talk. "Could you tell if it was a man or a woman?"

Adam pinched the bridge of his nose and squeezed his eyes tightly. "If I had to guess, I'd say a woman?" He took another sip of water.

"Why?"

He wiggled his fingers. "People have different

thicknesses and stuff, but these seemed too thin to be a man's hands."

"Finger nails?"

After thought, Adam shrugged. "I didn't really get much of a look, just a flash, so this is just an impression. I'd say not long ones for sure. Definitely strong hands to jerk me back so fast." He waved a hand up and down the length of him. "I may not be tall or stocky, but I'm still a hundred sixty pounds of person to try to choke."

"Is that why the doubt?"

"Doubt?" Adam croaked.

"You said you'd 'guess' it was a woman. I just thought that meant there was some doubt in your mind or you would have phrased it differently."

"You're right. I don't know. I can't say for sure, but there just was something about her—"

Rhette hurried to her side, interrupting. "Alexa! I'm sorry I didn't get to talk when you came in. The store keeps having these waves of thrill-seekers. You'd think with our proximity to the higher end shops of the Mile, we'd avoid this kind of sensationalist garbage, but…"

"Well, people are people, regardless of their bank accounts, aren't they?" Alexa smiled. "How is everything else going?"

"Sales are good—not as good today, of course—but steady. You just missed Rod from Delta Advertising. He's worked out a great campaign for the collection."

"You'll have to show me tomorrow. I just came to see for myself that Adam really is all right. And, of course, I have to talk to Darrell about the books."

Rhette and Adam exchanged worried looks. Rhette spoke for both. "Um, did Detective Romano mention anything about that?"

"He said Darrell turned himself in for embezzlement and a co-conspirator with Silva."

A comical look of relief covered Rhette's face. "We didn't know what to do when the detective called us. I mean, with everything going on, we thought maybe you'd just pull out."

"I don't know how much Silva told you about the set up, but I committed to this. The funds have already been released to a separate account with my financial management company. You had nothing to worry about."

"Oh. I wanted to hire a new general manager—to take Silva's place—but then I was afraid to."

"Why? You need one. Hire one."

Rhette glanced at Adam for support before she confessed, "Because I want to hire my older sister, Rhonna. She's great at this kind of thing, but I didn't know how you'd feel about that after everything that's happened lately. I just don't know who to trust."

Alexa suggested that they meet for dinner and go over the business issues then. "We can talk about Rhonna and what else the business needs to get us through this." She nodded to Adam and added, "You too, of course." To Rhette she said, "I can certainly understand why you'd want to hire someone you can trust. There's nothing wrong with that."

Adam's smirk earned him a gentle kick to the shins by Rhette as he said, "See, I told you she's not petty that way."

"Can I call her and ask her to come in for an interview while you're in town?"

"No."

Rhette gaped at her, visibly disappointed. "I'm sorry—"

"Don't be. If you want her, hire her, but don't expect her to race over her just so I can interview her. I won't have to work with her every day. Have Adam do it if you want a second opinion."

Alexa pulled out her phone and checked the time. "Well, now that I know Adam's doing all right, I suppose I need to go talk to Darrell."

"Before you go, do you want to see the box of stuff Mrs. Peters sent us?"

"Oh! Absolutely! Laidie always does such amazing work."

Rhette led her to a storage closet and pulled several ensembles from the rod. As she did, she said, "You know, I called her Laidie once, and she nearly bit my head off. She said, kind of stuffy like—I can't think of the word—"

"Primly?" The word fit Laidie perfectly.

"That's it!" Rhette exclaimed, nodding. "She said, 'Miss Hartfield calls me Laidie, but my name is Adelaide to everyone else.'"

"How funny... I wonder if it offends her. I'll have to ask."

"I don't think it does," Rhette insisted. "It sounded more possessive than offended—like when a little kid gets mad because you called *their* mom, 'mommy.'"

After the business dinner and her bath and bedtime routine, Alexa curled up under the covers, clicked on her Vivaldi playlist, and forced herself to relax to the opening strains of the Spring Concerto. As the second movement began, she picked up her phone and dialed Joe's number.

"Hey, how'd it go?"

The sound of his voice gave her the confidence to share the thoughts she wished she didn't have. "Good and not-so-good."

"Hold on. Let me turn off the TV. I took a pounding on the basketball court tonight."

Amused, she asked, "High school or junior high this time?"

"High school." She heard him swallow and realized he must have just walked in the door. Before she could offer to call back later, he asked about Darrell.

"Let's talk about him in a minute. I've got a theory and well—"

"What kind of theory?" he asked.

"Walk me through my thought processes. My mind keeps going places that I don't want it to go."

"Okay..." Joe hesitated. "Lex, are you all right?"

"I'm safe, if that's what you mean. I'm not sure about all right. Let me set up a scenario."

"I'm listening…"

Alexa began explaining her theory. "A Wisconsin farm wife is almost the sole seamstress of a clothes horse—"

"Tell me that you're not trying to make a case for Mrs. Peters."

She continued as though he hadn't interrupted her. "After several years of lucrative business, the clothes horse begs for extra sewing help one year. The woman—let's call her Adelaide, because pretending otherwise would be ridiculous—is nervous at first. After all, if the business is a success, she could be out of a job."

"Adelaide didn't really think—"

Without pausing to answer, Alexa set her stage and made her case. "She did, but I told her—honestly I might add—that while I love the line, I prefer my own things that she and I come up with. Anyway," Alexa swallowed a sip of water, hating the next part. "Anyway, after all that work on the clothes for the business, Adelaide has a bit of loyalty to it—pride in it perhaps. But then, things happen and they discourage her."

"Things such as…" The skepticism in Joe's tone, much to her surprise, encouraged her.

Alexa crawled from the covers and paced her hotel room as she described her scenario. "Then, one day she's talking to Silva on the phone and Silva gets another call. Adelaide expects to hear silence, but instead, overhears Silva and Darrell discussing how they are robbing from the business. Suddenly, that pride and loyalty to the business is transferred solely to me. After all, I've been her primary customer for years."

"But how could she have killed Silva?" Joe protested. "She was too sick to come to your party; remember?"

The twinge of doubt in Joe's voice encouraged her, but Alexa had to continue—to be sure. "She *said* she was too ill. Now, I don't doubt that she was truly sick. I can't imagine her lying about that. How sick, however, is another story. I think she used her husband's absence, the fact of her illness, and her proximity to Chicago to set up the fake appointment with

Bergdorf's."

Joe protested immediately. "She lives in Wisconsin! It's not that close!"

"Two or three hours, Joe. I think, if I remember right, she's two or three hours from the city. She could easily drive here, make that call from here in order to avoid it being on her phone records, and then go knock on the door. Silva met her once when she delivered a box of stuff that we needed A-S-A-P. Silva would have recognized her and let her in."

"Just a minute. I have to get some aspirin. My brain refuses to wrap around this idea." The sounds of cabinets opening and closing preceded a plea for help. "Do you know where Wes keeps aspirin?"

"Kitchen pantry top left in the first aid box."

"So," the bottle rattled as Joe retrieved the pain reliever, "what about the note? It was mailed from Chicago."

"I don't know about that—too many options. She could have driven into the city to mail it, but an six-hour car ride for a note seems excessive. She could have given it to someone to drop off, or she could have sent it to someone else who mailed it for her."

"None of them solid ideas."

Alexa agreed. "I think she just drove it. It's the only safe choice."

"So you think she tried to kill Adam too?" Joe talked as he worked in her kitchen. "I miss your house—how you had it. Bright cabinets, counters, an always-fresh pot of coffee waiting..."

"I'll buy you one of those one-minute single cup machines. I hear they are wonderful for people like you."

"Oh, be quiet and tell me about Adam."

"I think she has to be responsible for that too. No one else makes sense. I think she saw my interview, realized that I was still trying to figure out who had done it, and decided to scare me off once and for all—for my own good, of course."

"Oh, come on, coffee pot. Give me cranial relief," Joe moaned. "Look, it sounds good, Alexa. It's the only thing that has made any sense so far, but it has one serious flaw."

"No evidence." She sighed. "I know." Alexa crawled back under the covers and wriggled her toes. "That's going to be the difficult part."

"How do you plan to get it?" He sighed. "You know that I should not say that, right? I should say, 'Take this all to Detective Romano and stay out of it.'"

"But you won't." She laughed at his silence. "You would if it was a Fairbury crime."

"You know I would." He asked the question again. "So how?"

"I'm going to ask her. I think she's still loyal enough to tell me if I do, so I'll just ask." Alexa swallowed the lump that grew in her throat and sighed. "I think she's worked herself into a mental state that isn't quite… stable. She's probably nearing a nervous breakdown." Tears choked her as she added, "And I probably sent her there."

"You'll never convince anyone to get her off on an insanity plea. Favorite seamstress or not, this is murder we're talking about."

Alexa gazed at the perfect stitching and embroidery on the sleeve of her nightgown and sighed. "It's not that. The Laidie I knew last year would never have done anything like this. I couldn't have imagined it—not the slightest bit. But Joe, somehow, I know she did this."

"You can't go there and ask her point-blank. What happens if—"

"Joe, she'll know that others know I'm there. Tim—her husband—he'll probably be there."

"Take someone with you anyway."

A smile—a bittersweet one—tugged at her lips. The protective edge in Joe's voice comforted her. "Joe, I can't. I appreciate the concern—more than you know—but I just can't. Pray for me tomorrow. I'll call you when I leave there, but it might take a day or two. I'll probably wait until she's in custody."

"What do you think is going to happen? I can't believe—"

"I hope to convince her to turn herself in and confess. I'll personally ask for a psychiatric evaluation of her."

"Lex?"

"Yeah?" She grabbed a tissue from the box on the nightstand.

"Are you okay?"

"No." She muffled the phone and blew her nose. "Hey, Joe. I've got to go before I fall apart here—just pray."

Hours after she disconnected the call, Alexa lay in bed, praying. She needed wisdom—compassion—and Joe needed peace. Morning came just as sleep took her captive.

Chapter 28

Alexa pulled up to an automotive shop and parked the rental. The few businesses she'd seen all seemed closed, but an enormous door open to a garage bay gave her hope. She stepped up to the door and leaned in, watching as a mechanic drained oil from a late model Chevy truck. "Sir, can you tell me where to find the Peters farm?"

The man stepped around the vehicle, wiping his hands on a rag. "Oh, Tim and Adelaide's place is down that road about two miles. Then you turn left at the highway. Go about four miles or so until you get to the first dirt road. Turn right, and their house is at the end of the drive."

"Two miles, left four, right to the house. Thank you." Alexa smiled and turned to leave.

"Hey, are you that writer lady Adelaide sews for—Hartfield?"

"How'd you guess?"

The man missed the rhetorical nature of the question and answered quite seriously. "Them clothes. My wife just loves it when Adelaide is workin' on your things. She drives out there whenever she can to see what Adelaide is up to."

"Well, I'm glad she likes them." Alexa hoped it was an adequate response. "Thanks for the directions."

Few cars passed her as she drove to the highway and made the left turn that should lead her to Laidie's. Right at the four-mile mark, a dirt road appeared with a single word on the sign. "Peters." Alexa turned into the driveway and drove slowly down the dirt road. The rental agency would likely wonder why she'd taken a Cadillac off-roading. "I'm glad I changed the contract to let me take it out of state, or they'd be furious," she muttered to herself. It took another five hundred feet to realize she'd been speaking aloud again.

After a mile, Alexa wondered if she had turned on the wrong road, but suddenly, the road curved behind a grove of trees, and she found herself fifty feet from a barn. The house was another several hundred yards back. Alexa pulled up behind a car—Laidie's, she assumed—and parked.

It took a few seconds to gather the courage to open the door, but she climbed from the car and picked her way to the walkway.

A screen door swung open, and Laidie, needles woven in her apron and a bundle of fabric in her hands, stepped onto the wrap-around porch. "Miss Hartfield? Alexa? What are you—"

Without another word, Laidie turned and disappeared into her house. Alexa stood on the walkway, uncertain of what to do. She waited for a minute or two, but outside the occasional lowing of cattle—somewhere—or what sounded like a hen fight in the chicken yard, she heard nothing.

Determined, she mounted the steps and knocked on the screen. Laidie's voice called her from inside. "Come in, Miss Hartfield."

Unnerved by Laidie's reaction, Alexa felt for her phone, her hand ready to punch the emergency button if necessary. "Laidie..." She pulled open the door cautiously. "Are you all right?"

The voice came from the back of the house. Alexa stepped through the tidy living room and into the doorway of the kitchen. Laidie glanced over her shoulder as she reached for potholders. "I'm fine. Deep down, I always knew you'd come. I hoped you wouldn't figure out it was me, of course, but I knew. You're too clever not to see through me."

Alexa watched as Laidie pulled bread from the oven and rapped the bottoms of the tins to make them release from the pan. That done, she set them on racks to cool and grabbed a shopping list pad from the fridge. Minutes passed as she made notes, worked on things here and there—as if she never expected to leave.

"Laidie..."

"I'll be ready to go in a little bit. I have to finish a few things first. And, I want to see Tim." The woman choked on her husband's name. "He's on his way home."

Another item went on the notepad. She invited Alexa to follow her upstairs as she packed. Alexa's throat went dry at the idea. Upstairs is where she sewed. Scissors, rotary cutters—all seemed like dangerous items to be near if Laidie snapped. Still, Alexa followed.

Laidie filled a box with fabrics and articles of clothing. "Why don't you go put that in your car? You'll have to find someone else to sew them now." The woman mopped her eyes with a Kleenex before filling another box. "These... I wonder who she'll find to finish these..."

Alexa listened as Laidie explained about the bridesmaid's dresses. "Do you have paper? I'll have Tim ship them to Rhette. It's the least we can do."

"Oh, that would be nice. Thank you."

Note written, Alexa attached it to the box and carried her box out to the car. Just as she stepped back into the house, a truck bounced over a hidden road by the pasture to the south of the farmhouse. Laidie tensed. It must be Tim.

"Can you explain to him for me? I don't think I can stand to see his face. He's going to be so confused and disappointed in me."

The words sounded hollow—empty—as if someone else spoke them. Alexa's throat constricted, but she nodded. "I'll try."

"Thank you."

Tim raced up the steps and found Laidie standing just inside the door, holding a small suitcase. "Adelaide, what—"

"Alexa will explain. I'm so sorry. I hope you will forgive me."

Tim Peters' face contorted in shock and dismay as his wife clung to him for several seconds before she calmly stepped out the door and strode to Alexa's car. "Miss Hartfield? What is this all about?"

"The woman she was sewing for? The one who was killed?"

"Yeah—Silva, right?" Tim didn't look at her; instead, his eyes followed his wife as she climbed into the car and set the suitcase on her lap.

"Yes. Silva. Laidie killed her—and tried to kill Adam."

"No!" He pushed open the door. "She'd never—she couldn't—"

"She did, Tim. When I realized—I can't tell you how horrible I feel. I don't think she's in her right mind. Truly. I think we've all pushed her until she snapped."

"Where are you taking her?" He spoke in a daze—as though compelled to ask the questions but uninterested in the answers.

"I'll take her to Chicago. I don't see any reason to make her sit in a cell here—to be humiliated that way. She left a list of things for you—bills coming due and orders not finished."

"Oh, this can't be right." Tim wiped his forehead with his arm. "I—"

"She confessed, Tim. I didn't even have to ask. I walked up and she just confessed." Alexa saw what her presence did to the man and decided she should go. "Look, she said one of those boxes is for a wedding at your church. The box is on the cutting table in her sewing room. If you get permission from the bride and ship the box to the address I put inside, I'll get Rhette to finish it up for her. Laidie bent over backwards for us; we can do this for her."

Tim stood on the porch as Alexa and Laidie drove around the curve and down the long driveway. Alexa knew it would only be a matter of seconds—a minute at most—before the shock wore off and he raced after them. Laidie wiped away a few silent tears but fought to maintain control. Alexa took her hand a few times, but nothing could ever truly help.

As they drove past the outskirts of town, Laidie stared at her lap. "What happened to my suitcase?"

"I put it in the seat behind us when I got in. It would be uncomfortable to ride all the way to Chicago like that."

"Thank you."

Eight miles on the other side of town, Laidie stiffened. Her breathing grew shallow and rapid. "Miss Hartfield, dear."

"Hmm? Are you okay?"

"Please turn this car around."

Struggling to keep her voice even and unalarmed, Alexa slowed the car and pulled off the highway, noting that Tim's truck advanced on them from just a mile or so back. "Is something wrong?"

The expression on Laidie's face unnerved her. The woman seemed to be fighting for self-control. "I feel it coming again—that sense of panic and anger. I don't trust myself when I get this way." The woman turned cold eyes on Alexa and added, "I didn't used to do it, you know."

"Okay... how can I help?"

"Just turn around and take me back to town. Trevor Holmes can lock me in his cell until someone else can come get me, or maybe he can take me to Chicago." Tears splashed onto the woman's face. "Hurry, dear. I feel half-crazy now, but I know I'd go truly insane if I hurt you when I got like this."

Alexa did a three-point turn and headed back for the little farming town she had tried to avoid, trying not to let her hands tremble. Terrified for her friend, she met Tim's eyes as he passed. The truck burned rubber as he forced it to make too sharp of a turn.

Laidie frowned. "He'll ruin the tires."

For just those few seconds, she sounded normal again, but the strange terror fell over the woman demeanor again. A minute or so later, Alexa identified it. Laidie was afraid of herself. "Is there anything I can do to help?" she whispered.

"Do you think the girls will bring the children to visit me in prison? I can't imagine not seeing those babies grow up."

"I don't know, but if you were my mother and I had children, I would bring them to visit you."

"I'm so scared, Alexa." The use of her first name unnerved her even more. Laidie rarely did that. The older woman talked *about* her as "Alexa" but when speaking *to* her, she nearly always said "Miss Hartfield."

"It'll be okay. We'll get you help."

"I don't think you should talk to me, dear. I think I'll do better if I just keep silent and think of nice things. My goats, my chickens, my forsythia bush…"

Five minutes later, Alexa watched, broken, as the sheriff and Tim Peters helped her friend from the car and into the station. After a few minutes, she started to follow, but the sheriff met her at the door and said, "Mrs. Peters asks that you leave now. She says you'll understand."

Alexa nodded. "Tell her I'll be praying for her."

"I can't believe what she told me."

"It's true," Alexa mumbled miserably, "but I sure wish it wasn't."

The sun set three hours before she arrived home. The darker the world became around her, the harder she struggled to keep her composure. The desire to collapse into a fit of weeping threatened to overwhelm her, until she neared Rockland. No longer to contain herself, and desperate to avoid an accident, she pulled over to the side of the road and sobbed. She railed, cried, and screamed hysterically at the effects of sin in her world.

Once she finally arrived at home, Alexa hurried inside, dumped the keys in the tray by the door, and ran upstairs to her nook. Seated in her favorite corner of the couch, she curled up with her softest afghan, grabbed a box of tissue, and punched the remote for her CD changer until the plaintive, sonorous tones of the saxophone filled the room around her.

In time, her stomach growled, but she ignored it, feeling content that her misery was now complete.

Joe drove past on his rounds. By the time he noticed the unfamiliar car in the drive, he'd passed her house. Anxious, he circled the street, returning to check out the driveway once more. Lights on in the house and the strange car in the driveway bothered him. When he saw the Illinois plates and the rental agency's name on the license plate frame, he pulled into the drive and parked.

He bolted from the car, letting himself into the house and calling her name. "Alexa?"

"I'm—" she sniffed. "—up here." The sound of her blowing her nose punctuated the announcement.

Joe took the steps two at a time, wincing at the horrible sounds emerging from her speakers. As he reached the top, his heart twisted at the sight of her curled into a ball, sobbing. To his astonishment, she flung a blanket from her, vaulted over the back of the couch, and flung herself at him, weeping.

"Oh, Lex. I'm sure it was awful. Are you okay? Is she okay?"

"She was so scared, Joe. Of herself, more than anything." A hiccough interrupted her. "You've never seen anything so awful."

He led her back to the couch and tucked the blanket in around her. "Are you thirsty?"

Looking small and vulnerable with just her head peeking out of her blanket, Alexa nodded. "Hungry too."

Amused at her not-so-subtle hint, Joe promised to return as quickly as he could. He hurried downstairs and frowned at the empty fridge. After a moment's thought, he filled the electric kettle and then dashed outside. Minutes later, he returned with a sandwich, chips, and a brownie, compliments of Mr. Goldberg at The Deli. He flipped on the kettle and found the box of Chamomile tea.

"Where is your tray?"

At her reply, he pulled it from the pantry and set her food on it. The water boiled, the tea steeped, and Joe carried the tray upstairs, setting it on the couch beside her. "You have to take your arms out of the blanket or you can't—"

"I'll get cold."

The temptation to tease struck him hard, but he ignored it. Without a word, he climbed the stairs to her room and searched everywhere—closet, bathroom, even her bed—until he found a bed jacket hanging in a cupboard in the bathroom. Once back downstairs, he coaxed her into the jacket and handed her the tea.

The saxophone had to go. She needed something soothing but not quite so morose. Joe flipped through the CD changer, pausing once he found a CD of Irish music played on the violin. While not exactly his taste in music, it didn't send fingernails-on-blackboard shivers up his spine.

"Eat something, Alexa. Drink your tea."

She sipped at the tea and took a small bite of her sandwich to appease him, before ignoring the tray again. Joe pulled the ottoman close to her and tried to encourage her to take a bite, a sip, and another bite, until he thought he'd go crazy trying to get some food into her. Seeing her rub her temple, he retrieved her brush from her dressing table and set it in her lap.

Alexa took the silent cue and removed a dozen hairpins, handing them to Joe as she slowly freed her hair. "Oh, that feels better. Thank you. Would you put them away for me?"

A lump welled in his throat as his fingers closed over the pins. It took every ounce of his will power not to reach out and smooth her hair. His heart constricted at the thought of her silky hair sliding through his fingertips.

Without waiting for an answer, she took another bite of her sandwich, another sip of her tea, and sank deeper into the couch, as though permanently rooting herself there. Unsure what else to do, Joe retraced his steps upstairs and put away the brush and pins. An idea occurred to him as he turned to leave the room.

He pulled out his cellphone and dialed Wes' number, praying that the man had returned from whatever the assignment had been this time. "Wes. Are you home? Good. Look, Alexa's back. She's acting a little... strange. I think she's in shock—sort of." Joe listened for a moment, nodding. "Right. Hey, I have to get back to work, but I don't like the idea of leaving her alone."

Twenty minutes later, Joe hugged Alexa and forced

himself to leave. He climbed in the cruiser, backed down the driveway and onto the street. The mental picture of Wes holding her as she sobbed out the heartbreaking story of Adelaide Peters and her skewed sense of loyalty sent waves of pain through him. He wanted to stay—wanted to be the one to comfort.

Chapter 28

Four times that day, Joe drove past the house, watching for some sign of life in there, but unlike the cottage, the life inside didn't intrude into the yard and onto the street. He couldn't hear sounds of her off-key singing, signs of her working in the garden, or her head peeking up over the windowsill as she worked on the couch. The reflection off the large second floor windows made it impossible for him to see into the nook on the landing. The car hadn't moved.

On the third pass, he'd called Wes and asked about that car. "Does she have to drive it back, or—"

"No. She arranged for Jason to pick up her things at the hotel, fly down to Rockland, and drive it back. It's all good."

Joe disconnected the call relieved and disappointed. Jeremy could have done it. She wouldn't have had to pay him. That thought made him smile. Like the couple hundred dollars would make a difference to her.

After the fourth pass, Joe went home and pulled out running clothes. He hated running but needed the outlet. He started slow, waving as he passed Judith on beat. He worked his way to the highway, to the turnoff to the lake, and then down to the sand. His legs burned as he pounded the damp sand around the edge of the shore. He didn't see any evidence of her on the terrace.

"Pathetic," he gasped as he pushed himself to go further, faster. "Coward."

The words unnerved him. They weren't true. He knew it. What bothered him was that they *felt* true. Feelings were things he carefully avoided. Frustrated, he turned toward home, his eyes sliding toward her deck across the lake. No ant-sized Alexa filled the lounge chairs or moved about, fussing with pinpoint sized pots.

By the time Joe reached home, perspiration poured down his face and soaked his shirt. He didn't even stop for clothes. He snatched a towel from the closet and stumbled into the bathroom. The spray hit him, and with it, the built-up tension slowly evaporated.

Once dressed again, resolve formed in his heart. Time. It was time. They'd planned on a movie. After…

He grabbed his keys and locked the door behind him. As if on autopilot, he drove through the town. Two streets past The Market, he made a U-turn. Fresh sourdough bread from the bakery rack, two steaks, bag of salad — perfect. Hopefully, she didn't have anything already cooking.

Just outside the store, he glanced toward The Pettler. Wayne hadn't closed yet. Joe stepped in and glanced in the case. Wayne's assistant, Wendy, stepped up to the counter. "Hey, Joe. What can I get you?"

"Alexa needs flowers, but I don't know what she wants. Do you know what she usually gets?"

The girl nodded. "Over there. She likes the mixed bunch, and sometimes she gets the red gerberas — says they 'pop' in her kitchen."

Joe nodded. "Red it is. I can see that in there."

"How many…"

He shrugged. "Whatever is in there is fine."

The price nearly choked him, but Joe paid and waved. "See you next time."

"I leave for school Saturday. Won't be back until Christmas. See you then!"

The kids were growing up. He remembered when Wendy first entered the high school and now she'd be leaving. For the first time since he'd moved there, Joe considered Fairbury to be his "hometown."

"Have a safe trip."

"Thanks. Night!" Wendy waved as Joe stepped out the door with his bag of groceries and fistful of wrapped flowers.

Nerves attacked him as he neared Alexa's house. His hands shook, his heart pounded, his mouth went dry — until he stepped inside her door and heard the familiar off-key notes drifting down from the third floor.

Joe set the meat in the fridge, grabbed a vase from the cupboard, filled it, and stuffed the flowers inside. He took the stairs two at a time and the spiral stairs as quietly as possible. The noise-masquerading-as-song came from the closet. He crossed the room and leaned against the doorjamb, watching as she sorted clothes, covering some with dust protectors and pulling others out of storage.

Her skirt swayed as she worked, swishing around her ankles. The dress, one of his favorites, clashed terribly with the red-gingham headscarf. He'd never seen Alexa wear something so incongruous.

"So, is this a new trend you're starting—Aunt Jemima meets Guinevere?"

Alexa jumped, squealed, and spun in place. "Joe! Oh, boy." She gasped for breath. "I am going to throttle you."

"I suspect that would get you twenty years to life."

"It might be worth it," she muttered.

"What are you doing?" Joe's eyes swept the room. "Season change out?"

"And inventory." Alexa shifted another dress to what seemed to be a reject pile. "I thought playing with my clothes might take my mind off...everything," she whispered more to herself than to him it seemed. She leaned against the center rack. "I talked to James, Martine, and Elise today. They all agreed that I can't be seen in the same outfit too often or it loses the appeal."

"Since when do you dress for publicity?"

A smile grew. "I don't. I just had a fit of conscience for spending so much money on clothing. I thought I'd cut back and be less extravagant. Then I wondered if perhaps I could justify it somehow..." She winked. "A girl will do anything to justify what she really wants. And they said that the variety is good for my image—even James admitted it." Alexa snickered. "Man that must have hurt him to say. I should send him a bottle of his favorite scotch." She glanced out the window. "Early for the movie, don't you think?"

"I thought you might not feel like cooking, so I brought steaks."

"And that's what I love about you. Stick 'em on the grill. I'll come down and see what I can find to go with it."

"I bought a bag of salad. It's not the same as yours, but it's less work."

He didn't hear half what she said. The words, *'what I love about you'* mocked him. *She sees you as a friend—only a friend. Don't make a fool of yourself.*

"Great. I'll be down in a minute." Her hands reached up to untie the kerchief. He lingered for just that moment—hesitating in spite of himself. There it was; her hair spilled down her back and over her shoulders. Joe swallowed hard.

When had a great friend become so much more? How had he not seen it coming? Should he have tried to prevent it? As he made his way through the house and into the kitchen, Joe questioned everything. His thoughts, his emotions, his decisions, and even his sanity.

He rubbed the steaks with the seasoning mix he loved and carried them out to the grill. When he returned, Alexa stood at the counter, admiring the flowers, the red contrasting beautifully with the chocolate of her dress. She'd left her hair down—for him? Joe didn't imagine it likely, but the idea appealed to him.

"They're beautiful, Joe. Thanks."

"I thought you might need something cheerful."

She smiled up at him. "I did. Thanks."

Every move, every thought—he wanted to try to show her how his feelings had grown and changed. Nothing seemed natural. He waited. They had time. Dinner would take a while. The movie would last for a couple of hours. Maybe by then…

"Want me to wash the greens?"

She shook her head and turned to the fridge. "I've got it. Thanks. Why don't you set plates out there—or is it too cool?"

"It's a bit cool. Not uncomfortably so, but our steaks…"

"Okay, then maybe set the table in here."

"In here, here? Like the kitchen or in the dining room?"

Alexa turned, half-open bag of salad in her hands, gaping at him. "Why would we eat in the dining room? We never do that."

"Just making sure." Joe glanced at the French doors. "Better go turn over those steaks."

He felt her eyes on his back as he hurried outside. Self-recriminations pounded his mind. As he examined the steaks, he took a deep breath. *Okay, Lord. I need help here. I've lost my mind. It's gone. So, if you'd just keep me from making a fool of myself until **after** the movie, I'd be 'much obliged,' as the chief always says.*

Never had frivolous prayer been so swiftly and thoroughly answered—well, not for him. The moment he stepped inside with a plate of sizzling steaks, everything seemed normal again. She talked about her latest plot idea, and he told about finally getting through to one of the junior high kids. Camaraderie, routine—normality. Life was good again.

"Dishes and then movie, or movie and then dishes?" Joe stood, plate in hand, waiting for the verdict.

"Dishes first."

"I should have known." He took hers and carried it to the sink. As he flipped on the water, Alexa nudged him out of the way with her hip.

"Move it. I'll do it."

"But—"

"Put the salad dressing away if you need something to keep you out of trouble."

Laughing, he went to clear the rest of the table. "You seem more like yourself tonight."

"I feel better." She grabbed utensils and rinsed them before loading them in the dishwasher.

"I was worried about you, Lex."

"I know. Thanks for calling Wes. I really didn't want to be alone, and I knew I couldn't ask you to stay."

That she wanted to, encouraged Joe. "You could have. I would have called for someone to take my shift—even the new guy, Chad. He could have done it."

"Well, you did the next best thing. Thanks."

Wes was *next best* — next to him. That had to be good. "I'm just glad you're fine now."

"Wes says I was really out of it. I suppose I was," she admitted. "I don't really remember the drive home." She rinsed the last plate and set it in the dishwasher rack before wiping a damp tendril from her eye.

"I asked Detective Romano to call when they book Laidie. He says they'll handle her gently — planning to hold her in a private cell of the psychiatric unit for evaluation."

"Thanks, Joe. I—" She wiped her forehead again and sagged against the cabinets, leaning on them for support. "I just wasn't prepared for—for any of it."

"Who would be? I mean, what did you expect? Your friend murdered someone. No one is prepared to deal with that."

"I really thought I'd confront her, she'd be defensive but would turn herself in, and while painful, it would be simple. Sad, but simple. This was heart-wrenching." Alexa's pain-filled whisper nearly cut him when she said, "She was so confused and terrified, Joe — afraid of herself more than anything." She gripped the counter and added, "She said the spells lasted anywhere from a few minutes to a few days."

"And the days were when…"

She nodded. With a final swipe to the counter, Alexa turned an apologetic face to Joe. "Hey, would you mind if I renege on our movie? I'm just beat. I think I want to go to bed."

Wes' words echoed in his memory. *"Wouldn't it be nice to know you didn't have to go home?"* Buoyed with renewed confidence, Joe decided to try now. She wanted him to go home. That meant she wouldn't want him to stay and talk about it. Plant a seed and let it germinate. Joe groaned inwardly. *You sound like Tom Allen.*

"Are you saying you want me to go home?"

Alexa rinsed the dishcloth in the sink. "Well, I wouldn't put it that way exactly…"

Joe stepped behind her, wrapping his arms around her

waist. His jaw, prickly with evening stubble, grazed her cheek as he murmured, "But I don't want to go home."

She whirled, staring at him. "Well, you don't have that option, do you?" He grinned at the indignant expression on her face. Undaunted, she continued. "I'm going to bed; therefore, you are going home."

He watched as she sauntered to the door, untying her apron as she went. Just as she reached it, he sprinted across the distance and encircled her waist again, "But I don't want to go home," he murmured.

He felt her stiffen. Perfect. Irritation laced her voice as she shoved him from her. "I don't really care what you want right now, Joe. I can't believe—"

"If we were married, I wouldn't have to go home."

That statement halted her reply. She turned and leaned against the front door. "Married?"

"Sure. If we were married, I could come and go as I pleased."

"But you do anyway! I'm not complaining," she added quickly. "I like how you drop in whenever it's convenient. It's a little Knightley-ish of you, and you know how I love *Emma*, but—"

Joe leaned one hand against the door. His face drew closer as he murmured, "But, as you've made very plain, I have to go home at some point. If we were married…"

Alexa ducked under his arm and walked to the stairs. "Let's talk."

Grinning, Joe followed calmly behind her. Instead of taking his accustomed spot on the opposite corner of the couch, Joe sat cross-legged at her feet—or where they would have been had she not tucked them beneath her. Once comfortable, he waited, confident. She'd be fine—eventually.

Her eyes sought his. "What's going on? We both know you don't want to be married. We're both fine with that. You have plans for your life that don't include a wife, and that's okay. I thought *we* were okay."

"We are okay. I didn't mean to imply—"

"Joe, this is ridiculous. I blame Wes for this. He's been

badgering you again." She frowned. "Or is it the dumb thing with Darrin. I'm not dating Darrin, Joe. For that matter, I don't intend to date anyone, okay?"

"Lex…"

"No, listen to me. I'm perfectly happy with my life as it is, and I know you are as well. We don't want to destroy this friendship with both of us trying to become someone we think the other expects us to be."

Joe protested, "That's not—"

"Hush and listen," she growled. "I'm not a Proverbs thirty-one or Titus two gal. I'm just not. You aren't mister patriarch. I can't have children, and neither one of us want them." She leaned forward, smiling. "It's okay for us to be friends. We don't have to marry. We don't have to follow whatever expectations people might have for us."

Joe reached for her hand. "Honestly, Alexa, sometimes you act like you think your lifestyle is unbiblical. It isn't. God made you who you are."

"But—"

"Now *you* hush," Joe teased, squeezing her hand. "Your childlessness might have been because of His plan for you, or He might have made this plan for you because of what happened. I don't know. That doesn't make you in opposition to Scripture."

"Well, if I married I would be." His eyes questioned her, and she shook her head. "Joe, there's that little part about submitting to your husband 'as unto the Lord?' Well, let's just say that I'm certain I would fail—terribly."

"You're still seeing the idea of your marriage through your mother's lens. There isn't just one pattern for a marriage. They play out in lots of different ways."

"But the Bible is the Bible, Joe. You can't dismiss that it says, 'sumit—'"

"But, Lex," he protested, "what if submission means that you live your life as you do now? What if submission to *your* husband means nothing changes except that I don't go home?" He smiled as she began shaking her head. It would take a bit to sink in. He needed to go and give it time.

"But if I'm living my life as I do already, why change it? Why get married at all?"

Joe pulled her to her feet and led her downstairs, his fingers laced in hers. At the door, he waited to meet her eyes. The seconds ticked past, but he said nothing. At last, her eyes rose to meet his. "Why, Joe?" she whispered.

There. The best opening for further thought he could have asked for. He brushed her cheek with the back of his hand, leaned forward, and murmured, "Because, Lex, I don't want to go home anymore." With that, he opened the door, stepped onto the porch, and closed the door behind him. Smiling.

Wes looked up from his laptop as Joe stepped in the room. "Hey, you're back early." Something in Joe's face looked off. "Did you and Alexa have another argument?"

"Yep."

Wes' eyes widened at Joe's grinning face. "Well... what about?"

"Marriage."

For a moment, Wes assumed they'd been talking about his engagement. "What's it to you? You have a problem with it?"

"No," Joe said, sinking into the couch looking utterly relaxed. "That's why I said I thought we should do it."

Wes blinked. "You what? You're kidding!" Shaking his head, he added, "You proposed? What did she say? Dumb question, I know what she said. Congrat—"

"I didn't propose, and she didn't accept anything."

"You—What?"

Grinning, Joe kicked off his shoes and propped his feet on the arm of the couch. "I merely told her that I didn't want to go home."

Wes' outrage came on cue. "You did *what?* Joe, I can't believe you would do something like that."

"Well, it worked—"

"Joe!"

He couldn't help it; he howled. "It broke the idea to her anyway—reasonably gently, too. After she misunderstood me, twice, almost threw me out, and gave me a lecture on why we weren't suited for marriage, she asked why I mentioned such a ridiculous idea."

"And you said?"

"Because I don't want to go home."

The men's chuckles grew into guffaws. Wes shook his head. "Oh, man. That was good. That was really good."

"It should be," Joe snickered. "I stole it from you."

Wes' eyes widened. "You did, didn't you? Man, I'm smart. First a profound statement that I can't even remember, and now this. Do you think she's figured it out yet?"

"She's not dumb, Wes."

"Think she'll say yes?"

Joe shrugged. "I'm not going to stop suggesting it until she agrees that it's the brilliant idea that it is."

Chapter 30

Saturday morning, Joe and Wes sat outside Fairbury's best—not to mention only—jewelry store. Joe dug for his phone. "What time is it?"

Wes glanced at his watch and opened the door. "It's ten now. I'll go knock. George gets working and forgets to unlock the door sometimes."

"Here." Joe passed a wad of bills to his co-conspirator. "Make sure it's right..."

"I know, I know. It's not like you've told me a million times this past hour."

"It's just—"

"Knock it off. You're being juvenile about it. I should make you go in there and get it yourself."

"No way. In this town, buying a ring is equivalent to announcing a wedding. I won't risk irritating her by making her conspicuous."

Wes erupted in delighted chuckles. "Alexa? Conspicuous? Never!"

"Not like this she isn't. I have no doubt she'd tell me to go give it to Shannon—and mean it—" Joe grimaced at the thought, " —if someone got to her before me."

Wes crawled from the vehicle. "Then you'd better hurry. Her neighbors have two-story windows and telephones."

"Wha—" Joe began, but Wes slammed the door shut and strolled down the sidewalk.

Joe twiddled his thumbs, drummed his fingers on the steering wheel, tapped his toes, and shifted continuously in his seat. What seemed to take several hours, took exactly four point three minutes. Wes returned, thrusting a tissue stuffed gift bag into his hands. "There. I hope she likes pink. He couldn't have shoved another handful in that bag if he tried."

"My change?"

A much smaller roll of bills landed in Joe's palm. "Get me out of here. I've got to tell Heather about this. Oh, and for the record, I think Alexa is arranging an engagement party for next week. I'd suggest getting Saturday night off, or she'll kill you."

"It would kill me to miss that much good food," Joe muttered as he turned toward home.

Wes jumped from the Jeep as Joe pulled up in front of Heather's house. "I'd offer to pray for you, but I wonder if I shouldn't be praying for her…"

"Get out of the car. I've got to do this before I lose my nerve."

Joe's engine roared as he pulled away from the curb drowned out Wes' laughter. At the corner, he took a deep breath and forced himself to calm down. It shouldn't be a surprise. She had to be expecting something. All would be well—eventually.

Citizens waved. Aiden Cox darted out across the street on his skateboard, with Chad chasing close behind. A snicker escaped. "Welcome to Fairbury, Chad," he muttered as he turned toward Alexa's side of town.

At Alexa's house, he pulled up to the garage and glanced at the pink bag on the console. "Time to shake things up even more," he muttered, grabbing the bag and striding toward the house.

Inside, as he reached the kitchen, he heard her planning a menu with someone on the phone. "I expect around seventy-five people, and…" Without a word, he leaned over her shoulder and dumped the little gift bag on the notepad before her.

Alexa shoved it aside before he moved his hand. "… I don't want a traditional sit-down meal. I want substantial finger foods so people can walk about and mingle." He slid the bag in front of her again, but she brushed it out of her way and continued speaking as if uninterrupted. "I want vegetable… somethings, um… hot… somethings… fruit somethings, and some bread.. um… stuffs. Yes, I are articulate."

She winked at Joe. Joe dumped the bag back in front of her. For the next ten minutes, as Alexa worked with a caterer about the party, Joe repeatedly pushed the bag under her nose, and Alexa shoved it back again. By the time she disconnected her call, Alexa gasped with suppressed laughter and threw her pen at Joe.

"We can't have a party, you fool, if you won't let me plan it."

"How can I tell the world that I'm moving in if you don't open that bag?"

"Rocks and metal?"

He shook his head. "Not quite. Mollusks and metal. Is that any better?"

At the mention of mollusks, Alexa dumped the contents of the bag onto the counter, pulling apart the tissue as she did. The little gray ring box gave away the contents, had any doubts lingered. "I almost got a bracelet—just because it's easier to remove, but—"

As she pried open the lid, Alexa glanced up at him. "It's perfect. Really, but mollusks?"

"That's where mother of pearl comes from."

Alexa slipped the ring on, twisting it as if to gauge how comfortable it would be. "Hmm… I always thought abalone. How interesting." Joe's laughter filled the kitchen. She glanced up at him, curious. "What?"

"You'll be researching all shellfish that produce that stuff that makes mother of pearl inside twenty-four hours, and I have no doubt that you'll discover abalone makes it as well—either that or you'll discover that abalone is a mollusk." He leaned over the counter and brushed her ring with his thumb.

"Am I really so obnoxiously know-it-allish?"

He tugged her hand, lead her around the counter, and sank into one of the kitchen chairs, pulling her onto his lap. "I'm not pushing you away this time. This time," he added, his eyes never leaving hers, "I'm not letting you go until you agree to sign a license for me to move in."

Smiling at him, Alexa gently pulled his arms from around her waist and stood. Joe watched, confused, as she walked slowly from the room. So much for his assertion that he'd "not let her go." He had expected some kind of protest. She'd want to be certain of him before she agreed, but he had never imagined that Alexa would just walk away from him as though she had laundry to pick up from the cleaners and nothing better to do than go get it at that moment.

A minute or two later, he raced up the stairs, feeling like an idiot as he realized the problem. Alexa sat on the couch, still wearing the ring and twisting it around her finger absently. Joe hesitated before he sat next to her, taking her hand in his. "I feel like a fool."

"Well..."

"Laughing, Joe shook his head. "Don't say it. As true as it is, don't say it. I think my Friday genes have kicked into overdrive."

"You said it, not me."

"I'm so comfortable with you, Lex... I," he hesitated. "You're just one of those people who understand me most of the time, so I forget that some things need to be said—not assumed."

She tried to act affronted, but the repressed giggle and smile gave her away. "You got that right."

"I love you."

"I know. I just wonder if you're prepared for the changes you're suggesting. I wonder if either of us is."

Alexa's lack of response to him sharing his heart left him spinning. Had he misunderstood her? Maybe she truly did regard him as only a dear friend. He'd laid his heart on the line with absolute confidence, and now—Another thought occurred to him. "Hey, Lex..."

"Hmm?"

Joe couldn't stand to meet her eyes, so he pulled her close. Resting his head on her hair, he said, "I just realized that it could seem like all I want is a convenient friendship." He swallowed the lump that rose in his throat. "I know I did this... differently. I tried to ease you into the idea, but if I made you think I don't want it, you're wrong. I could buy us a house and do it the more traditional route if you wanted. I just think of you as here or at the cottage, but—"

"But what?"

"But I just want to be wherever you are whenever I can."

"But that's just what I said the other night. You already are. You already fill your spare time here. We both do that— spend our free time together. I think sometimes you even choose coming here over being with the kids."

Joe nodded. "I do. I like to be with you. That's what I'm trying to tell you."

"So if we're already together all of the time, why change the dynamic of our relationship now? That's what I don't understand."

"Because I love you." Joe tried to interject every note of meaning he could into the words, hoping to remove all of her doubts.

"Well, I heard you the first time, and that means the world to me, Joe, but I still have to ask—"

Irritation welled up in him and he interrupted. "C'mon, Alexa. You're not that naïve. I love you, and I don't want to go home anymore. How difficult is that to understand?"

"It isn't, but I think you're trying to say something you're not, and I refuse to make assumptions in that direction. I will not put myself in that kind of vulnerable position."

"But I have to—"

Alexa whipped her head around to meet his eyes. "That's how it works. Sorry if you don't like it, but that's how it works. Women risk a level of vulnerability when they marry that men can't possibly fathom. Just Biblically, it's huge. So, the least the guy can do is give her a reason to believe he understands how scary that is."

"You're my best friend, Lex, and I love you. But I don't want to be just your best friend anymore. I want to be your husband. I don't just want you to be Alexa Hartfield. I want you to be my Lex. My wife."

"Alexa Freidan. That could take some getting used to."

Excited, Joe tried to sound nonchalant. "Stay Hartfield, for all I care. It would probably be a publicity nightmare anyway."

"I can be both. That's why they have pseudonyms. I'll be Alexa Freidan, and I'll wear the name proudly, but—"

"But what?" Something in her tone told him he was in for teasing.

"But I might decide to call you Jordan when you irritate me—just to keep you in line, you know."

Another lazy afternoon passed as they watched the boats on Lake Danube. This time, rather than silence, they found much to discuss. As dinnertime approached, Alexa stood and smiled down at a very sleepy Joe. "I love you."

"I was wondering," he murmured without opening his eyes."

"Well, now you don't have to anymore."

Downstairs, she pulled marinated chicken from the fridge, arranged it in a baking pan, and went to rinse her hands in the sink. Joe's arms stole around her waist. "I think," he murmured, "I should be able to kiss my fiancée…"

Music—the kind both Alexa and Joe despised—pulsated and wailed through the house as the party shifted into full swing. People mingled, offered congratulations to both couples, and engaged in semi-rhythmic jerks around her foyer—jerks that appeared to be attempts at dancing. Joe cringed and watched Alexa as she welcomed new guests and bade goodbye to Judith. He owed that woman for taking his shift.

Her scarlet evening gown flowed with each shift of her body, giving it the appearance of liquid. Era—he had no idea, but it amused him that he considered it at all. So much of his life had already acclimated to hers in the past year.

From across the room, Alexa caught his eye. She jerked her head slightly toward the spiral staircase on the second floor landing and held up five fingers. Mrs. Varney, unaware that she'd interrupted a mimed tête-à-tête, asked for directions to the bathroom, leaving him barely able to nod his agreement.

By the time he arrived upstairs, Joe found her picking up little articles of clothing and personal effects. "Hey, it's a rousing success," he said, "but we both knew it would be."

"Wes seems happy. I just wish our parents would have come—for his sake anyway. I sent tickets right out of Inyokern, but they sent regrets, with a nice note saying," her voice turned clipped—almost snide. 'We hope he's happy and that God's blessing is on this union.'"

"That sounds so very sincere. Were those your voice inflections or theirs?"

"Both, I imagine."

A slower dance number followed the latest pop song, and Joe pulled Alexa into his arms, dancing with his fiancée around the furniture of her bedroom. "So, when do you want to do this thing? I'm guessing you'll need time for a largish wedding—"

"Oh, no! Joe, no! Where's the nearest justice of the peace? Isn't there some place other than Vegas where you can get married without being a resident and without a waiting period?" She rested her head on his shoulder. "I don't want to wait," she whispered.

"I know Los Angeles is just as easy as Las Vegas. I overheard Wes and Heather talking about that, but, Lex…"

"Ew, I'd rather go to Vegas. What about Atlantic City? Is it easy there?"

He led her down to the landing again, before someone misinterpreted their absence. "Lex…" Joe gave her a slow spin, pulling her close again and turning an old Beatles song into a Texas two-step. "I don't get it. I thought you'd want a chance for an incredible dress, and you're talking about going to a courthouse. That doesn't fit you."

They danced for several minutes before she sighed, resting her head on his shoulder. "A dress is almost too good to pass up. You can only do that once in a lifetime—or one would hope."

Joe nodded. "Yep, and if I were you, I'd take advantage of that."

"Oh!" she exclaimed as if she hadn't heard him, "and that staircase. Can you imagine—" Joe grinned as she pulled a pen and paper from the end table and started jotting down notes. "Come check this out, don't you think…"

At that moment, Joe realized that he'd just ensured that a simple wedding became a fairly elaborate affair. "And I pride myself in not talking too much," he muttered as he followed Alexa to the terrace. "When, Alexa?"

She turned, smiling. "December."

"That's three whole months."

"Early December then." Alexa stepped close and wrapped her arms around his neck. "I just want to decorate my house for Christmas and have it fit the wedding too. Trust me."

With an uncharacteristic huskiness to his voice, Joe said, "But that means I have to keep going home."

She kissed him, heedless of those who might be watching. Seconds later—it seemed like hours—she stood on tiptoe and whispered, "For now."

The Hartfield Mysteries: *Two O'Clock Stump* (Book Three)

Chapter One

Just after one o'clock, sleep finally overtook Alexa. Her room, at the back of the hotel, buffered any latent noises from the sleepy desert town. A siren wailed somewhere outside—the merest trace of it piercing her subconscious. She stirred—and relaxed.

The ting of the small room refrigerator didn't affect her. The air conditioner clicked on, buzzing and sending a fresh wave of cool air over the room. Her hand pulled the blanket up closer to her face.

The red glow of clock numbers tried to burn themselves into her eyelids. 1:59. She didn't stir. Seconds passed. Slowly, the incessant bleeping of a clock ripped away the cocoon of sleep and woke her. Bleary-eyed, she tried to focus on the clock. 2:01.

Who would set an alarm at this time of morning—in a town like Ridgecrest? That's just weird.

As much as she tried to ignore it, the rhythmic blare of the clock refused to let her sleep. She glanced at hers again. 2:04. *If that thing changes over to 2:05, I'm calling the front desk. Some maid probably muffed it when she was cleaning.* She hadn't finished the thought before the clock rolled over another minute. 2:05.

Alexa grabbed the room phone and punched the operator button. Several rings passed before a sleepy-sounding clerk announced with fake chipperness, "Front desk, how may I help you?"

"Yes, I'm in room 204 and there's an alarm going off in the room next to me. I can't sleep."

"An alarm? In 202 or 206?" The clerk didn't wait for a response. "That doesn't make any sense. There's no one in either room. I'll send up maintenance."

Alexa sighed, relieved. "Thank you."

Ten more minutes, each second of which was punctuated with alarm blasts, passed before she finally heard keys in the lock of the room next to hers. Alexa's body relaxed. Her eyes closed as she shifted, adjusting her pillow for perfect comfort.

Alexa bolted upright in bed as a scream—too masculine to be a woman and too high not to be utter terror—echoed in the room next door.

Books by Chautona Havig

The Rockland Chronicles

Noble Pursuits
Discovering Hope
Argosy Junction
Thirty Days Hath…
Advent
31 Kisses

The Aggie Series *(Part of the Rockland Chronicles)*

Ready or Not
For Keeps
Here We Come

The Hartfield Mysteries *(Part of the Rockland Chronicles)*

Manuscript for Murder
Crime of Fashion

The Agency Files *(Part of the Rockland Chronicles)*

Justified Means
Mismatched

Past Forward- A Serial Novel

Volume 1
Volume 2
Volume 3
Volume 4
Volume 5

Historical Fiction

Allerednic (A Regency Cinderella story)

The Annals of Wynnewood

Shadows and Secrets
Cloaked in Secrets
Beneath the Cloak

The Not-So-Fairy Tales

Princess Paisley
Everard